RELIQUARY

The spiral design in the center of the chamber floor was moving, becoming three-dimensional as the little metal tiles forming it shifted fluidly. The whole floor was still vibrating, making the glass and metal debris jump and dance. Something groaned again below their feet, and the spiral began to sink into the floor.

Standing at John's elbow, McKay glared at Kavanagh, his mouth twisted in annoyance. "What did you do?"

John wasn't thrilled either. "Some warning would have been nice, Doctor."

Teyla and Ford watched the spiral uneasily, Kolesnikova a few steps behind them. Kavanagh shook his head, his eyes still on the metal sinking into the floor, his gaze rapt. "I wasn't sure it was really here, if the power source was still active. If I was...imagining it..."

The groaning rumble of metal parts undisturbed for ages was growing louder, and John wasn't sure he had heard right. "What?" he said, having to raise his voice over the din. "Why did you think you were imagining it?"

"I was imagining what?" Distracted, Rodney stepped sideways, moving along the edge of the shaft, craning his neck to watch the spiral's progress.

"I wasn't talking to you," John shouted back, "I was—"

"Wait." Rodney straightened up suddenly, looking at John. "It occurs to me that something may come out of here that could kill us."

John swore and yelled, "Fall back, now!"

STARGATE ATLANTIS™

RELIQUARY

MARTHA WELLS

FANDEMONIUM BOOKS

An original publication of Fandemonium Ltd, produced under license from MGM Consumer Products.

Fandemonium Books
PO Box 795A
Surbiton
Surrey KT5 8YB
United Kingdom
Visit our website: www.stargatenovels.com

STARGATE
ATLANTIS™

METRO-GOLDWYN-MAYER Presents
STARGATE ATLANTIS
JOE FLANIGAN   TORRI HIGGINSON   RACHEL LUTTRELL
RAINBOW SUN FRANCKS   and DAVID HEWLETT as Dr. McKay
Executive Producers BRAD WRIGHT & ROBERT C. COOPER
Created by BRAD WRIGHT & ROBERT C. COOPER

WWW.MGM.COM

ISBN: 0-9547343-7-8

Printed in the United Kingdom by Bookmarque Ltd, Croydon, Surrey

Author's Note

Many, many thanks go to Julie Fortune, for encouraging me at just the right moment, to Irina Kolesnikova for her name, to Liz Sharpe for the title, and especially to Margie Gillis, Katrien Rutten, Seah Levy, Naomi Novik, Nancy Buchanan, Lisa Gaunt, Troyce Wilson, and Rory Harper, for critiquing, encouragement, beta reading and being my auxiliary backup brains. .

CHAPTER ONE

John Sheppard pivoted, eyes narrowed critically as he examined the large round chamber. "I don't know, Ford. I don't think we could mount a backboard on these walls."

They were a pearly white ceramic, ornamented with three wide silver bands that had a faint hint of sea greens and blues woven into their metal. The sunlight that fell through the cathedral-like stained glass panels high in the peaked roof made the whole room opalescent. The floor also had translucent white-on-white patterns, long lines that were abstract and floral, sort of Art Nouveau. It was a subtle and beautiful space, but for Atlantis, that was hardly unusual.

"Major," Lieutenant Ford said regretfully, shaking his head. "You are obsessing on the basketball. I'm thinking this would be a great place to play handball. Or racquetball. We're in another galaxy here. You have to think outside the hoop."

John lifted his brows, considering it. "Racquetball, huh? You may be on to something." He doubted anybody had brought a set of rackets along as a personal item, but they could probably make them. He might even be able to talk one of the Athosians on the mainland into carving a set out of wood, which would bypass the whole 'using limited materials for recreation' issue. "McKay, what do you think?"

Rodney McKay and Radek Zelenka were both deep in the innards of the pillar device at the center of the room, occasionally muttering inaudible comments to each other. John thought of it as a pillar device because at the moment they didn't have a clue what it did except look like a pillar. It was silver and waist-high with the typical crystalline touchpad controls on the flat top. So far, poking at it and pressing the touchpads had done nothing, but that wasn't atypical for Atlantis, either.

McKay's voice answered from inside the device's guts. "I think you should stop exchanging facetious random babble with Ford and try to use your obviously overrated gene to make this damn thing work."

John obligingly leaned an elbow on the unresponsive pillar. Most of the Ancients' technology had to be either operated or initialized by someone who had the Ancient gene, which was rare even on Earth, where the Ancients had spent a lot of their time when they weren't traveling between galaxies. There was a mental component to it too, which was sort of cool when you could turn lights on with your mind, and lifesaving when the puddlejumpers responded to your urgent need to make a course change or fire a drone before you could physically reach the controls. "I don't think that's the problem. If it won't work for me or your half-assed gene, then it's probably a lost cause."

McKay had the gene artificially through the gene therapy retrovirus Carson Beckett had developed. It worked for much of the Ancient tech, but some things just needed the natural gene to initialize. "Oh please, nothing is a lost cause. It's just a matter of— Are you thinking at it?"

"I'm thinking it's broken," John admitted. It was kind of hard to turn something on with your mind when you had no idea what it was supposed to do.

"That's not helping!"

"So if it is broken, can we use this room for recreation?" Ford put in hopefully.

McKay extracted himself from the pillar's guts, twisting sideways to avoid elbowing Zelenka in the head. Annoyed and sweating from working in the close confines of the device, he said, "So not listening to you, Lieutenant." He picked up a tool, nudged the grumbling Zelenka over, and plunged back into the pillar again.

"Hey, recreation is important," John said, just to keep the argument going. Standing around cradling a P-90 while watching other people work on something he couldn't help with bored the crap out of him, but moving on to another room while the others were occupied was out of the question. This wing wasn't part of the secure area patrolled by the Marine detail and hadn't even been thoroughly explored yet. It was distant enough from the center section that the only sound was the constant wash of the sea against the floating city's substructure far below their feet. Nobody was supposed to be here without a military escort, and two scientists, deeply distracted by recalcitrant Ancient machinery and oblivious to the world, definitely needed somebody to watch their backs. Or their butts, which was about the only part of them visible most of the time.

But John really didn't mind. It wasn't that it beat beat being up in the operations tower, debating the different ways to replenish their dwindling stores of ammo and toilet paper; exploring Atlantis was one of the coolest things he had ever done in his life, and he didn't expect that to change anytime soon, no matter what wonders they found traveling through the 'gate.

"Yeah, recreation is important. For team-building, and exercise. And for morale," Ford agreed earnestly. Or at least he was doing a good imitation of earnest.

"Morale, that's a good one." John gave Ford an approving nod. "We'll use that when we talk to Elizabeth." John and Ford had both been hoping to find an area that could convert to outdoor space closer to the center section of the city. They had found several big rooms that could have been meant for theaters, lecture halls, or even ballrooms, and the others had searched for controls while John had stared hopefully up at the ceilings, thinking *retract, please*. But nothing had happened.

Since Atlantis had been built for underwater use, space travel, and harsh land conditions like the Antarctic, John could see why the inhabitants hadn't gone for an open football field. But there were balconies, so it seemed like they might have wanted a larger outdoor area occasionally.

And, with the city's shields inoperable, any large space able to open to the air could function as a landing field for an intruder. John wanted to know about that, too. At low power, with so many of its Ancient defenses useless, Atlantis was nearly helpless against Wraith attack.

McKay grunted and emerged from the pillar again, wiping sweat off his forehead with his sleeve. "Nevertheless, you're out of luck. This is some kind of projector, and it must use the walls to display images. Throwing a ball around in here could damage the surface. And, to be absolutely clear, it's a stupid idea."

"You're a spoilsport. Literally," John told him.

Rodney McKay did not work and play well with others. Even the science and technical teams of the expedition, the people who had spent their whole professional lives dealing with brilliant and creative personalities, had trouble with him. Some of that probably stemmed from the fact that Rodney was right so much of the damn time, and that just had to chafe.

But the fact remained that a tense situation just made McKay think faster. You could probably phrase it as an equation, where the increasing awfulness of whatever tight spot they were in was directly proportional to the speed of McKay's ability to think a way out of it. He was so reliable on this point that John had stopped counting the number of times McKay's brain had saved their asses.

Some people were intimidated by that, and it made for a lot of yelling on occasion. John wasn't intimidated, and neither was their other teammate, Teyla. Ford, twenty-five years old and barely out of kidhood, was learning not to be. And John had realized early on that he and Rodney had eerily compatible senses of humor. That probably wasn't a good thing, but it made for interesting conversations.

McKay was steadily getting better on the fieldwork aspect as well. It helped that nobody ever had to tell him to be careful; he knew better than anyone just how dangerous any kind of alien technology could be and just how many things there were out there besides Wraith that wanted to kill you.

"And if this is just a big projector room, it's not new. We've already found plenty of projectors," John added, just to mess with Rodney a little more. A lot of the living quarters had small theater rooms; the science team had already been able to use parts from a damaged laptop to convert one to play the DVDs people had brought along in their personal items.

Still sitting on the floor, McKay gave him a withering look. "This is a holographic projector," he corrected pointedly as Zelenka struggled out of the pillar.

"We found one of those already, too."

"Oh, hey." Ford looked intrigued. "Maybe this is a holographic game projector, for virtual reality games. That would be cool."

"You watched too much *Star Trek*," Rodney told him.

Ford snorted. "Oh, like you didn't."

Before John could add that a virtual reality game room would be awesome, Zelenka said, "I don't think this is for entertainment." He sat back on his heels, looking thoughtful and adjusting his glasses. Zelenka was Czech, short, with a fuzzy halo of brown hair, and probably the most brilliant person in Atlantis next to Rodney. He had had the Ancient gene therapy, but he was one of the forty-eight percent of the population that it didn't affect. "There is no place to insert media. It will only play what's contained in the memory core." He eyed the pillar without satisfaction, then shrugged philosophically. "Perhaps it's meant to be a museum display."

"Whatever. Let's try it again." McKay shoved to his feet, wiped his hands on his pants, and slapped a touchpad.

The walls started to glow with a mild white light. Then it suddenly flashed and dissolved in a bright flare of fuzzy three-dimensional static. The pillar made a constipated burping noise that just couldn't be good. "You broke it," John told Rodney. The gray static stood out about a foot from the walls, and the shimmery three-dimensional quality of it was already giving him a headache.

"Oh, I did not." McKay rolled his eyes, still poking touch-pads.

"I don't think you should have substituted those crystals from the—" Zelenka began.

The pillar burped again, and the walls flashed, but this time John happened to be looking in the right spot and saw it had displayed an actual image, just for a second, before dissolving into static again.

"Whoa, did you see that?" Ford asked, flinching away from the brightness.

"What was it?" McKay demanded, pivoting to stare around the room.

"Those were symbols for a 'gate address." Intrigued now, John stepped up to the pillar, hoping the thing was stuck in some kind of memory loop. Just as the pillar burped again he hit the biggest touch pad.

The walls blurred into motion, blazing with light and color. For an instant John got an impression of dark stone walls and towers, a storm-gray sky overhead. Then it all flashed into the bright liquid static again and vanished. John winced and rubbed his eyes; his retinas felt as if they had just gotten a tan.

"Ouch," Ford commented, grimacing. "That wasn't good. I think it's wrecked."

"Okay, all kidding aside, now you really broke it." Irritated, Rodney flung his hands in the air.

John threw him an annoyed look. "I did not. It was already broken when you were screwing with it."

Zelenka waved his hands, glaring up at them from his seat on the floor. "Hush, enough! I'm tired of watching the Major play Bugs Bunny to McKay's Daffy Duck."

McKay frowned down at him. "Hey, why is he Bugs Bunny?"

"It's the teeth." Ford nodded seriously.

John turned to him, saying earnestly, "What did you say,

Ford? You want to go to the mainland and dig irrigation ditches for Halling? Why, yes, that can be arranged!"

Swearing, Zelenka dived into the pillar console again, his voice muffled. "Recriminations later. Let me try..."

This time there was a muted flash and an image froze, stretched across three-quarters of the wall area. It was the seven symbols of a Stargate address, displayed in three-dimensional blue figures a couple of feet high.

"Huh. What do you know about that?" McKay frowned thoughtfully at the pillar. "What's so special about this address that it gets its own kiosk and a holographic display?"

Zelenka growled from inside the device. "If I could just get past this damaged section of power input, I might be able to- Though perhaps the memory core itself is damaged, maybe when crystals were drained." He pulled his head out to look at the address, brow furrowed. "We need to figure out a way to make it play the whole thing. It must explain itself."

"Or," John put in, studying the address thoughtfully, "there is a quicker way to find out."

The address wasn't one that Teyla recognized, which meant it wasn't a planet that the Athosians had ever visited on their trading trips. Peter Grodin was trying to find it in the Ancient database, but that could take forever. John pushed for his quick solution, and Elizabeth Weir, the expedition's leader, agreed.

Standing on the control center gallery level of the 'gate room, John impatiently watched the techs get the MALP ready. The self-contained probe would tell them if this was an orbital 'gate or a planetary one, check for radiation and other hazards, and the video telemetry would let them know if there was a bunch of Wraith waiting around for lunch to show up. The address had already been dialed into the 'gate, and the event horizon was a lucent pool of liquid blue glittering invitingly inside the ring.

The 'gate room was large and light and airy, designed

with practicality and aesthetics in mind, like most of Atlantis. The soft copper-colored walls were inset with the elaborate geometrical patterns of stained glass that decorated all the living areas, and the 'gate itself was in the lower level of the room, with a wide sweep of stairs leading down from the gallery level to the embarkation floor. Unlike the 'gate room at Stargate Command on Earth, there was no protected area that could be sealed off if a hostile force came through; Atlantis' 'gate room had been built at a time when the city expected only friendly visitors. The only defensive measure was a force shield over the 'gate itself that, like the trinium iris on Earth's Stargate, prevented unwanted arrivals. The puddlejumper bay was directly above the 'gate room, with a floor and ceiling that could retract, allowing the little ships to drop into a launch position for the 'gate or lift up to leave the city.

Teyla, Zelenka, and McKay had gathered to watch, and Elizabeth Weir was standing beside John, arms folded. John thought everybody was acting like it was Christmas and Santa was about to arrive through the 'gate. Elizabeth must have thought so too, because her mouth quirked, and she glanced at him, saying, "So what are you hoping for?"

John shrugged, pretending he wasn't just as intrigued as everybody else. What they were all hoping for, of course, was a place that might have a Zero Point Module. ZPMs were the only thing that could fulfill Atlantis' huge demand for power, and the last of the city's resources had been nearly used up bringing it to the surface. Now the expedition was using the naquadah generators they had brought from Earth to keep the city partially powered. This mostly worked, but it wasn't enough to raise the city's shields or power the Stargate for a wormhole back to Earth, so they couldn't get supplies or new personnel, report that they were in a hell of a lot of trouble, or retreat. John just said, "Oh, I don't know. A puddlejumper dealership and repair outlet?"

Below, the techs cleared the floor and the blocky shape of

the MALP trundled through the wormhole's event horizon. Peter Grodin, one of the British scientists, was seated at the console that acted as the dialing device and monitor for the Stargate. "And there we go. Yes. We have a safe arrival." He shifted over to the laptop that would receive and interpret the MALP's telemetry, glancing up over his shoulder at Elizabeth. "It's a viable destination, at least."

Teyla, standing to the side, said with a smile, "I would hope it leads to another lost city of the Ancestors, with many ruins to explore." Teyla was the leader of the Athosians, the first group of humans native to the Pegasus galaxy that the expedition had met. The Wraith had arrived on Athos not long after that first meeting, and Teyla's people had had to flee and were now living on Atlantica's mainland. She was a beautiful woman, with red-brown hair and a lovely smile, and she could kick John's ass in Athosian stick combat, which was one of the reasons he had wanted her on his Stargate team.

"We haven't even fully explored this lost city of the Ancients yet," Zelenka pointed out with a mock frown.

McKay said a little wistfully, "A planet with coffee plantations would be nice."

And no Wraith, John added mentally. No one had said it, but it was there, hanging over all of them like a headsman's ax. He could see from Grodin's console that the MALP was running through its initial program, transmitting streams of data. Then the screen lit up with static as the MALP's camera switched on. John nudged Rodney with an elbow. "Maybe it'll be a ZPM factory next to a coffee plantation."

Rodney threw him an annoyed look. "Don't tease."

The static resolved into a grainy black-and-white view of an ocean as the camera panned across a rocky coastal landscape. Attracted by the movement, it zoomed in on waves rolling up a beach. Then it panned across an open plain and stopped abruptly as it found a structure in the distance.

John heard a collective indrawn breath from everybody watching. It was a huge structure. As the MALP focused on it, he could make out a high wall, curving away to make a round bastion, and above it three towers, each resembling a flattened version of the onion domes you saw on old Russian palaces. "Cool," he muttered. The pillar's address hadn't been a bust, at least; there really was something interesting there.

"Oh my God," Elizabeth said suddenly. She grabbed Grodin's shoulder, leaning in beside him to study the image. "That looks like— Am I imagining the resemblance—"

"You're not." McKay shouldered forward, unceremoniously shoving Zelenka aside and stepping on John's feet. "It's very similar. Grodin, can you—"

"Pull up the description so we can compare it, yes." Grodin had already turned away to another nearby laptop, typing quickly. Even he looked quietly excited.

"What?" John demanded. "What is it?"

Watching intently, Zelenka explained, "It is like the description we have of Heliopolis, the repository found in the first year of the Stargate program."

"Seriously?" John's brows lifted, and he whistled softly. "Hot damn." He hadn't been in the SGC before Atlantis, but he remembered the story from the Stargate Command mission reports that were available to all expedition members.

"Heliopolis?" Teyla echoed, leaning in to listen. "What place is this?"

Zelenka told her, "It was one of the first indications we had that the Goa'uld did not build the Stargate network, that they were parasites using the remains of an earlier civilization. It was later concluded that Heliopolis was a meeting place where the Ancients shared information with the other great races of the time, the Asgard, the Furlings, and the Nox. There was a database designed for interspecies communication, that if we could have studied it—" He waved his hands helplessly.

"They lost it when a big storm came up and the building collapsed into the ocean," John finished the story for Teyla.

"They barely got out in time, then when they tried to redial to see if the 'gate was still there, they got nothing."

Teyla nodded understanding, her expression intrigued. "Then this could be a wonderful discovery."

"The resemblance isn't exact," McKay was saying, "but the shape of those towers, the height of the walls, even the fact that it seems to be near a sea, it's all very suggestive. We have to check this out."

Elizabeth nodded slowly, but a smile tugged at her mouth. "If it is another Heliopolis—"

McKay's grin was smug. "Then maybe we did find a ZPM factory."

They geared up for the trip in record time, with McKay actually changing into his field uniform in the puddlejumper bay while John was running the preflight check. But it was late in the day on the destination planet, and the jumper shot out of the Stargate into a cloud-streaked sky already reddening with sunset. John dropped speed, guiding the little ship up to give them a sweeping view of the area. He thought about sensors and the jumper obligingly popped up holographic life sign and energy detector screens.

In the near distance he could see the building that they hoped was a repository, the dark stone standing out against the lighter grays of the sky, the storm-colored sea, and the rocky shore. It was about a mile from the Stargate, maybe a little more, standing in the center of a scattered complex of dark stone ruins on a flat rocky plain. The sea curved around it, bordered by a wide gravel beach. Inland, past the edge of the ruins, grew a sparse forest of tall slender trees with light green leaves. Nothing stirred, except a small flock of gray and white birds, startled into flight by the jumper's arrival. The screens confirmed it, showing only the little flickers that meant local fauna.

In the shotgun seat, Ford said, "See that? Somebody's bombed the crap out of it."

"Hell, yes," John agreed, sparing a look out the view port. "That's not encouraging."

This close, the damage was more evident than it had been on the MALP's camera. John could see big bomb craters in the surrounding ruins, and the spires in the onion dome towers had cracks or holes, the exposed girders bearing a distinct resemblance to skeletal remains. He grimaced, but it wasn't a surprise; the Wraith didn't like their food source to get uppity and fight back, and the Ancients had fought back until they had been nearly exterminated.

"The Wraith must have attacked here, perhaps after the Ancestors left," Teyla commented from the other jump seat, her tone regretful. "But still, you can see what a beautiful place it must have been."

McKay was less impressed. "No energy readings. And it's far more damaged than we thought, but the MALP's image was so pixelized, it could have been sitting in the middle of Miami Beach. This is probably a waste of time." He sounded bitterly disappointed.

"Oh, stop it." Splitting his attention between the port and the HUD, John banked the jumper back around toward the Stargate. It sat on a large elevated stone platform, about twenty meters high. At one time a stairway had led up to it, but now it was just a pile of rubble. The MALP had trundled itself off to the side, out of the path of the wormhole's blowback, its camera still pointed toward the ruins. John told McKay, "You're just still mad because you're not the one who made the new holo-thingy work."

"The new holo-thingy is broken, Major," McKay reminded him pointedly. "If it weren't, we might know exactly who attacked this place. And if this repository had anything like Atlantis' full defensive capacity, it had to be one hell of an attack."

"Grodin was right, there's no DHD," Ford pointed out, studying the area around the 'gate. "The Wraith must have destroyed it. Funny, we've never found a damaged 'gate like that before."

"My people never encountered damage like that either." Teyla added wryly, "Fortunately, since we would not have been able to return through the 'gate."

The jumpers came equipped with their own Dial Home Devices for the Stargates, right between the pilot's and copilot's seats, so the MALP's inability to locate the DHD hadn't been an impediment to coming here. "That's weird," John said, as the corollary occurred to him. "Why would anybody bother to blow up the DHD when the Ancients probably did most of their 'gate traveling in the jumpers?"

"Major, down there," Ford said suddenly. "They must have taken a direct hit."

John craned his neck, hearing Teyla make a startled exclamation. As the jumper came around the far side of the big complex, they could see that the outer wall of one wing was partly missing, revealing a mass of arched girders and partial stone walls. But it all looked a little too neat to be bomb damage. "No, I don't see any rubble. I don't think that section was finished."

Rodney snorted derisively. "That doesn't bode well for us finding a cache of ZPMs or another Ancient database."

"Cache, schmache," John said, though he thought McKay was probably right. "I'll be happy with one ZPM. So will you."

"That's true," Rodney admitted grudgingly.

John put the jumper down on a flat and relatively clear stretch of paving near the base of the repository's wall, in a section with terraces and a big doorway that seemed to be the main entrance. He lowered the ramp, and Teyla bailed out of the back first, walking out onto the cracked pavement of the plaza and pivoting for a look around, cradling her P-90. John joined her a moment later with Ford and McKay.

The air felt damp, smelled of sea salt, and was warm enough that the cool breeze off the beach was welcome. There was also a faint foul odor underneath, like rotten fish. The building itself stood on a slight rise, so they had a good view of the field of scattered stone ruins where it followed the shallow curve of the beach.

It had been a large city at some point. Many of the buildings still had slab roofs that were mostly intact, though any other features had been stripped away by time and the violence of the long-ago bombing. Some were just roofless stone boxes, some only the outlines of foundations, but John could see where the streets had been laid out, where there were open squares that might have been anything from outdoor meeting areas to shopping malls.

Teyla was studying the ruins, her brow furrowed. "It is very... I want to say empty, but that is rather obvious."

Ford was surveying the area with his binoculars. "The word you're looking for is 'spooky.'"

"Or 'creepy,'" John added, frowning. The dark oblongs of the empty doorways and windows looked too much like eyes that were staring at you. He turned toward the building, and glass, broken and ground nearly to powder, crunched under his boots; it gave him a weird feeling for a moment, that somebody-walking-over-your-grave sensation. He shrugged it off, glancing over at the others. McKay was studying the handheld Atlantean life sign detector, his hard mouth twisted into a grimace. John stepped in to look over his shoulder. "Anything?"

"No. Go away." McKay, who hated people reading over his shoulder, elbowed him.

"I am not sensing the presence of any Wraith," Teyla said, sounding thoughtful. She had the hereditary ability of some Athosians to know when the Wraith were nearby; it gave you just enough time to bolt for cover or the nearest Stargate and was a valued survival trait.

It wasn't an ability that the expedition had any scientific explanation for so far, but it was definitely real, and it had led to some initial suspicion of Teyla, at least on the part of

Sergeant Bates, whom Elizabeth had appointed head of city security. John preferred some level of paranoia in the person who held that job, but Bates had never trusted the Athosians in general and Teyla in particular, and it had gotten in the way. Even before Bates had accused Teyla of betraying them to the Wraith, Bates had made a snide comment about John wanting his new friend on his 'gate team. Unsure at the moment whether Bates meant Teyla or Rodney, John had pretended to think that Bates meant Ford, and told him not to talk that way about the lieutenant or he would put Bates on report, and things had gone downhill from there. Now Bates' paranoia just made John paranoid, mainly about Bates.

"No Wraith, that's always encouraging to hear," McKay muttered, still studying the detector. It wouldn't identify the presence of hibernating Wraith, just conscious ones. They had found that out the hard way.

"We're not going to have much time to look around before dark." John went to the end of the plaza and up a short set of steps to the big double doorway. Through it he could see a hall, littered with blown sand and powdered glass, quiet, dusty, and dead. No bodies, but then this was old destruction; any remains would have long ago rotted away. Still, it just looked like a place where John would have expected to see bodies.

The two doors had both been blasted off and lay on the paving. One had tumbled down so the outer side lay face up; it was unadorned except for some embossed circles, which didn't necessarily mean anything. The Ancients hadn't been big on brand names, or even just labeling stuff. He started inside, the others following.

Inside the big foyer, McKay paused to take some more readings, and John stopped beside him, frowning, trying to get a feel for the place.

At the far end a giant spiral stairway curved up into a large shaft. It was made of cracked slabs of stone and charred metal, still mostly intact, but John wouldn't have wanted to

chance it, not without climbing gear. Still, he would rather
trust stairs than the transporter/elevators, if there were any
and if there was anything left to power them. Behind the
stairway was a big triangular archway, opening into a passage toward the center of the repository. It had all been grand
and lofty once, but the dark gray stone of the walls and floor
was scarred where broken pieces of the stairway's elaborately
curled metal balustrade had shattered and slammed into it.

"I thought I had something for a second," Rodney muttered, glaring at the detector. "An energy signature."

John frowned at it too. "From where?"

"Couldn't tell, it wasn't there long enough for the detector
to get a direction." Rodney grimaced. "Let's try that way." He
nodded toward the triangular passage and gave a mock-shud-
der at the stairway. "Better than climbing that deathtrap."

"If we search this whole place, we're going to have to
tackle the deathtrap levels sooner or later," John pointed out.
He caught Ford's eye and, with a jerk of his head, told him to
watch their six.

"We?" McKay's brow furrowed, his attention still on the
detector. "We who, kemosabe?"

John led the way through the foyer and the big arch, Teyla
coming up to walk beside him. Ahead he could see the corridor opened into another large space, streaked with light and
shadow. John flicked on the light attached to his P-90.

They reached the triangular arch at the end of the corridor
and saw what lay beyond. John said softly, "Wow. I guess
they didn't get any time to pack."

The eight-sided chamber was huge and shadowy, bigger
than Atlantis' gate room, with three levels of open gallery
above it, all intact. At the highest level, the walls curved up,
meeting in a point overhead. Long diagonal open spaces had
once held skylights, the glass long shattered by the bombing,
allowing in dimming light from the overcast sky. Directly
across from the archway, a bunch of giant silvery tubes like
the top of an immense pipe organ stretched up and away,

vanishing into the ceiling high above. The place was littered with debris: broken consoles that had been ripped off their platforms, smashed crystals, twisted metal, bits and pieces of Ancient technology, scattered and smashed like a trash heap. On this level alone, a dozen archways led off in all directions, into dark rooms that seemed to be filled with odd-shaped equipment.

McKay looked up from the detector and his jaw dropped. "Oh, oh yes, this is going to take a while."

CHAPTER TWO

The sun was already setting over the sea when they took the jumper up and dialed the Stargate back to Atlantis to transmit a report to Elizabeth. After a three-way radio conversation between her, John, and Rodney, they decided to go back for the night and return with a larger team when it was morning on the planet. This Heliopolis, ruined or not, was in no danger of falling into the ocean.

The next morning, John put the jumper down in the plaza near the entrance again, saying, "Everybody out. Last one to Heliopolis II is a rotten egg."

Unbuckling her seat restraints, Teyla stared at him, smiling incredulously. "What?"

"It's an old joke," he explained.

"Don't worry if you don't get it, it's not funny." Rodney dug the life sign detector out of his pack and headed for the ramp.

Ford and the other two Marines exited first to walk a perimeter. Both Kinjo and Boerne had field experience on Bates' recon team, and Boerne had received the Ancient gene therapy and had been training to fly the jumpers. Locking down the console, John heard Boerne's startled "whoa" at the view of the repository and the ruined city spread out at the end of the plaza. Sitting in the back of the jumper, most of the team hadn't been able to get a good view of it from above. John followed McKay and Teyla out, while Kavanagh, Corrigan, and Kolesnikova were still picking up their packs.

John paused on the plaza, taking a deep breath. The sun was out this morning, and the sea gleamed blue, though the color was duller than the sea around Atlantis. It didn't have that crystal-clear morning of creation quality, of a world that had never been touched by pollution. Then the breeze turned and John winced and coughed. "Damn." *Atlantis doesn't have that, either.* The odor of rot was stronger today, worse than the dead fish smell usually associated with sea ports.

Dr. Kavanagh emerged from the puddlejumper, his expression torn between curiosity and wary disgust; John figured that was probably from the smell. Kavanagh was a tall thin man, with glasses, a high forehead, straight hair pulled back into a tail, and a sort of permanently pissed-off expression. He watched Rodney pace around with the life sign detector, asking sharply, "Anything?"

"Yes, there's an entire horde of Wraith about to descend on us, I just failed to mention it because I was waiting to be asked," Rodney snapped. "There's no life signs except us. I'm checking for energy readings now."

Kavanagh snapped back, "If you can't answer a simple question, McKay, then don't bother." Kavanagh wasn't exactly the best team player in the expedition, but sometimes biting McKay's head off was the only way to deal with him. John frankly preferred scientists who bit; McKay had some of the less aggressive science team members cowed into hysterical submission, not counting the ones with Stockholm Syndrome.

"Boys, please, we've only just arrived." Irina Kolesnikova shaded her eyes, looking up at the dark wall looming over them. She added worriedly, "Yes, the destruction is far more severe than the MALP indicated. We have a large job ahead of us." Kolesnikova was short and plump, with a round plain face and short dark hair. She also had a deep voice for a woman, sort of like Lauren Bacall with a thick Russian accent, and John could have listened to her all day. Like McKay and Boerne, she had had the ATA gene therapy. This was her and Kavanagh's first trip away from Atlantis; Corrigan was an archeologist and had been going out on 'gate missions with Sergeant Stackhouse's team.

All the scientists were dressed in tac vests over the blue science uniform shirts and tan pants, carrying a small pack for tools and other supplies. It was warm enough in the ruin for John just to wear his tac vest over a t-shirt, and he was leaving his BDU jacket in the jumper. He also carried a P-90, like Teyla, Ford, Boerne, and Kinjo. The scientists had been issued 9mm sidearms, though Corrigan and McKay were checked out on the P-90; McKay just didn't like to carry one, saying he could run faster without it.

John used the binoculars, scanning the ruined buildings around them, but there was no hint of movement. They hadn't taken the time to look at the city much yesterday. Today the contrast between the bright sunlight and those empty dark windows reminded him of something straight out of a post-nuclear-holocaust or disaster movie.

Teyla came up to stand beside him. Surveying the scene with a preoccupied expression, she said, "I am not sure I like this place, Major Sheppard."

"Oh, what's not to like?" John teased her. She lifted a brow at him, her mouth set in an unamused line, and he gave in. "Yeah, I know. It's going to be a logistical nightmare trying to explore this thing, even if there aren't any...monsters and whatnot. I wouldn't worry so much if it was just our team." He looked back at the group by the jumper, frowning a little. The last time he had gone on a mission with inexperienced scientists, it hadn't ended well. They had been investigating an Ancient Lagrangian Point satellite in orbit around the second planet in Atlantica's system and found a downed Wraith supply ship on the planet's surface. Unfortunately, there had been one last surviving Wraith, hibernating after having eaten all the stored humans on board and then all his Wraith friends. John and Rodney had managed to survive; the two scientists with them hadn't. "Kavanagh and Kolesnikova don't have any experience with field work, and keeping people from getting hurt in all that debris is going to be hard enough."

Teyla nodded. "And I admit, I am glad to find this place deserted. If there are people who would choose to make this sad ruin their home, I do not think I would like to meet them."

McKay arrived in time to hear Teyla's comment, juggling his equipment to check for power signatures and to keep one eye on the life sign detector. "In most movies, a place like this would come equipped with a horde of cannibalistic mutants, possibly with psychic powers."

"Oh, that's ridiculous." John snorted. "It would be zombies, flesh-eating zombies."

Teyla sighed a little and refused to take the bait.

Corrigan joined them, using a small camcorder to film the wall of the repository. He lowered it, frowning. "This is a little odd. The surrounding structures aren't Ancient, or at least not Atlantean. The Ancients might have built this place with help from another culture."

Ford, Boerne, and Kinjo returned from their quick survey of the immediate area. John lifted a brow at Ford, who shook his head, saying, "Nothing, Major."

"Good. Boerne, Kinjo, I want you out here with the jumper."

John caught a flicker of disappointment on Kinjo's face. He was Asian and looked nearly too young to be here; John knew he was one of the volunteers from the SGC, and probably hadn't been there very long before the chance to join the expedition had come up. Boerne was big, blond, and older, and if he was disappointed, he kept it hidden behind a very correct poker face. "Yes, sir."

McKay turned to yell at the other scientists, "Let's get a move on, people, we're on a schedule here!"

"Don't shout, McKay, we can hear you perfectly," Kolesnikova said, shouldering her pack and coming to join them with Kavanagh.

"Still nothing?" Kavanagh demanded, craning his head to look over McKay's shoulder at the sensor. "No energy readings?"

"No such luck. If there's anything still intact in there, it's been shut down." McKay eyed the repository grimly, apparently forgetting that he had just tried to eviscerate Kavanagh for asking nearly the same question earlier. "We're going to have to do this the hard way."

John nodded. He wasn't surprised; the hard way was the way they did everything. He made everybody do radio checks, then used the remote to tell the puddlejumper to close its ramp and set its cloak. The little ship obediently sealed itself, then vanished. The cloak would keep it invisible to the naked eye and to any non-Ancient instruments, and each team member had a remote to allow them to open the ramp and enter. Those precautions, plus leaving the two Marines on guard, made John reasonably sure the jumper would still be here when they came back—possible Wraith, flesh-eating zombies, and mutants notwithstanding. "Right, let's go," he said, and started up the steps to the entrance.

Once inside, McKay paused to take some more readings, and the others spread out a little to look around, Corrigan still filming, moving close to the walls to get detailed shots.

John led the way on through the foyer and into the big triangular corridor. The bright daylight outside and the broken skylights made it possible to see the big control area at the opposite end, and he could hear the scientists' awed reactions.

"Well, here it is," McKay said as they reached the entrance. He didn't sound as enthusiastic as John had expected. Normally something like this would have caused McKay to go into a near hysterical frenzy of excitement. He should almost be able to smell the ZPMs that possibly lurked in the bowels of the building's power systems. Instead he sounded almost resigned. "I'm still not getting any readings—most of this is probably too damaged to tell us much—but this has to be the control center for the structure."

"The only thing missing is the Stargate," Kavanagh put in. Corrigan was still filming, and Kolesnikova was already moving toward the intriguing heaps of dead machinery, both as eager as kids in a toy store. Kavanagh was frowning at a spiral design in the center of the floor, directly below the peak of the ceiling. It was too obscured by dust and debris for John to make out much, but it looked as though it was made of little silver tiles. Kavanagh shook his head. "The Heliopolis in our galaxy had an interior 'gate. The one here must have been removed at some point."

"You think?" McKay glanced up, intrigued, studying the chamber again. "It would have to be here in the center, and I'm not seeing anything like a well or a platform safety zone. Though it could be—"

"If there was a 'gate here, we'll find evidence of it," Kavanagh cut him off.

"Listen up." John raised his voice to make sure they all heard. They had gone over this with the new kids before leaving, but he wanted to emphasize the point. "Everybody remember the rules. Especially the one about not going anywhere alone. Stay in sight of me, Ford, or Teyla at all times. If you see something interesting in another room and need to take a closer look, tell one of us and we'll come with you. At the moment we have plenty of time, and there's no point in not practicing safe science."

"He means," Rodney added, digging through his vest pockets distractedly, "Don't do anything stupid and get killed. This is an alien planet, possibly filled with things that will try to eat you. Listen to the man who had a giant bug attached to his neck, he knows."

John rolled his eyes. *I am never living the giant bug thing down.* He asked Rodney, "Can you not bring that up every time we go out with new people?"

Rodney already had a power bar unwrapped and shoved into his mouth. He said around it, "It makes an excellent object lesson."

"We know what he means, McKay," Kavanagh snarled and started toward the nearest pile of debris.

Leaving Ford on guard in the central chamber, John and Teyla did a brief survey of the dozen or so connecting rooms. Their flashlights revealed nothing but more shattered glass and twisted metal, bits of the crystalline material the Ancients had used for their circuitry and wiring, the remains of incomprehensible machines, melted lumps of plastic-like substances and ceramics. Everything was so wrecked, John suspected that it wasn't just the random destruction of a bombing and a surface battle. It looked methodical and deliberate, as if someone had been careful to destroy every working console, to leave nothing intact. "The Wraith must have been very angry at this place," Teyla commented, sounding sober and a little regretful.

"We don't know it was the Wraith." John flicked a look at her, but it was too dark to read her expression. He was glad to hear she thought the destruction was unusual too, that it wasn't just his imagination. "But yeah, whoever it was definitely had anger issues."

They came back through the center chamber to find Ford keeping a wary eye out, Kolesnikova and Corrigan hard at work, and McKay and Kavanagh having a loud emphatic discussion that was probably another one of Kavanagh's attempts to challenge McKay's position as alpha male of the science team. John trusted one of the others to break it up if it progressed to the hitting stage. He decided to risk a set of wide stone stairs that still seemed stable and do a quick sweep of the upper galleries.

There was no sign that anything alive had been in here for decades, despite the open access through the doorway and the broken skylights. Up on these levels, an undisturbed layer of dirt and dust coated nearly every surface, made thick and corrosive by the moisture and salt in the air. There wasn't even anything like bird or rat droppings, no spider webs or other signs of insect life. The local fauna seemed to be carefully avoiding this place. It was quiet, except for his and Teyla's footsteps and an occasional exclamation or clatter from below. *Creepy*, John thought, and felt glad to rejoin the others on the main level.

Once they were back down in the center chamber, Teyla moved off to tell Ford they hadn't found anything, and John went over to Rodney.

He was crouched down, already half-buried in the center control station near the giant organ-pipe-tubes, taking what was left of it apart. John knew he was trying to get some idea of what the connections to the power system were like, hoping for a clue to where a ZPM might be hiding. McKay was also assembling a little pile of useful spare parts to drag back home to Atlantis.

"Hey, you think this damage looks deliberate?" John asked him.

Rodney snapped automatically, "If I look busy it's because I am!" Then John's question must have penetrated, because he pulled his head out of the console to stare up at him. "What, you think it was accidental? Somebody tripped and accidentally pushed the 'bomb our own city back to the stone age' button?"

"No, no, I do not." John held onto his patience. "I mean, like somebody came through here with a crowbar or the high-tech equivalent and made sure nobody would ever be able to use any of this stuff again."

McKay sat back on his heels, poking into his pack for another tool. "Wrecking whatever human technology they can find still intact is probably standard operating procedure for the Wraith, Major. What are you getting at?"

"I know, but this looks different." John gestured helplessly, giving up. He didn't know what he meant.

He left Rodney to get on with it and paced, trying to keep an eye on everybody, feeling a little like a hen with too many chicks. The back of his neck kept itching, but he didn't see how anybody or anything could be watching them. Ford was helping Kolesnikova shift some twisted pieces of metal to get to the crystals and circuits underneath, Corrigan was making notes on his PDA, and Teyla stood across the big chamber, watching the corridors that led off into unlit areas. She didn't look like she was having a great time, but it wasn't like she wouldn't have mentioned it if she started sensing Wraith. And— *Where the hell is Kavanagh?*

Gritting his teeth, John keyed his radio on and said into the headset, "Dr. Kavanagh, come in, please."

He heard a distant crackle from the headset, then nothing. *Crap.* "Kavanagh, come in."

McKay looked up, frowning. "What? What's wrong?"

Frustrated, John took a moment to say, "Rodney, is your name Kavanagh? Then shut up." The others had heard him on the radio and were starting to look around. He called, "Teyla, Ford, did you see where Kavanagh went?"

Ford started across the chamber. "He was right over there, sir, looking at the stuff over in that back— There he is."

Kavanagh was coming out of the shadowy passage to a side room, his face distracted. John waved Ford off, crossing over to say pointedly, "Uh, Dr. Kavanagh, why didn't you answer your radio?"

Kavanagh looked up, startled. "Did you call me? I didn't hear it." He fumbled his headset off. "It was working earlier."

"Yeah, I know." John looked past Kavanagh. The passage the man had come out of led to a room with side areas sectioned off by empty metal panels that had probably once held colored glass. The only thing interesting about it was a round swirly design in the floor. John was pretty sure Corrigan had already filmed anything in here that looked like a decoration or a symbol. "Look, you need to stay in sight at all times. I know this place seems safe—"

Kavanagh blinked, his glasses reflecting the dim light. "Sorry. I was only gone a moment. I thought I heard something, but it must have been my imagination."

John let out his breath. He had cleared that room himself earlier, something Kavanagh probably knew and was refraining from pointing out. "Right. Just...be careful about that."

John sent Ford back to the jumper to get another headset

for Kavanagh. When that was taken care of and everyone had gone back to work, Ford pulled John aside to say, "Sorry I lost him, sir. I'm used to keeping an eye on Dr. McKay, and Dr. Kavanagh moves faster than he does."

Rodney, who had a preternatural ability to know when people were talking about him, popped out from under a wrecked console and glared at them.

"It's okay," John told Ford. "Just stay sharp."

Everyone kept working and they expanded their explorations, making their way across much of the ground floor, with cautious forays up into the more stable upper levels. Corrigan confirmed that some of those levels had unfinished sections, where construction had stopped at some point before the bombing had occurred. After a couple of hours they took a break, going back out to the plaza to let the scientists regroup and to refill water bottles and pass out MREs. The day was still warm and pleasant, and they sat down on the steps up to the repository's outer door. It was a good spot, allowing a view of the beach and the sea, and the distant Stargate.

As they ate, the dust from knocking around inside the ruin was making everybody sniffle, even John, who didn't normally have allergies. He felt it was probably because he had gotten too used to Atlantis, with its automatic cleaning systems and fresh air.

Poking at her MRE thoughtfully, Kolesnikova said, "Have you boys got any idea yet what this place was for? It can't be simply a repository. They had more equipment in that one room than in the operations tower at Atlantis, systems that must have supported weapons, communications. Yet the 'gate is well outside the complex. This looks very much like a support or control center for something, but for what?"

Kavanagh's brow furrowed. "I'm finding a great deal of monitoring systems, possibly meant for the unfinished upper levels of the towers, though with so much damage it's hard to tell." He seemed uncharacteristically hesitant, especially for a man who regularly got in Elizabeth Weir's face about how

she was running the expedition and who had nearly as practiced a turn for tearing people's heads off as Rodney. "I think
this facility was meant to include a hospital."

"Abandoned hospitals are inherently creepy," John said.
Teyla lifted a puzzled brow, Ford nodded emphatically, and
McKay looked at him as though he wanted to ask if John had
forgotten to take his lithium or something. Everyone else was
too busy considering Kavanagh's suggestion to notice John's
comment.

"Atlantis wouldn't need an offsite hospital for its own
inhabitants, of course," Kolesnikova said slowly, thinking it
over. "But if they meant this to be a meeting place for many
cultures—and that large space in the unfinished section certainly seemed intended to be an auditorium—a hospital may
have been part of the services provided. Or if this world is
perhaps inhabited—or was inhabited—by another human culture..."

"We didn't pick up any communications from the puddlejumper, and neither did the MALP," Corrigan pointed out.
"But if the people of this world have been bombed back
to primitive conditions by the Wraith, they might not have
recovered enough to have radio traffic yet."

McKay eyed Kavanagh narrowly but didn't comment on
the hospital theory. The word John had gotten earlier from
Ford was that Kavanagh had found some intact control crystals in one of the pieces of equipment near the center shaft
and that McKay hadn't found any; McKay was undoubtedly
still constructing his game plan for getting them away from
the other scientist. McKay asked Corrigan, "You still think
this place is Ancient?"

Everybody stared, even Boerne and Kinjo, who had been
having a separate conversation about city duty shifts. Corrigan frowned doubtfully, as if he suspected McKay of setting him up for something. "The writing on the consoles is
Ancient, and so is the design of the equipment. The building itself resembles Heliopolis. But...". He shrugged, looking

around again.

"It doesn't look like Atlantis, at least from inside that main control area," Ford said, glancing at the big doors behind them. "Even in the technical areas, Atlantis is made to look pretty. This is all just mostly functional."

"I agree," Teyla said. She had finished her meal first because McKay had talked her out of the brownie and was neatly tucking the remnants back into their foil bag. "This place does not have the same..." She hesitated, looking thoughtful. "The same feel as Atlantis. I do not think the Ancestors were here for very long."

"Well, part of that could be because the structure is unfinished," Corrigan told her, "But that triangular archway, the way the walls are put together, the colored material in those skylights—those are Atlantean design. It could be another branch of Ancient culture—"

McKay shook his head. "I doubt that. The technology that created that equipment was inferior. It isn't integrated with the building's superstructure in the same way the Ancients would do it. A lot of it was added after construction. And Irina's right, there's too much of it for just a repository and meeting area—far more than was recorded in even the brief examination of the original Heliopolis conducted by SG-1." He sniffed, possibly in disdain, possibly from the dust. "I think this place was taken over before it was completed by scavengers who had access to Ancient technology."

Kavanagh looked annoyed. "What kind of evidence have you seen for that?"

Kolesnikova shook her head. "I don't think we've seen enough to make that call. Why would a culture advanced enough to understand and use this technology need to scavenge?"

"What do you think, Major?" Ford asked.

"It's sort of Atlantean. And sort of not," John admitted.

"Oh, that's helpful." Rodney snorted. "I'm glad we have a consensus." He leaned toward the spaghetti MRE John had been picking at. "Are you going to finish that?"

"Yes." John shifted it out of range.

They finished up, everybody packing the remains of the meal away into the trash container on the jumper, to be taken back to Atlantis for recycling. This was part environmental policy, part safety; it would be dangerous to leave indications of their recent presence to any Wraith that might come sniffing around after them. John always found the practice a little depressing; it made him feel like the rabbits in *Watership Down*, trying to keep from luring foxes to their burrow, helpless to defend themselves against a stronger enemy. *War and Peace* had its share of issues, but he was glad he had brought it to Atlantis instead.

Corrigan wanted to do a survey of the city ruins, so John sent Boerne and Kinjo with him, both men seeming glad to have something constructive to do besides watch the inert Stargate and the empty sky. John scanned that sky one more time, then went inside with the others, heading back through the cavernous foyer toward the control area.

As they passed it, John cast a thoughtful look at the big and apparently unstable spiral staircase. From its position in the building, it probably led up into the damaged spires, which the galleries above the control area weren't connected to. If nobody turned up any clues to where a ZPM might be soon, they would have to search up there, and it might be better if he and Teyla started on that now. But he found himself still reluctant to separate the group to that extent, even with everyone wearing a headset, even with Boerne and Kinjo outside, even with Ford standing watch over the others. *Just because the last time you left a couple of scientists on their own Abrams got eaten and Gall ended up offing himself in front of Rodney,* he thought bitterly. *Yeah, let's make that mistake again.*

McKay, walking along beside him, still messing with his pack, muttered, "This is a waste of time."

Surprised, John stopped him at the top of the corridor while the others continued into the control area. "Hey, what's with you? Why are you so pissy now about exploring this place? You were as enthusiastic as Corrigan and Kavanagh when we saw the image on the MALP."

"Pissy?" McKay lifted his brows, but John just continued to watch him inquiringly, and he finally sighed. He admitted, "Okay, fine. I was as gung-ho as the rest of you at first, but I just wasn't expecting— The state of disrepair—" He stopped, mouth twisted as he thought it over. "I have no idea. Maybe I'm coming down with something."

"Oh." John nodded, and decided reluctantly that he had started the conversation, he might as well finish it. "I asked, because I was gung-ho too when we got here, and now I'm creeped out, like I'm walking in a vandalized graveyard, and I have no idea why." He jerked his chin at Teyla, who was watching them with a puzzled expression. "And you're acting the same way. As soon as we got here, you were talking about the flesh-eating zombies."

"That was you," Teyla corrected firmly. "I do not even know what flesh-eating zombies are. Nor do I wish to know, so please do not explain."

"I know that," John persisted, "But you said you didn't want to meet anybody who'd choose to live here, and that started the whole zombie conversation."

"I take back my earlier agreement," Rodney said unhelpfully, "I think you're insane."

Teyla tilted her head, looking thoughtful. "Many people must have died in the attack that destroyed this place. Why shouldn't we feel as if we walk on their graves?"

"Because they're not here." John gestured broadly, taking in the big shadowy room beyond. Kolesnikova was getting tools out of her pack, and Kavanagh had moved on to the center of the room, back to the spot where it looked like a Stargate should be but wasn't. "It's not like we're finding any kind of human remains. We've been to lots of ruins from before the last Wraith culling, and this is really no different. Except in the creepiness factor. Which is fricking off the scale."

"Do you have a point?" McKay demanded.

"Yes! No." John gestured in frustration. "My point is that I know for a fact that the three of us wanted to come here and investigate this place, and as soon as we started, we all changed our minds and thought it was a bad idea." He shook his head, gesturing helplessly. "It's oddly...odd. That's all."

"All right, all right." McKay considered it, or at least pretended to consider it, it was hard for John to tell. "If that isn't just a sign that we three have a more highly developed sense of survival than the others, what is it? What does it indicate?"

John sighed. "I don't know. If I knew, I wouldn't need to irritate myself by asking for your opinion."

"Oh, well, thank you, Major! Here I was—"

Metal cracked and groaned and the floor vibrated under John's feet. He swore, lifting the P-90, looking frantically around. From across the control chamber, Kavanagh shouted, jumping up from the console he had been digging into, staring down. John ran toward him, skidding to a halt when he saw what had caused the disturbance.

The spiral design in the center of the chamber floor was moving, becoming three-dimensional as the little metal tiles forming it shifted fluidly. The whole floor was still vibrating, making the glass and metal debris jump and dance. Something groaned again below their feet, and the spiral began to sink into the floor.

Standing at John's elbow, McKay glared at Kavanagh, his mouth twisted in annoyance. "What did you do?"

John wasn't thrilled either. "Some warning would have been nice, Doctor."

Teyla and Ford watched the spiral uneasily, Kolesnikova a few steps behind them. Kavanagh shook his head, his eyes still on the metal sinking into the floor, his gaze rapt. "I wasn't sure it was really here, if the power source was still active. If

I was...imagining it..."

The groaning rumble of metal parts undisturbed for ages was growing louder, and John wasn't sure he had heard right. "What?" he said, having to raise his voice over the din. "Why did you think you were imagining it?"

"I was imagining what?" Distracted, Rodney stepped sideways, moving along the edge of the shaft, craning his neck to watch the spiral's progress.

"I wasn't talking to you," John shouted back, "I was—"

"Wait." Rodney straightened up suddenly, looking at John. "It occurs to me that something may come out of here that could kill us."

John swore and yelled, "Fall back, now!"

Everybody scrambled back toward the shelter of the main entrance corridor. Kavanagh didn't move immediately but came along readily enough when Teyla took his arm and pulled him away. That was another good thing about civilians used to dealing with alien technology, John reflected, backing rapidly toward the corridor and making sure everyone was clear—when you yelled *Run!* no one stopped to ask why.

John halted in the shelter of the archway. The metallic groaning and thumping continued, and McKay looked at the detector again, chewing his lip. "Now I'm getting power readings," he said, sounding peeved about it.

"Well, I assumed this wasn't some kind of Rube Goldberg device," John told him, watching the effect warily. He couldn't see much from here, but it sounded like the spiral had originally been an elevator platform, and was now ponderously lowering itself down its shaft. Maybe Kavanagh had been right in the first place, and this had been a Stargate operations chamber, with the 'gate itself in a safety well on a lower level.

McKay spared John a glare. "If there's shielding in this floor and no active power sources in any of the equipment we found, how did Kavanagh manage to activate it?"

Kavanagh stood a few steps away, staring intently at the

sinking floor. John pointed out, "You could ask him."

"I'm thinking out loud!" Rodney snapped. Asking Kava-nagh for information was apparently a fate worse than death, to be resorted to only under the most extreme conditions.

Which meant John had to do it. "Kavanagh, how did you find this thing?"

He shook his head. "It was an accident. I must have trig-gered a circuit that still had power, even if it wasn't showing up on the sensors."

The rumbling stopped. McKay consulted the detector again, brow furrowed. "Still no life signs. I am getting low-level power signatures."

"Right." Not taking his eyes off the dust cloud above the spiral, John said, "Teyla?"

"Yes, Major Sheppard?"

"We're still negative on sensing any Wraith, correct?"

Teyla sounded grim. "If that changes, Major, you will be the first to know."

"Just checking. Everybody stay where they are."

Moving forward cautiously, John heard Kolesnikova mut-ter, "I want to be the first to know, I need more time for run-ning than the rest of you."

Ford told her, "Don't worry, we'll take care of you."

It was the right thing to say, and Ford sounded like he believed it; John just wished they could make those kind of guarantees. Kolesnikova had told him once that it was unlucky to be Russian and to be in the Stargate program. When John had finished reading the SGC reports he had understood why. Most of the scientists, techs, and field operatives in the origi-nal Russian program had been killed. The ones who had come over to work in the SGC hadn't fared well either.

John got close enough to look down into the spiral's shaft. It was round and carved from the rock substructure, with bands of a dull-gray metallic material. He reached the edge, where he could shine the light on his P-90 directly down, and saw the spiral had come to rest about fifty feet below. Small lights gave off a faint blue glow. They looked like emergency lights, meant to function under low power and guide the inhabitants out in a blackout. The air coming up from the shaft was cool and dry, laced with a musty odor. Oddly, it carried that hint of rot underneath that John could smell outside. He had thought it came from dead fish or other sea life washed up along the beach, but maybe not.

Shining the light around, John saw there was actually a ladder, set in under the edge of the floor, in the wall of the shaft. It was narrow, partly carved from the rock, with metal rails and treads, and it looked stable. *But that first step is still a killer.* This was obviously meant for emergency use only. "Guys," John said, "We got a bunker here."

CHAPTER THREE

After the Genii, John regarded all bunkers with suspicion on principle, but the detector still wasn't finding any life signs, just the low and intermittent power readings. With that evidence, it wasn't likely anybody had survived down there; or if they had, they had long since departed the area, and maybe the planet.

John sent Ford back to the jumper for some climbing rope and carabiners, then the others stood or crouched around the opening as he, John, and Teyla rigged a safety line. They had lost enough expedition members to dangers that couldn't be avoided; John would be damned before he lost somebody because of a stupid fall.

"That's a waste of time," Kavanagh said, arms folded, his face tight with impatience.

Saving John the trouble, Rodney said, "There's no way you're getting me or anybody else—which includes you, whether you like it or not—on that insanely narrow ladder without something to grab on to when it inevitably gives way."

"There could be a ZPM down there. A half a dozen ZPMs," Kavanagh snarled. "We need to get down there and find them."

His expression deeply sardonic, McKay drew breath to answer, but Kolesnikova cut him off by pointing out mildly, "There might be a hundred ZPMs, but they aren't going anywhere in the next fifteen minutes."

John checked the line where it was secured to a heavy pillar supporting the gallery. He still didn't like splitting the team, but in this case there wasn't much choice. Besides, he could tell Kolesnikova was nervous of the whole idea, and while John was willing to drag Rodney protesting and predicting their imminent deaths into these kinds of situations, he wasn't willing to do it to the other civilians. At the moment, when they didn't even know if there was anything useful down there, this was for volunteers only. "Ford, you'll stay up here with Kolesnikova. Keep up the regular updates with Boerne's group."

A flicker of disappointment crossed Ford's face. The kid was the poster boy for gung-ho; he actually wanted to go down into the dark hole to see what was there and hopefully kick its ass. But he said sharply, "Yes, sir."

Kolesnikova just nodded, relieved. John could tell she had been willing to go if ordered to, but was more than glad to stay up here. "You will call us if there is anything of interest?"

Rodney leaned over to look down the shaft, his mouth set with distaste. "Call, scream, whichever seems more appropriate at the moment."

Climbing down one by one with the safety line clipped to a harness was slow but uneventful. John went first and checked out the bottom of the shaft with the P-90's light while he waited for the others. There was a big space at the bottom, with eight corridors leading off it. The walls were dark gray, metal bonded to rough stone, with the little blue globe lights set high in the ceiling. It was warm, but the air wasn't as stale as it should have been; some kind of recycling system must still be minimally functional. The odor of rot came and went, drifting on some barely existent breeze. As McKay reached the bottom and extracted himself from his harness, John said, "Searching this place may take a little longer than we thought."

"Always look on the bright side, Major." McKay came over to join him at the entrance to the nearest corridor, getting the detector out of a vest pocket. He checked it again, then rolled his eyes. "Except there is no bright side. Power signatures are still present but intermittent. If there is a ZPM here, it's turned off, drained, running on minimal capacity, or actively trying to play hide and seek with us. We're going to have to find it the hard way."

"Color me surprised." John tapped his headset. "Ford, can you hear me?" No answer. "Crap." He moved back into the shaft, into the fall of light from above. Kavanagh was nearly down, and Teyla was starting her climb, moving lightly and easily down the awkward ladder. "Ford?" he tried again.

The radio responded immediately, "Here, Major."

"It looks like the shielding up there is interfering with our communications. We'll come back here and check in on the hour."

"Yes, sir. Be careful down there."

McKay picked a corridor before Kavanagh could dispute the selection. John led the way, putting Teyla at their six. "The construction is more primitive down here than on the upper levels," Kavanagh pointed out, as John moved his light over the walls and ceiling.

"More support for my theory." McKay said this in a little singsong, calculated to drive Kavanagh insane.

It worked. "Your theory is crap," Kavanagh snapped, his eyes on his own detector. "It could have been built later, when their resources started to fail."

"Kids, don't make me separate you," John said, keeping his attention on the corridor ahead. "Or beat you unconscious." Privately, he thought Rodney was right. The blue light gave everything a spooky glow, but their flashlights showed that the metallic material in the walls was rougher, with rivets and seams. There were gray-green patches that might be some kind of mold, creeping in wherever the metal met stone.

"It is very odd," Teyla said from behind them. "There is just something that is not..."

Something that's not right, John finished. *Yeah, that too.* He found himself straining to listen, but all he could hear were their own movements and the whisper of air in ancient vents.

About twenty paces down the corridor the walls widened into a large circular chamber, with the walkway forming a bridge across a lower level. The platform held a couple of big work stations, the screens shattered and the metal melted from a blast by an energy weapon. Warily, John flashed the P-90's light across the level below, but all he could see were closed metal doors, three on each side.

Kavanagh immediately went to the first console, wrenching the top off and asking Teyla to hold a light for him. "Don't touch anything without gloves," he told them.

"No, really?" McKay said, playing his flashlight over the rubble. "I'll try to resist the urge to lick the debris."

John looked down into the well, at the nearest door. Something about this setup gave him a bad feeling. Maybe it was for storage. Volatile materials, something else that needed to be monitored. He looked at Kavanagh, intent on the damaged equipment, Teyla holding the light but still surveying the room warily, and Rodney, who was balancing his flashlight with the detector. The blue light washed out color and bleached skin, making them all look like they had drowned in cold water. John said, "Let's check this out."

Rodney just nodded grimly.

The metal steps creaked as they climbed down. John picked a door at random, standing back ready to fire, waiting for McKay to open it. But the circular handle was too stiff for McKay to wrench open on his own. John still felt uneasy about taking both hands off his weapon to help, even with no life signs on McKay's detector. He was glad Teyla was up on the gallery above them, keeping watch.

John had to put his shoulder to the handle, with McKay hauling from the other side before it squeaked hesitantly into motion. "I saw this in a movie once," Rodney said through gritted teeth. "Everybody died."

"I saw this in fifty movies, and it's never a great idea," John told him, his voice grating as he struggled with the wheel. He felt the click as it finally gave way and the heavy door shifted a little.

McKay backed away as John swung the P-90 up and pulled the door open. He flashed the light on a little cell, maybe ten by ten, bare stone walls streaked with mold.

The air was dead and stale inside, but it had been so many years the odor of rot was just a ghost, barely enough to make John wince. He was pretty sure he knew what the crumpled little bundle in the corner was.

He stepped inside reluctantly, pausing to note there was no mechanism to open the door, no handle, button, or lever, from the inside. Moving closer he saw the skull and the rib bones, lying in a pile of residue that was all that was left of the rest of the body, flesh and clothing rotted together. "Don't touch it, or get too close," Rodney cautioned him from the door, low-voiced. "Sometimes there's still bacteria, even after years of being sealed in like this. You could get a fungus."

John had seen enough, anyway. It was human, or close enough to make no difference. He stepped back out and pulled the door shut again. The blue emergency lights showed him Rodney's expression, his mouth twisted down, his eyes grim. Rodney said, "This was not a hospital."

Kavanagh was leaning over the gallery rail above, demanding, "What did you find?"

They found corridors, and rooms with more broken equipment and blasted consoles, floors littered with glass and broken ceramics, giant pipes emerging from the ceilings and disappearing into the floors, sealed chambers filled with empty racks for little containers, other rooms that might have been frozen storage. There were also what looked like living quarters, or at least rooms with the stark remnants of metal furniture and no locks on the doors. And there were lots of little cells with monitoring equipment outside; after the first few, they stopped checking for bodies. As Rodney pointed out, it wasn't like they were going to find anybody alive and waiting to be rescued. The ones they saw that were empty, the doors standing open, were a relief. Imagining what was behind the closed doors was in some ways worse than actually seeing it. "We should be finding bones out in these corridors, too," Kavanagh had said at one point, "But there's nothing. That's anomalous."

"Everybody who wasn't in a cell could have escaped," John had suggested. "Or the people who were locked up were already dead when the attack started. Like the World War II concentration camps, where they'd start trying to gas the prisoners faster when the Allies—"

"Yes, I'm aware of that practice, Major, and thanks so much for the image." McKay had glared at him. "Why don't you just hold the flashlight up under your chin and make spooky noises while you're at it?"

And Kavanagh had said sharply that they didn't know these were cells, they could have been quarantine rooms for plague victims, and Teyla had said "World War *two*?" in an appalled and incredulous voice, and the discussion had veered off into unproductive areas.

They had also found stairwells leading down to even lower levels, telling John that the place was far more complex than they had hoped. The first hour stretched into four, then six, then eight, and John returned to the shaft periodically to check in and let the others know they were still alive. He could tell from Ford's voice that the younger man no longer regretted being left behind.

That intermittent odor of rot and decay was starting to get on John's nerves, especially since, in the few cells they had opened, the remains had been too desiccated to have much of an odor at all. It made him wonder just what the hell they hadn't found yet. John had firmly banished all thoughts of zombie movies, and McKay didn't bring the subject up either. Kavanagh was too intent on the search, and just didn't seem like the kind of guy who would have been into cheap horror flicks. Teyla was culturally immune. Though she admitted that she would rather be doing just about anything else, including helping Halling and the other Athosians build latrines in their new village on Atlantica's mainland.

Now she and Kavanagh were checking out the lower part of a large room full of equipment that looked like it was for synthesizing something. John and McKay, having finished their section, waited on the gallery above.

Groaning under his breath, McKay sat down on the metal floor to consult his PDA. He was making a map as they went along, trying to deduce where the main power generator, whatever it was, might be. McKay and Kavanagh had told each other at least ten times that nothing except a big naquadah generator array or a ZPM could have kept these emergency lights powered for so many years. They had been trying to identify main power conduits, testing them to see which were still hot, and trying to figure out where the cables were coming from. It allowed them to mostly skip the areas where the emergency lights weren't working, except when one of their flashlights caught something Kavanagh or McKay found fascinating and they just had to go explore.

John sat on his heels beside McKay, rolling his head to ease the tension in his neck. The air still wasn't stale, but the smell was getting steadily worse. It made him wonder how many people had been down here when the surface bombing started, if the shielding had protected them or just delayed the inevitable. From the peculiar taint in the air, he figured it was the latter. Of course, considering what they could have been doing to the people in those locked cells, that might have been no loss.

And your imagination is out of control, John told himself grimly, trying to shake off his mood. He was beginning to think it was time to call it a night. According to his watch, it should be getting dark up on the surface. The MALP's telemetry data had told them that it was summer in this hemisphere and that the night should only last about seven hours. Besides, his stomach was starting to grumble, and McKay, who had hypoglycemia, had bummed the last power bar a half-hour ago.

McKay put the PDA away in his pack and sat back with a sigh, looking at the others below. "Kavanagh might just get a gold star for working and playing well with others today after all."

John eyed Kavanagh. Once they had gotten down here, the man had settled down and concentrated on the task. At the moment he was examining something deep inside the remains of a dead work station, addressing an occasional remark to Teyla, who was holding the light for him. They seemed to be getting on well enough, probably because Teyla didn't fall into any of the normal categories of military, civilian scientist, or technical support personnel that Kavanagh was used to dealing with. He treated her like a respected professional in another field. "He gives Elizabeth enough trouble."

"Yes, that, of course, but he's usually very cautious when it comes to risking lives," Rodney said. "His own, true, but also everyone else's. Especially stupid unnecessary risks, like climbing down that ladder without a safety rope. And triggering that power surge that opened the shaft. He had no idea what that was. Never mind the possibility of electrocution, he didn't know what it was going to do. It could have been an intruder destruction sequence. Elizabeth could be sending somebody with a bag to collect what was left of us right now."

John pretended to consider it. "I don't think they'd use a bag. I think they'd be more respectful than that."

Rodney gave him a withering look. John relented and added seriously, "Maybe he's overcompensating. From what Grodin said, Elizabeth did practically hand him his ass." John and Rodney hadn't been there to see it. That had been during the infamous bug-neck incident, when their puddlejumper had been stuck halfway through a Stargate and they had only had the thirty-eight minute duration of the active wormhole to figure out a solution. Kavanagh had thought the jumper would explode, and the force would be transferred through the wormhole and take out the 'gate room. Somehow, in all the tension of the moment, this had led to a public dressing down from Weir.

Whatever Kavanagh had been on about, John didn't think Elizabeth should have lowered the boom in public. John had had more than his share of public dressing downs, and it wasn't a command style he preferred. It was only going to cause more problems, but when it had happened Elizabeth must have been feeling the time pressure intensely. Apparently she had been stiff with Halling about something too, and he was easy-going to a fault.

But whatever had happened, John wasn't sure he felt comfortable pointing fingers about it. He wasn't exactly the sterling example of good chain-of-command relationships at the best of times, and he had made more than his share of mistakes. Big mistakes. "You know Kavanagh's still chafing. He's just going to have to get over it."

Rodney was frowning thoughtfully. "Yes. But the man did a stint in the SGC, I can't believe he never had his ass handed to him before. That place is practically the ass-handing capital of the world."

"I got that impression." Ford and many of the others had been part of the SGC, but John had first found out about the Stargate program in Antarctica, about fifteen minutes after nearly crashing a helicopter with General O'Neill as a passenger while being chased by a stray energy drone accidentally launched from the Earth Atlantis outpost. His military career had been fraught enough that he really hadn't been all that surprised by it. He also thought the SGC needed a sign outside that said *You don't have to be crazy to work here, but it helps*. Of course, as someone who was for the moment permanently stationed in Atlantis, he wasn't in any position to criticize.

Below, Kavanagh finally extracted himself from the tangle of wrecked equipment. John pushed to his feet to call down, "Hey, we need to pack it in for tonight. It's getting dark up top."

Kavanagh stared up at him for a moment, squinting in the dim blue light, his expression blank. Then he said, "Oh, yes, of course."

They made camp outside the repository, in a half-ruined structure facing the plaza where the cloaked puddlejumper rested. It was made out of cut stone blocks, its roof one big still-stable slab. There was a little crumbling around where the door had originally been, but otherwise it was mostly intact.

Corrigan was saying, "I found some indications that part of the city might have been in place before construction started on the repository, but most of it is about the same age. We're not looking at an intrusion into a long-term occupation site." He had found writing carved into some of the buildings, some in Ancient and some that was completely unfamiliar. Teyla hadn't recognized it, either. There had also been some decorative carving, mostly worn down to nothing by the weather, just a few ghostly traces of leaves and vines. Corrigan continued, "I think the Ancients were building this place with the help of another group. Whether they were humans or not, whether they were native to this planet or not, I have no idea."

They were sitting around a battery lamp, the bedrolls and other supplies for the night stacked against the wall, the life sign detector out to make sure nothing crept up on them in the dark. John would have preferred a campfire, but it was really too warm for one, and the lamp was an adequate if less comforting substitute. They could hear the sea from here, the distant roar of the waves rolling up the rocky beach; after months of living in Atlantis, it was a deceptively homey sound.

Listening to Corrigan, Kolesnikova had been drawing patterns in the dirt with a finger. "I think we are all hoping, after what our friends found down in the bunker, that the people who did that were not the Ancients." She looked up, regarding them all seriously. "Are we not?"

"Yeah. We are. At least I am." John looked at Teyla, who just nodded soberly.

Kavanagh's mouth was set in a grim line. "I still believe what we found was part of a hospital. And considering that, there may have been a pressing need for it, which explains why it was built inside the repository."

John had settled across the battery lamp from Rodney, so he had a good view of the elaborate eye roll, the rubbing the hands over the face, and the exasperated gesture to whatever deity might be listening to grant something, possibly patience or strength, to deal with Kavanagh's boneheaded stupidity. At least, that was John's interpretation of what Rodney was doing over there.

"But with the Stargate, this place is only moments away from Atlantis," Teyla said pointedly. "If these people needed medical help, why not take them back there?"

"Whether it was built by the Ancients or not, the underground was not a hospital, or not just a hospital," Kolesnikova told her. "There are devices similar to the quarantine system in Atlantis, rooms that must have been laboratories, also the remains of defensive capabilities, of weapons manufacture."

With a snort, McKay picked up the pack of MREs, digging through it and holding the bags up to read the labels by the lamplight. "A hospital, quarantine laboratories, and weapons development. What does that sound like to everybody, dead people in little cells aside?"

"Biological warfare," John said, setting a water bottle aside. He saw Ford exchange a troubled expression with Teyla, and Kinjo gazed out the empty doorway toward the repository. The òthers just looked grim.

Kavanagh frowned. "Not necessarily."

"Oh, please." Still flipping through the MREs, McKay threw him a sour look. "You've been theorizing in advance of your data since we got here."

"Atlantis has literally miles of laboratory space," Kavanagh said, his voice acidic. "Why would they need to put a biological weapons development laboratory out here, in a structure meant to house a meeting place for other races or other human civilizations?"

"They didn't," McKay told him. He had finally selected an MRE and proceeded to rip the package open. "True, the working laboratory space on Atlantis is phenomenal. If they were pursuing a bioagent to use against the Wraith, we'll find it there. This just supports my point that the lower levels were not built by the Ancients, or at least not the Atlantean Ancients."

It was Kavanagh's turn to roll his eyes. Kolesnikova rescued the supply pack from Rodney and briskly started to pass out the bagged meals, putting an end to the conversation with, "Let's speak of something else while we eat, shall we?"

John thought that was the best idea he had heard all evening, and cut off Kavanagh's attempt at a rebuttal by turning to Teyla and explaining loudly what chicken tetrazzini was and why she probably wouldn't like it.

Earlier, John had taken the puddlejumper up to dial the Stargate back to Atlantis and transmit his report, updating Elizabeth on what they had found, their inconclusive conclusions so far, and what Rodney and Kavanagh had said about the possibility of finding a ZPM. He had practically heard her reserving judgment over the suggestion of an Ancient facility that might have experimented on humans. And she must have read more in John's voice than he had intended, because she had asked, "How much more time do you think we should devote to this?"

John had let his breath out. "At least another couple of days. Seriously, from what McKay and the others are turning up, there's every chance there is a ZPM down there somewhere. What state it's in is another story. But if we can't find it in the next couple of days, I'd recommend bringing in another team for a longer stay. We just can't pass up this opportunity."

"Yes, I agree. We'll reevaluate in twenty-four hours, if any-thing happens to change your opinion." There was a pause. "You sound resigned, rather than enthusiastic."

John hesitated, considering asking her if she had ever seen *Dawn of the Dead*, or read *The Stand*. No, probably not. "Well, you haven't seen the working conditions. I'm going to complain to my union rep."

"I see." She had sounded amused, which was good.

Now people were digging into their food with the usual range of reactions from disgust to dogged tolerance. McKay actually claimed to like MREs and never complained about them; it was one of the things about him that made him an unexpectedly low-maintenance companion on field mis-sions.

Kolesnikova was asking Corrigan about Earth's Atlantis myths. "How did the stories of Atlantis come to center on the Greek islands, when the actual city landed in the Antarctic region? Or was the word carried to Plato somehow, and he set his version of the story in the land he was familiar with?"

"That's always been my theory," Corrigan told her, warming to the subject. "Now, the island of Thera was always associ-ated with Atlantis, usually because of a volcanic eruption that destroyed the Greek settlement there. Part of the island still exists today, with a giant hole in the center where the eruption occurred." He looked absent for a moment. "There's a huge number of myths about Greek vampires—Vrykolakas—asso-ciated with the modern island, which is called Santorini. I hadn't really given that any thought until we came here and encountered the Wraith, but the association with Atlantis, and vampires, is a little...indicative, if you think about it."

Kolesnikova sighed. "Perhaps the Atlanteans visited Thera, and left some warning about the Wraith there, that was per-haps destroyed by the eruption. Cretan civilization was also thought to be very advanced, was it not?"

McKay was listening skeptically. "It's probably a coinci-dence." He turned to John abruptly, asking, "Do you still find this place incredibly disturbing? Again, dead bodies in little cells aside."

John lifted his brows, surprised at the abrupt turn. "Yes. It's creepier during the day than Atlantis ever has been at night, including during the time the Darkness creature was drifting around eating power sources and attacking people."

McKay nodded. "Right. I've got a theory about that."

"A theory?" John stared at him, brows drawing together. "Earlier today you said I was insane."

"That's beside the point." McKay shifted forward, explaining intently, "We know the Ancient technology responds to humans who have the Ancient gene, either naturally or artificially with the ATA therapy. We know the receptors must emit some kind of field that allows them to interact with the human nervous system, even though we can't isolate it yet. And though it often seems to work best when the operator is in physical contact with the device, it's not always necessary. So that field must be broadcast continually all over Atlantis, from the lights to the stations in the operations tower. You've gotten used to the presence of that field, even though you're not consciously aware of it. The lack of it is affecting you here because parts of this place are built with the same type of materials that were used to build Atlantis, even if the construction is inferior. Those materials may be affecting your perceptions, making you expect to experience the field when it isn't there, causing a cognitive dissonance. Or—" McKay interrupted himself, staring distractedly into the distance. "Maybe these people tried to duplicate the field for their own purposes, and it's broadcasting in a different range, causing us— you— to—"

"Hold it." John put that Freudian slip of 'us' together with the way McKay had shut down the conversation about Corrigan's vampire theory, which, if you had to pick one or the other, went a lot better with dinner than the hospital versus biological warfare development lab argument. He said accusingly, "Dammit, Rodney, you feel it too. Why didn't you say something about it when I asked you earlier?"

"It was Dr. McKay who first mentioned the cannibalistic mutants with psychic powers," Teyla contributed helpfully.

McKay frowned at her in a wounded *et tu, Brute* way.

The others looked confused. "Cannibalistic mutants what?" Ford demanded.

Kavanagh was still stolidly eating his MRE. He shook his head in disgust. "I wonder about you people sometimes."

Corrigan was pretending to be engrossed in his field notes, and John caught Kinjo mouthing the word 'sometimes?' at Boerne.

Kolesnikova held up her hands placatingly. "All that aside, I have had the gene therapy, and I too feel something is not right about this place. I haven't had as much experience with exploration as you all, so I had put it down to that. I thought it was normal to be afraid all the time."

"It is, but I don't think it's just that," John told her.

"Which is what I just said," Rodney insisted.

"Maybe it's something else that's making you guys jumpy," Ford said. "Maybe something in the air down there." He threw a cautious look at Kavanagh, apparently not wanting to be caught in the middle of the earlier argument. "If they were experimenting with chemical or biological warfare..."

"There may be dangers down there our equipment can't detect," Kolesnikova added.

Rodney said, not helpfully, "If there was anything airborne, it was too late the moment that shaft opened."

Kavanagh shook his head. "The air down there isn't stale," he said, obviously giving it serious consideration. "It's being recycled, and must be drawn in from outside. There were probably scrubbers in the system, though it's unlikely they would last this long. But the air movement has been constant; anything released in the destruction would have been flushed away long ago. We should, however, avoid opening any more of those sealed cells. If there's a contagion, it's in there."

Teyla nodded, her face sober. "Yes, there must be a constant source of fresh air. There is no odor of mold or rot."

"It does stink down there," John countered, surprised she hadn't noticed, and that Kavanagh hadn't mentioned it. "Kind of musty, and rotten. Really rotten. You could smell it when the shaft opened, and it got worse the longer we stayed down there. Just like you'd expect from..." Everybody was staring at him quizzically. "What?"

Kavanagh was frowning slightly at him, the way you did when you thought someone was making an inappropriate joke. "There's no odor, Major."

If it hadn't been Kavanagh, who didn't have a sense of humor at the best of times, John would have suspected they were screwing with him. He still suspected it. "Oh, come on."

"It is true, Major Sheppard," Teyla assured him carefully. "There is no odor of death. Salt from the sea, rock, metal, dust, but nothing foul."

Ford nodded agreement, and none of the others objected. John looked at Rodney for help, always a mistake. Rodney was squinting at him with deep suspicion. "Are you seeing things? Or hearing things? You know olfactory and auditory hallucinations are a sign of—"

"Stop. It." John glared at him, then grabbed his pack, firmly stuffing his water bottle back in. "We need to get some rest, people. We've got a long day tomorrow."

Teyla stood out on the plaza under the stars, breathing the sea air. She was on the third watch, after Major Sheppard and Lieutenant Ford, and was rather enjoying the peace and quiet. Like Atlantica, this planet had two small moons, one nearly full, the other just a rising sickle shape, and they lit the plaza and the old ruins with a gentle pearly glow. She thought Sheppard was right; there was something in the air about the repository, something wrong in the building's very walls. Something that didn't seem inherent to the ruined city, or the sea and the plain beyond it. Even this small distance away from the structure, her spirits had lifted a little. Enough that she was able to enjoy the night air and the sky, to feel comforted by the small sounds her friends made as they slept in safety.

A footstep on the pavement made her turn and she saw a figure step out of the doorway of their shelter. She moved toward it, recognizing him by his height and the way he stood. "Dr. Kavanagh? Were you unable to sleep?"

His head turned toward her, and he said a little uncertainly, "Yes, I just needed some fresh air. It's all right."

Teyla's brow knit in concern, and she stepped closer, trying to get a better look at him in the dim light. "You do not sound well. If you are ill, you should tell Major Sheppard and return to Atlantis immediately. If there is some contagion in the lower levels—"

"No, no, it's nothing like that. I'm not physically ill," he assured her so readily that Teyla believed him. "It's just..." He gestured helplessly. "I'm not sure what it is. Just restlessness, I suppose."

Teyla could understand that. She felt restless herself. "Do you truly think... I cannot believe that the Ancestors would use this place to experiment on humans, even if they meant to find a way to destroy the Wraith."

Kavanagh didn't hesitate. "They wouldn't. McKay's an ass, but he's right about that. Frankly, they wouldn't need to. Their science was so advanced, they could run their experiments as simulations on artificially created genetic material. They wouldn't have needed human test subjects at all, much less unwilling ones."

Teyla nodded, feeling a flash of relief. It was just one other learned man's opinion, but from what she knew of him, Kavanagh was a very unsentimental person. She thought that he didn't romanticize the Ancestors the way her people and many of the expedition members did.

He took a deep breath, putting his hands in his pants pockets. "There's some other factor here. Something we aren't quite understanding, or interpreting correctly. You know, I thought I had it earlier today, but now I'm not so sure." He shook his head, started to turn away back toward their shelter.

Teyla heard stone click and slide, and reached out to steady him as his boot slipped. He caught her arm, leaning heavily on it for a moment, then found his footing. "Sorry," he said. He lifted a hand to his head, saying a little vaguely, "Maybe I'm more tired than I thought."

"You should go back and rest," Teyla urged him. Like McKay, like all the scientists, Kavanagh would work himself to exhaustion if allowed to. "We have another long day tomorrow."

"I will," he said, still sounding distracted. "Good night, Teyla."

"Good night, Dr. Kavanagh." Absently scratching her arm, she watched him make his way back toward their shelter, just a dark shape in the shadows. He had spoken of 'another factor' and she thought he was right. There was something here they just didn't understand yet.

CHAPTER FOUR

"This is odd." Rodney crouched near the lip of the shaft, frowning at the life sign detector.

John, checking the safety rope for today's descent, looked up sharply. "What?"

Rodney gave him that look. "Again, I point out that if I had seen indications of a ravening horde of something, I would have said, 'My God, Major, run!' rather than, 'This is odd.'"

John rolled his eyes and deliberately turned his attention back to the safety rope. "Fine, then. Golly gee whiz, Dr. McKay, what's so odd on this lovely morning?"

So he was still jumpy. Last night hadn't helped. John was used to Marines and airmen, who slept when it was time to sleep. Scientists who got up every five minutes and wandered around, he would never get used to. McKay's ability to function on little or no sleep for long periods of time was great when lives were in danger, irritating when he was standing on the edge of your sleeping bag chewing loudly on a power bar and contemplating the meaning of life and time or whatever the hell he was doing in the middle of the fricking night. What made it intolerable this time was that Kavanagh and Kolesnikova shared this bizarre behavior. John had stopped asking people where the hell they were going when Kolesnikova had replied with some annoyance, "I'm going to pee, Major, and I didn't think you all would like it if I did it in here."

And it also didn't help that it was a lousy morning. The sky was dark and overcast and the white-capped sea like dull pewter. The forest on the other side of the Stargate's platform was a brighter green against the purple-gray clouds, and the wind blew sand through the ruins and across the plaza. John had taken the jumper up into the atmosphere to look around and check the long range sensors, making sure this coast wasn't about to be hit by a hurricane or a tropical storm. All he had found were ordinary rain clouds, and he had landed again feeling inexplicable disappointment.

Kolesnikova had told him earlier that she had seen all there was to see in the repository's command center and wanted to tackle the lower levels with them. He hadn't argued with her, having the feeling that she thought she had let them down by not going yesterday. Corrigan was actually gleaning far more information in the city's ruins, and wanted another day out there. John was leaving Boerne and Kinjo up top again, to keep watch and back up Corrigan. Ford had been chafing at the inactivity yesterday and he wasn't needed on the surface, so John was adding him to the belowground group. Hopefully more searchers meant faster progress. And maybe with Kolesnikova's engineering background, she would see something that McKay and Kavanagh had missed.

"I'm getting more pronounced energy readings," McKay said, finally answering the question.

That got Kavanagh's attention. He nearly dropped the pack he had been sorting through and strode to the shaft, pulling out his own detector. McKay lifted his brows and sat back on the floor, making a production out of waiting for Kavanagh's assessment.

Fortunately for team harmony and John's already depleted supply of patience, Kavanagh didn't notice. "You're right," he said, also failing to notice when McKay took an ironic half-bow. "This is markedly different from the readings we took yesterday."

"Thus the choice of the word 'odd' in my original statement," McKay added. He pushed to his feet. "Something changed down there."

"Maybe you guys tripped something without knowing it," Ford said, leaning out to peer down into the shaft. "Set off something that increased the emergency power, or activated some other stuff."

"But there appeared to be no changes." Teyla shook her

head. "We took readings throughout our search, and before we left, and there was no increase in power at that time."

"What she said," McKay added.

Ford shook his head, gesturing helplessly. "Maybe it took a while to get going."

For some reason, everybody then looked at John. He shrugged, pretending this new development didn't make him uneasy. "We're not going to figure it out up here."

Once they had gotten down to the bottom of the shaft, the readings were stronger. "This way." His eyes glued to the detector, McKay pointed them toward a corridor John knew they had tried yesterday. They hadn't found any cells along it, just debris from laboratories smashed so thoroughly that McKay and Kavanagh had only been able to make guesses as to what their original purpose had been.

The blue emergency lighting glittered off the wreckage of twisted metal and the unidentifiable stains on the stone walls on either side of the broad walkway. John had a bad feeling about this; he remembered what else they had found down this corridor and he had a strong suspicion of where the detector was going to lead them.

McKay dug out the PDA with the map he had made yesterday and wordlessly shoved it at Kavanagh. Bringing up the map, Kavanagh scanned the screen hurriedly. "Damn," he muttered, obviously coming to the same conclusion John had just drawn. "I wouldn't have expected that. Our suppositions about the layout of the active power conduits must have been—"

"Wrong." McKay's voice was grim. He stopped next to a round opening in the walkway, where metal stairs curved down into a dark well. They hadn't bothered to search down there or in any of the other dark areas yesterday, believing the power source would be where the active power grid lay. McKay let out his breath, looking up and shaking his head in exasperation. "Well, this is just fantastic. It's pitch dark down there."

John stepped to the lip of the well, shining the P-90's light into the depths. Teyla moved up next to him, leaning over to peer downward. He estimated the stairs descended about forty feet; the light reflected off a metallic floor. If he had a choice of where to lead their little group, a dark hole in a ruined bunker was about the last place he would pick.

Grimly resigned, he took a moment to get the infrared night-vision goggles out of his pack, Ford doing the same. They would rely on the flashlights since the scientists' field packs didn't include the goggles, but John wanted to be ready in case something attacked them and they needed to kill the lights. Everybody else used the time to check their handlight batteries. When everyone was ready, John looked them over. He knew McKay had too much awareness of his own mortality to wander off in the dark, and Kolesnikova, uneasy but game, would stay as close to Ford or Teyla as she could without actually holding hands with one of them. "Now everybody stick together. Do not go off on your own, under any circumstances. Do not stop to examine anything without letting me know. And yes, I'm mainly talking to you, Dr. Kavanagh."

John went first, testing the stairs cautiously with each step, the P-90's light revealing a passage larger than the one above, high-ceilinged, with a jumble of the large opaque pipes branching down. The pipes joined up with another set and ran off along the far wall. The sinuous shapes were almost organic, their material gleaming faintly in his light; John was uncomfortably reminded of movies where aliens exploded out of people's chests. The smell, which he had been trying to ignore, was distinctly worse. "What the hell are those pipes, did we ever figure that out?" he asked, exasperated. "It's like the damn *Nostromo* down here."

Kavanagh, just stepping off the stairs and pausing to give Kolesnikova a hand, said, "It's part of the air system, Major." His tone was laconic but still managed to have an element of *are you stupid?* in it.

The others made their way down, and John leaned over to look as McKay consulted the detector again.

"It's stronger now. This way," McKay said, jerking his chin toward the other end of the large passage. "Back toward the center portion of the building."

"That makes sense," John said. McKay threw a look at him that he couldn't quite read in the reflected glow of the detector. "What? The power source would be under the main part of the complex."

"It makes as much sense as anything does," Kolesnikova answered for him. "This signal is strong, you should have picked it up yesterday."

Kavanagh shook his head, watching his own detector. "We must have activated something. Like the lights and the other systems that came online when we first arrived in Atlantis. It just took some time to power up."

"That's what I thought," Ford pointed out.

John had to admit it was reasonable, but it didn't make him feel any less uneasy. Still studying his detector, McKay grimaced suddenly and said, "I think the floor above us is shielded. And there seems to be some electromagnetic field activity— Check your radios."

John tried his headset and got nothing but static. From what he could hear from the others, he wasn't the only one. He swore. "Oh, that's all we need." The detectors were Ancient technology and wouldn't be affected, but their communications equipment was all good old-fashioned Earth-manufacture.

He took the lead with McKay to guide them with the detector, and put both Ford and Teyla to watch their six. Ford was leaving route markers with a reflective spray paint to keep them from mistaking the way. Their lights seemed to make the shadows even darker, and the detector led them into one branching corridor, then another. The giant pipes veered up the walls and over the ceiling, and they caught sight of more piles of wreckage.

The uselessness of the radios was making John's nerves jump. As they moved through the large dark space he had to suppress the impulse to make everybody choose a buddy and hold hands. If they lost somebody down here, if someone fell in a hole, got lost, wandered off... And the more ground they covered, the worse that odor got.

Finally, after they had been threading their way through this giant maze for about twenty minutes, he couldn't ignore it any more. He said, plaintively, to McKay, "Look, seriously, are you sure you don't smell that?"

"No." McKay threw another opaque look at him. "I have a theory about that."

"Oh, right, that theory. I'm really beginning to resent the implication that I have schizophrenia. I—"

"I did not say you had schizophrenia. I said—" McKay stopped abruptly, staring at the detector. "Hold that thought, I think we're here."

"Where?" Kolesnikova asked anxiously.

"There." McKay flashed his light on a section of wall and John made out the shape of a large blast door. The pipes that ran along the walls swooped in from across the passage and above to end in the wall around the door.

"A bunker within a bunker," John said. "That's...vaguely disquieting." He steadied his light on the door as McKay's flash flicked around wildly for a moment, then settled on a panel to one side.

"Vaguely?" Kolesnikova questioned softly.

"It makes perfect sense," Kavanagh said, his voice tense with suppressed excitement. "Extra shielding for their power source. We should have expected that."

McKay had already pried the panel open, holding his pocket flashlight in his mouth so he could see. John didn't see any control crystals, just a mass of dark wiring and circuits. McKay threw Kavanagh a hard look, taking the light out of his mouth so he could talk. "This panel is the only intact piece of equipment we've found so far."

"Hold it." John stepped closer so he could see Rodney's
expression. "Are you saying we shouldn't open this?"

John ignored Kavanagh's "Of course we should! Are you
out of your mind?" Rodney took a breath, his mouth twisted.
He looked distinctly uncomfortable. "There aren't any life
signs, just the energy signatures, and Teyla's not sensing any
Wraith. Of course, that means there could be anything in there
from evil cybernetic guards to people-eating nanites. But the
chances that there's a ZPM inside— We have to open it."

Sounding more frustrated than anything else, Kavanagh
said, "I don't understand why you two think there's something wrong here. It's an abandoned wreck of an Ancient
facility. That's all."

John didn't understand either, which was what worried him.
But Rodney was right, they didn't have a choice. And maybe
it was just something to do with the electromagnetic fields or
damaged technology trying to broadcast to the Ancient gene
that was making his skin creep. Fooling his brain into thinking he could smell rotting corpses when there was nothing
left of the dead but dry bones. He had a sudden image of
trying to explain this to Elizabeth and Bates and Grodin and
the others, that he had had a weird feeling and so they had
left a possible ZPM cache behind after wasting a day and a
half searching for it. He took a breath to tell Rodney to open
the door, when Rodney glanced at the detector again, did a
double-take and said, "Oh, no."

John recognized that tone. "What?" He grabbed Rodney's
wrist, angling the device so he could see the display. It was
reading life signs, a bunch of them. John did a quick mental
calculation to translate the distance reading and realized the
blips were only about a hundred yards behind them, somewhere in the maze of dark corridors they had just passed
through. The blips were all in a tight clump, and there were
too many of them; it certainly wasn't Boerne, Kinjo, and Corrigan following them down here for some reason. And they

were moving steadily closer.

Rodney said urgently, "Major, there's a ravening horde of something approaching."

"Thank you, Rodney, I got that already." John was already shining the P-90's light down the corridor, Ford and Teyla moving to flank him.

All their lights revealed was the slick blackness of the walls and conduits, but Teyla said softly, "Listen. Can you hear them?"

John stilled his breathing and listened. After a moment he heard movement far up the corridor. It was a weird soft sound, like a large group of people walking barefoot. *Or shambling,* John thought, suddenly struck by a half-buried memory of reading H.P. Lovecraft in college. *That's definitely shambling.* He looked at Ford. Brow furrowed, listening hard, Ford shook his head. Keeping his voice to a low whisper, he said, "That's not people, sir. Not human people. Animals?"

"Could be. It's not Wraith, at least." John glanced at Teyla for confirmation. "Is it?"

"No, it is not the Wraith," she said, shaking her head, baffled and worried. "Something that lives underground, in these tunnels?"

"I vote we open the door," Kolesnikova said uneasily.

John had to admit that the enigmatic door had started to look a lot more friendly in the past minute. If they tried to go further up the corridor, they might find themselves trapped in a dead end. A literal dead end. "Yeah. McKay?"

"I'm doing it," Rodney snapped from somewhere behind him. John heard a muted thump and a low power hum.

"Do you need help?" Kavanagh demanded.

"Of course not! If I can't hotwire one stupid blast door— That's probably been sealed for ten thousand years— With intermittent power—"

"McKay, be nice and let Kavanagh help," Kolesnikova told him, sounding anxious.

"Rodney, what she said," John ordered tensely. He could

hear a soft murmur echoing down the corridor now, even over their voices. There was something about it that made his skin crawl and his back teeth itch. He caught movement in their lights, something with gray and silver mottled skin that flicked hastily out of sight.

The low power hum from the door intensified. "Wait, wait!" McKay yelped. "I've got it."

John swung around to cover the door, gesturing sharply for Kolesnikova and Kavanagh to move to the side. Teyla and Ford stayed in position, still watching the corridor.

The blast door clunked again and a dark seam formed down the center, splitting it into two sections. With a deep bass groan, it began to cycle open, each section lifting up to reveal a large empty chamber lit by several white globes suspended from the high ceiling. There were big round pillars, either conduits for something or supports for the weight of stone and metal overhead. It was quiet and nothing moved.

John eased forward, wary, checking the nearest shadows with the P-90's light. McKay moved up beside him, his eyes moving from the detector to the room around them. "Power readings all over the place," he said, keeping his voice low. "But no life signs. From in here, that is," he added urgently. "The ones outside are holding steady."

"Right, everybody inside." John didn't have to say it twice. From down the corridor came a low hooting that was almost ape-like and a growl that made John's scalp prickle. Kolesnikova hurried in and Kavanagh followed, throwing an eager look around the big room. Ford and Teyla took up positions on either side of the door, and McKay was already prying open the control panel on this side.

McKay handed the detector off to Kavanagh so he could use both hands on the cables and circuits inside the wall, saying, "Twenty-five yards and closing, and in my opinion, that's way too close."

John agreed wholeheartedly with that. "You can get this door shut again, right? You didn't break it, did you?"

"Of course I didn't break it!" McKay snapped, then muttered something under his breath that John didn't quite catch.

Before John could demand further information on the door front, Teyla asked, "But why did the detector not show them before this?"

"There could have been some kind of shielding that blocked the detector." Rodney grimaced, digging a tool out of his vest pocket to tinker with the panel's insides. "Or they were too far away. But it's always worked before."

"Fifteen yards and closing," Kavanagh reported grimly, his eyes on the detector. "Some have broken off from the main group and are moving faster."

Ford told McKay, "You were distracted. Maybe you didn't notice them."

John didn't buy that. "He looks at that thing every two seconds, that's why we let him carry it. These guys, things, whatever, just appeared about a hundred yards away down one of these tunnels, however they did it." He threw a look around the shadowy chamber, hoping for inspiration. "When we close this door, they'll have us trapped in here," he added, thinking aloud.

"I don't think we have a choice," Ford said, keeping his eyes and his P-90 on the corridor.

"Not so much," John agreed. There was nothing in here to make a barrier across the door, no cover.

"We should see what they are first," Teyla added, stepping close to the opening, narrowing her eyes. "We cannot fight them if they are just noises in the dark."

With a gasp of relief McKay shut the panel and tapped at the controls. Ford and Teyla stepped back, and the big doors began to slide down and together. John breathed out in relief. "Right. We need to—"

Something struck the door, scrabbling at the rapidly shrinking opening at the center. McKay skipped back with a yelp, and John jerked up his weapon.

The light flashed off iridescent scales and white claws, just as the door slid shut.

John took a deep breath, feeling his heart pound. "Okay. That wasn't good." McKay backed away another few paces, and Ford shifted uneasily. Kolesnikova was breathing hard and fanning herself. Only Kavanagh seemed unaffected. A muted thumping sounded from the door, as first one something, then a lot of somethings, pounded on it. After a few moments, the pounding died away.

"It was unpleasantly close," Teyla commented, throwing John a worried glance.

McKay recaptured his detector from Kavanagh. "Fifteen yards? Thanks for the warning!"

"I read exactly what the screen said." Kavanagh looked around impatiently. "We should spread out and search for the power source."

"Not yet," John told him sharply. "After we check this place out. We don't know what's down here."

"Yes," Kolesnikova put in grimly. "As you may have just noticed, we have good reason to be wary."

"Whoa, whoa, we've got an abrupt increase in energy readings," McKay said suddenly, scanning the room with a worried grimace.

"Where, what? Nobody touched anything!" Kolesnikova stepped toward him, alarmed.

"The door opening must have activated something. It's this way." McKay started forward, face intent.

"Like activated as in turning all the lights on, or activated as in getting ready to blow up?" Ford asked as John took long steps to catch up with McKay.

"I don't know, that's why I'm trying to find it!" McKay snapped back.

McKay led the way past the pillars, through a triangular arch, and out onto a broad gallery opening into a darker space. A single overhead light emphasized the crannies and shadows in the rocky walls. The gallery was empty, but a broad metal stairway led down to an area with several open doorways that were more like the entrances to caves. McKay hesitated, grimacing at the detector, then started down.

John stopped halfway down the stairs, startled. He had just realized the odor of rot had faded, as if they had left it behind in the corridor. *That's weird. Either good weird or bad weird.*

Sounding concerned, Teyla asked, "Major, what is it?"

"Huh? Nothing." John hurried to catch up to Rodney at the bottom of the stairs. He saw lights flickering on in the room ahead, heard the low-power hum of a large installation coming online.

They both stopped in the arched doorway. The walls of the room were lined with panels and readouts and controls, but in the center there was a coffin-sized transparent case, set on a platform with more humming equipment. The inside was obscured by a white mist, but as John stared in consternation it cleared, revealing the body of a human man. It was hard to see much detail, except that he was dressed in a loose brown robe.

"What the hell?" John said, throwing a baffled look at Rodney.

"It's a stasis container." Rodney moved forward, staring as if uneasily fascinated, studying the readouts as the others gathered around.

"I can see that. What— Who—" Realizing he sounded like an idiot, John shut up. He just hadn't been expecting this. He had no idea what he had been expecting, but it wasn't this.

"I have never seen anything like this before either, Major," Teyla said, regarding the stasis container warily. "Could he be a survivor of the attack? Why did he not leave through the Stargate?"

Kavanagh moved forward impatiently, standing next to McKay to look at the readouts. McKay flung a hand in the air, saying, "In another minute, you can ask him personally. This chamber is cycling through an opening sequence."

"Now we'll get some answers," Kavanagh muttered, staring intently at the chamber.

"Ah, is that a good idea?" Kolesnikova looked worriedly from John to Rodney. "We think this place is a hospital, at least partly."

"Yeah," Ford added. "What if he's in there because there's something wrong with him, and opening it kills him?"

"I have no idea. What if he's in there because there's something wrong with him and opening it kills us?" Rodney ducked around the side of the platform to check the various panels.

"Can you stop it?" John demanded.

The platform clunked as bolts were released deep inside. Rodney hurried back to John's side. "I could, if I had half an hour and we weren't concerned about killing him."

John swore under his breath. That wasn't going to happen. "Everybody get away from it," he ordered, backing away.

Kolesnikova retreated hastily, Ford motioning for her to get behind him as he and Teyla retreated back through the doorway. Kavanagh stayed where he was, and John said sharply, "You too, Doctor."

Kavanagh shook his head, as if barely listening. "He's human, there's no danger. He could be an Ancient." He gestured, his voice incredulous. "Do you have any idea what that could mean? We could have all the answers to all the questions we've ever had."

"Yes, I understand that. But that man could be ill," Rodney said urgently. "He could be—"

White mist flushed through the clear part of the chamber and locks clicked; the low-frequency hum got louder.

"Well, it's little late now," Rodney muttered.

John caught Kavanagh by the collar and swung him bodily away from the stasis container, back toward Teyla. Kavanagh staggered, catching his balance against the archway.

A whoosh from the stasis container made everyone flinch, then the glass split smoothly in two, both sides rotating back and down into the platform. The occupant lay exposed on the opalescent material of the bed, still as death. John had a moment to think the point was moot and that the man was actually dead; his face was drawn and colorless in the wan light. Then he twitched and took a hard gasping breath. His eyes opened and he shook his head, gasped again, and suddenly sat up. He buried his face in his hands, as if sick or dizzy.

Beside John, McKay hovered uncertainly. "Well?" he asked, keeping his voice low. "If there was an airborne pathogen in that container with him, it could already be too late. If not... What do we do?"

"I have no idea," John admitted. The only thing he could think to do was ask. He cleared his throat. "Uh, hello?"

The man's head jerked up and he twisted to face them. He had a high intelligent forehead, short gray hair matted flat, and his eyes were blue. His gaze went to John, and he stared for a frozen moment. He said in amazement, "You're human."

"That's what we were about to say to you." John eyed him uncertainly. "You are human, right? Uh, who are you?"

The man lifted a shaky hand to his head. "I am called Dorane." He was turning paler by the moment. "I— It has been so long..."

John was starting to feel that using three P-90s to cover one frail unarmed man in a bathrobe was overkill. "Are you all right?"

McKay interposed worriedly, "We thought you might have been in stasis because you had a communicable illness, like, oh, some kind of plague, for example. You don't, do you?"

"What?" Dorane rubbed his eyes, as if he were having trouble focusing. "Oh, no. I placed myself in stasis, when the athenaeum— I was hoping my people would—" He tried to push himself off the platform and faltered, his legs refusing to support him.

John and McKay both started forward, but John let McKay

catch the man's arm and hold him up, just on the off chance that it had been a ploy to get near his weapon. Kavanagh lunged over to help, shouldering the man's other arm and saying, "We have so many questions—"

"Let us wait on that for a moment," Kolesnikova interrupted quickly. "Give him some time to recover."

"There is a room, just down the next passage," Dorane said, his voice strained. "Please take me there."

While the others helped Dorane, John sent Ford back to the gallery, to stand guard where he could keep an eye on the outer blast door. They found the other room a short distance down the cave-like passage that led off the doorway next to the stasis chamber. It was a little smaller, with a low couch built into the wall, padded with some slick blue-gray material. McKay and Kavanagh helped Dorane sit down.

John stood back in the doorway; he couldn't figure this. Everything they had seen in this area was intact, though he couldn't see why whoever had destroyed the rest of the place had left it behind. Surely that one blast door hadn't been enough to keep them out.

Teyla had paused beside him, and he asked, low-voiced, "Any thoughts?"

Kolesnikova sat next to Dorane, handing him her water bottle, and McKay retreated to join John and Teyla. "If that man is an Ancestor," Teyla said, watching Dorane uncertainly, "this could be far better than finding any number of ZPMs."

After taking a long drink, Dorane handed the bottle back and looked up at them all. His face already seemed less pale and strained. He smiled a little in confusion and asked, "Who are you, how did you come here?"

"We're peaceful explorers," John said. *Who are also looking for ZPMs and anything else we can haul back home to protect us from the Wraith,* he thought, but he wasn't going to say that aloud. Not just yet. "From a place called Atlantis. I'm guessing you've heard of it."

Dorane's brows drew together and he said uncertainly,

"Atlantis? But I thought...the city was abandoned."

Great, now he's suspicious of us. John looked pointedly at McKay, passing the diplomatic duties over to him. McKay gave John a mild glare, but faced Dorane squarely. "Ah, yes. Atlantis was abandoned. We come from a planet now called Earth, which is where the Ancients returned to when they left Atlantis. As you may know." Teyla cleared her throat, and he added, "Teyla there is Athosian, we met her people after we got here. We came to this galaxy through the Stargate to search for Atlantis. And we found it."

John added, "The Ancients were driven out by the Wraith."

"Hey, I'm doing this," McKay objected, frowning at him impatiently.

"You're doing it slowly." Then it belatedly occurred to John that maybe he should have broken that a little more gently. He said to Dorane, "You know about the Wraith, right? Because I'm starting to feel like we may be dumping a lot of bad news on you all at once."

Dorane made an absent gesture. "Yes, yes, it was the Wraith who attacked this place." He shifted on the couch, wincing. "It must have been a long time. I have few supplies left here, so I must remain in stasis almost continually. I set the container to open periodically, and I check the emergency communications systems to see if my people have tried to contact me, if anyone has returned. But I haven't been good at keeping track of the passage of years, the last few times I woke."

"Communications system?" That was the best news John had heard all day. Their radios might not be able to punch through the shielding and electromagnetic interference, but John bet an Ancient communications setup would. "Look, we were attacked on the way in here by some kind of aliens, creatures, something. Three of our people are still up on the surface, and we can't reach them with our radios to warn them."

"The Koan," Dorane said with a grimace of distaste. "I had hoped they were dead, after all this time. Yes, the communications system is there." He didn't look or gesture or anything else, but a metal section of the wall slid aside, and a light flickered on, revealing a cubby with a circular console. It looked a little battered, not as pristine as the Ancient equipment in Atlantis, but John could see lights and readouts blinking on as the system powered up. "We are safe enough in here. All entrances to this lab area are sealed blast doors."

"So you really are an Ancient?" Kavanagh said, getting to his feet and stepping up to the console. "You lived in Atlantis?"

"I don't think of myself as ancient," Dorane said, a little bemused as Kavanagh beat McKay to the console and took a seat there. "I did live in Atlantis, very long ago."

"Do the Koan go up on the surface?" Teyla asked, watching Dorane carefully. "We had seen no sign of them before this."

Dorane gestured helplessly, shaking his head. "They were nocturnal creatures and didn't go to the surface during the day, but that was when they first came here." He looked bleakly at John. "I thought their species would have died off by now."

John nodded, relieved. It wasn't midday yet, and Corrigan and the others would be outside, searching through the ruins; that gave them a little time. He said, "Kavanagh, if you can't get them on their headsets, try to call the jumper."

Dorane looked up, lifting his brows. "The what?"

"The ships that can dial the 'gate." McKay made gestures indicating something vaguely square.

Dorane lifted his brows. "Ah, you have a gateship from Atlantis."

McKay threw John a dark look. "I told you we should have called them gateships."

"Nobody cares," John told him firmly. He answered Dorane, "That was the only way to use your Stargate. The dialing console isn't there anymore."

Dorane shook his head, smiling in bitter amusement. "I wondered why I had no visitors. I had begun to fear that the Wraith had eliminated all human life in this galaxy." He hesitated. "As I said, I have lost track of the time. How long has it been?"

"It's been ten thousand years," McKay told him. "We have no idea what happened to the Ancients after they went to Earth. We have theories that they either died out or ascended at some point after that time, but there's no proof." Dorane looked up, startled, and McKay winced in sympathy. Low-voiced, he added to John, "This is a little awkward. I can see now why Elizabeth usually wants to handle anything more complicated than 'We come in peace and would like to trade with you for food and/or ZPMs.'"

Dorane was staring at nothing, shaken. He looked weary and old. "I see," he said finally. He shook his head and looked up, obviously making himself smile. "Then you are...our descendants. The children of my people."

"In a way. Some of us more than others." McKay asked Dorane, "Did the Ancients—your people—build this place? We thought it resembled an Ancient meeting place and repository in our own galaxy."

"Yes, we were building it with the help of the Thesians. They had agreed to be the caretakers of it, and they came from their own world to build a colony here and to aid us in constructing our athenaeum," Dorane explained. He looked away, his jaw set. "Then the Wraith came."

Teyla nodded in resignation, and John exchanged a grim look with McKay. The Wraith always came.

"But why did you stay here?" Kolesnikova asked in the sudden silence. "After the attack, I mean. You didn't know the dialing device was gone, so you never tried to leave? Were all the puddlejumpers—gateships—destroyed?"

"They were destroyed. But it didn't matter. I had nowhere to go," Dorane said simply. "The last message I received from Atlantis was that they were also under attack and could not come to our aid. I knew they meant to abandon the city if the Wraith's advance continued. After the attack, when they never came here or tried to communicate, I knew they were gone." He shrugged, glancing at Kolesnikova with a smile. "I know it sounds odd, and perhaps I am odd, after this long time of sleep and waiting. But if I didn't go to Atlantis, I couldn't find them dead. I could think of them as safe, somewhere."

Kolesnikova nodded slowly. John thought he understood what Dorane meant, it just wasn't a course of action that would ever have appealed to him, under any circumstances. Kolesnikova asked suddenly, "Why didn't you ascend?" Dorane stared at her, startled, and she actually blushed a little. "I'm sorry, but we know many of the Ancients ascended, either before or after leaving this galaxy."

Dorane hesitated, and John squashed the urge to intervene. It was probably a very personal question to ask on short acquaintance, but he thought they needed to know the answer. Then Dorane smiled, a little bemused. "I preferred to live and hope." He shrugged. "Hope that my people would return with a way to destroy the Wraith, that I could reclaim this world, all our work here." He added ruefully, "And I was given to understand that Ascension can be rather...dull. Not that my life here has been terribly exciting."

"Major, I'm not getting any response from the jumper," Kavanagh said, brow furrowed as he glanced up at John. "Or from their radios."

"Are you on the right frequency?" McKay demanded, stepping up behind Kavanagh to get a look at the board.

"No, I thought I'd just try a random frequency." Kavanagh glared. "Of course I'm on the right one."

"Crap," John muttered. He told Kavanagh, "Keep trying," then asked Dorane, "Is there another way out that doesn't involve going through that blast door into the tunnels? I need to get back up to the surface and warn our people."

"Yes, yes. This way." Dorane pushed himself up, accepting a helping hand from Kolesnikova, and started out of the room.

John headed after him with Teyla, Kolesnikova, and McKay following while Kavanagh stayed on the com system. John was going to take Teyla with him, and let the others stay behind to work on Dorane. Though the man seemed glad enough to see them, John thought Dorane was still a little confused, and probably suspicious of their motives. John didn't want to screw this up; if they wanted Dorane's help, they needed to make it clear they were intending to rescue him, not drag him off against his will.

John stopped to briefly update Ford on the situation, and when he caught up with the others again McKay was asking, "Just what are these Koan? Do they live down here in the tunnels? They showed up rather abruptly."

"They are an alien species, barely sentient, but clever, and they can be vicious," Dorane said, as he led them down a passage behind the stasis chamber, under more of the giant pipes, to where a metal wall met rough rock. He stumbled, and took the arm Teyla offered him with a grateful glance. "They were brought here from their world by the Wraith, to infiltrate our defenses from underground." He shook his head in exasperation. "I thought they would have died out by now. The last few times I went out to explore, there was no sign of them. I used this passage, so it should be safe. The access shaft is straight down it, at the very end."

Dorane stopped at a metal door, set deep in the stone. Mold and damp had crept in around the edges. As Dorane touched the control and the door slowly started to slide upward, John asked, "Do you have any idea how they managed to appear out of nowhere?"

Dorane shook his head. "They did the same to us, when they first attacked. I think the Wraith must have given them something to jam our scanning equipment, but surely the device cannot still exist."

McKay, in the act of handing the life sign detector to John, paused and they exchanged a weary look. "Oh, that's just great," McKay said, "Take it anyway—if the others are away from the jumper—"

"Yeah." John stuffed the detector into a vest pocket. There was no point in further speculation until they got to the surface. He gave Rodney a narrow-eyed look. They needed to talk Dorane into coming back to Atlantis with them, and bringing all his stuff, including any stray ZPMs he might have around. Rodney would know he should be taking care of that while John was gone, and hopefully he knew enough to let Kolesnikova and Kavanagh mostly handle it, and just kick them back into play if they got distracted by any other interesting Ancient technology. He just said, "Ford's in charge."

Rodney rolled his eyes. "Oh, no kidding. I'll try not to stage a coup while you're gone."

"Just play nice, Rodney."

Teyla was waiting beside the open door, and John stepped inside, flashing the P-90's light to give him a view of a long narrow corridor, dark and dank.

McKay watched them from the doorway, his face etched with worry. "Be careful."

CHAPTER FIVE

Rodney had a lot of questions he wanted to ask, and he needed to nudge the conversation toward ZPMs. But he kept getting put off, which irritated the hell out of him. First Dorane had seemed unsteady on his feet, so Rodney and Kolesnikova had helped him back to the main part of the lab area. Once there, Kavanagh had stepped out of the communications alcove to help Dorane sit down, and the alcove sealed itself up again. Rodney had objected, telling Kavanagh that they should be monitoring it in case Sheppard tried to contact them, but Kavanagh—now the team's Ancient communications expert because he had touched the damn thing once—had replied irritably that he had set it to monitor itself, and that it would alert them when Sheppard called in. Then Kavanagh had taken up more important question-asking time by apologizing for Rodney and Sheppard's behavior. Rodney had snorted derisively, but before he could comment on Kavanagh's behavior, Kolesnikova frowned at him and said in a whisper, "You and the Major talk to each other as if you are badly-raised eight year olds. Not everyone finds that attractive."

Rodney allowed himself a restrained sneer. "The fact that our professional communications function on a level that Kavanagh doesn't comprehend is not my problem." Focusing his annoyance on Kavanagh made it easier to pretend he wasn't worried.

Rodney had always hated relying on other people, who were inevitably fallible and wrong and usually stupid, but once they had arrived in Atlantis it had startled him how quickly he had come to rely on Sheppard. It had occasionally been difficult to reconcile the fact that the surfer/pretty boy type who qualified for MENSA but couldn't be bothered to join was the same person who had stalked and killed Genii in the city's corridors like they were cockroaches, could snap a man's neck, and was crazy enough to attack a super-Wraith with a belt knife. But Rodney was over that now.

"What is this part of the facility for, exactly?" Rodney asked, once he could get a word in. "This whole underground section doesn't look like it was part of the original design of the repository, athenaeum, whatever."

"We believed it was a hospital and medical research facility," Kavanagh told Dorane, and Rodney swore mentally. He wanted Dorane's version, in his words, uncluttered by any of their suppositions and suspicions.

"You are correct, the underground levels were a hospital, also a facility for biological research," Dorane told him, glancing up. He was seated on the couch again and still looked a little pale, sweat standing out on his forehead. "The settlement on this planet suffered from a sickness, originally created by the Wraith, in their experiments on their human livestock." He gestured around a little helplessly. "We were making some slow progress in defeating it when the Wraith attacked again."

McKay frowned. That wasn't a strategy they had heard of the Wraith using before. "Didn't you have have shields, like those on Atlantis?"

"We did, but—" Dorane looked up, brow furrowed in thought. "How long have you been here?"

"A little more than a day," Kolesnikova answered, watching him thoughtfully. "Why did the stasis chamber wake you now?"

"I had set the controls to wake me if any of my own people opened the blast door and entered the upper chamber." Dorane smiled around at them all. "You are our descendants indeed. Atlantis' children."

"Yes, yes, whatever, but what happened with the shields?" Rodney persisted. For some reason, Kavanagh glared at him. Rodney glared back. *Oh please, like you don't want to know too.*

"The Wraith used the Koan to infiltrate the outpost from within, and shut down the shields and other defenses," Dorane explained. He looked a little confused, as if he wondered what was so urgent about the question.

"Oh. So the shield generators could still function?" Rodney prodded. "We could turn them back on, protect this place from Wraith attack? Once we got rid of the Koan, that is." He wasn't personally fond of this place, but if something happened to Atlantis, it was essential to have a safe point to retreat to. Or if they couldn't turn the repository into a secure Alpha Site, they could cannibalize the working systems to shore up Atlantis' failing power grid.

Dorane shook his head. "Unfortunately, they were destroyed by the Wraith deliberately during the attack. But I have never needed the shields. The Wraith believe this planet to be uninhabited, and have never returned here, that I know of. I am safe enough, if isolated."

Kavanagh said earnestly, "You can't mean to stay here. You must come back to Atlantis with us. There's still much we don't understand."

"You could help us a great deal," Kolesnikova added. "And you would be returning to your home."

Dorane smiled at her. "Why yes, I would be happy to accompany you."

This was what Rodney had been waiting for. He added, "Hey, since you're coming with us, you can bring your ZPM. Your Zero Point Module? The subspace power source?"

Dorane gestured absently, as if it didn't matter. "If you like. I'm not sure how much power it has left." With a rueful expression, he added, "It has been working a long time."

Oh, hell. Rodney had nearly been able to smell that ZPM since they had first seen this place on the MALP's fuzzy transmission. He couldn't wait; he needed to find out now. "I need to take some more readings." He snapped his fingers impatiently at Kavanagh. "Give me your detector."

Kavanagh snorted in annoyance, but retrieved the device

from his vest pocket and handed it over.

Rodney ducked out, following the short passage back to the stairwell. He got a base reading and found the nearest power conduit, then started across the room. From the gallery, Ford asked, "Dr. McKay, what are you doing?"

Rodney barely glanced up. "I'm going to check out his ZPM."

Ford started down the stairs, whispering urgently, "You're not going to steal it!"

"Of course I'm not going to steal it!" Rodney rounded on him, glaring. "He's coming back to Atlantis with us, I presume he'll want to bring it with him since it would be criminally stupid to leave it." *You take one ZPM that looks like it's just there for no reason, and suddenly everyone thinks you're the mad ZPM bandit of the Pegasus Galaxy.*

"Oh." Ford stopped, shifting his weapon in a somewhat chastened way. "So why are you going to check it out?"

"To see if it's the only power source. It would be nice to be able to have lights on the way out. Hey, and you're supposed to be guarding, so guard."

"Okay, okay. I was just asking." Ford held up a placating hand, retreating back to the gallery.

Still huffy, Rodney followed the power conduits, tracing them back through the big room. He didn't know how useful Dorane was going to be; the man seemed a little off, a little confused, and Rodney thought the isolation here might have driven him over the edge.

Rodney had had nightmares that involved being the last one left alive in Atlantis after a Wraith attack, and they weren't pleasant.

It didn't help that it wasn't all that far beyond the bounds of possibility; Sheppard, Ford, Teyla, and the other military personnel would be on the front line, the operations team not far behind them, while Rodney, Zelenka, and the other scientists would be deep inside the city nursing the power grid or trying to get that damn weapons chair activated. Rodney didn't expect that witnessing the actual effect on someone unlucky enough to be a lone survivor would change any of his nightmare scenarios. He made a mental note to run some calculations on the possibility of placing triggers for the self-destruct sequence at multiple locations around the city, to see if it justified the risks involved.

He came to a landing with a short set of stairs leading down into an open bay with several hatch-like doors. Rodney followed the detector to the nearest, and tapped its control pad. It slid upward, revealing a small power room filled with bundles of what looked like jury-rigged conduit. Two Zero Point Modules lay in open metal cases on a low bench, and a third was seated in the round unit that tied it in with the power system. "Oh, oh, oh," Rodney whispered. "Oh, yes."

But after a few moments of examining them, he grimaced in disappointment. Dorane hadn't exaggerated the problem. The two ZPMs in cases were at maximum entropy and dead. The third one, still powering the system, was drained to only a partial charge. *That's a hell of a lot of power,* Rodney thought, studying the detector. Especially for a facility that had been drawing minimal power for ten thousand years or so. Atlantis' ZPMs had been in a similar state, but they had been maintaining systems that had held Atlantis stable on the bottom of an ocean, keeping the city intact and pressurized by tremendously powerful force fields. Even if most of this facility's power had been expended trying to defend against the Wraith... *Except he said the Koan shut down the shields before the attack started; that eliminates the major power drain.* All these ZPMs had been doing since then was running one stasis container and waking Dorane occasionally to putter around and check his com system, plus maintaining the minimal lights and air movement. *This...doesn't add up. Literally.* He started to take more readings, running some mental calculations.

The tunnel led out from the complex to the south, and the going was fairly easy. The floor was metal grating, the walls weren't overly dank, and the blue lights were set every twenty or so paces. Other passages branched off, curving away into darkness, but Dorane had said the surface shaft would be at the end of the main passage.

"I have never heard of a race called the Koan, or of the Wraith using another species to attack a human settlement," Teyla said, throwing John an uneasy glance, her face shadowed by the blue light. "I hope that is a trick they have forgotten."

"Maybe it was a one-shot deal," John said, though he didn't think that was too likely. The Wraith they had run into didn't tend to vary their methods of attack. Being at the top of the food chain didn't encourage innovation. "Maybe they ran out of Koan, ten thousand years ago. And maybe Dorane hasn't told us everything that happened yet." That sounded a little grim, so he added, "He seemed a little confused."

"I do not think he is...well. Despite his protestations. I could not live without knowing my people's fate, even if it meant giving up all hope that they had survived."

"Yeah," John admitted, "I didn't get that either." He hadn't gotten the impression that the Ancients had been that...distant. Atlantis was example enough that, as a people, they had liked color and light and life. But everybody was different.

After a short time the ground turned to uneven dirt and rock, though they still kept passing branching passages. John kept trying to reach Boerne and the others on the radio, but all he got was static.

Teyla said slowly, "I am beginning to wonder... When you saw Dorane, did you not feel any sense of recognition?"

"No." John checked the life sign detector again and saw the area around them was still clear. But with the Koan possibly having some kind of Wraith jamming device, that didn't mean much. He threw Teyla an odd look. "Why? Did you?"

"I felt something, as if I had seen him before, though that is impossible. And...it was not what I would have expected." She bit her lip, looking troubled, and asked, "Do you not think that you would recognize an Ancestor if you saw one? You have the Ancestor's gene from birth, not through Dr. Beckett's therapy, as the others do."

"I don't think so." Considering it seriously, John glanced down at her. "It's not like I'm psychic or anything. I just have a gene that lets me control the jumpers and turn on the lights and initialize the systems and stuff just by thinking about it." He considered that for an instant. "Okay, I know that didn't sound like it supported the argument I was trying to make, but you know what I mean. And you said 'if I saw an Ancestor.'" He stopped, regarding her seriously. "You don't think he is one?"

Teyla shook her head, then got what John could only describe as a very weird expression, as if something disturbingly strange had just occurred to her. But she said, "I— I cannot say."

"You cannot say? Huh? Teyla—"

She was a few steps ahead of him as they passed another intersecting passage, so John had a heartbeat's warning when the Koan dropped out of the shadows onto her shoulders.

With a yell, John surged forward. Teyla staggered but managed to flip the struggling Koan off her back. It snarled, clawed hands snatching at her as she kicked it in the chest. John fired up into the dark space above her, the P-90's flash catching another Koan just leaping out of concealment. He spun to cover the rest of the ceiling but the next Koan slammed right down on top of him.

Half-expecting it, John twisted to land on his back, getting the breath knocked out of him but still managing to slam the creature in the head with the gun's butt. It reared back, and he pulled the P-90 down and triggered it, catching the Koan nearly point blank in the chest. It toppled back, and he shoved it off his legs, rolling to his feet. *God, these things smell foul.* Teyla was already firing down one cross-passage, and John turned to fire down the other just as a dozen dark shapes charged toward him. The first three fell. The others yelped and scrambled back.

John caught movement out of the corner of his eye and ducked. A heavy metal rod split the air right where his head had been. He got off a three-shot burst as the Koan lifted the rod for another blow; one bullet caught the creature in the upper thigh. It bellowed and flung the rod at John's head.

John fell backward, deflecting it with his shoulder. He lifted his weapon but his light showed the Koan was already fleeing back up the cross passage with a kind of limping gallop, the others in full retreat ahead of it. He decided not to waste the ammo. It looked like the Koan had changed their minds about the ambush.

Teyla had shot her first attacker and was covering the other two passages. "Are you all right, Major?" she asked a little breathlessly. Her arms had long shallow scratches from the creature's claws, but she wasn't bleeding too badly.

John took a long look around. There was no movement in the shadows down the corridors. His shoulder hurt, but nothing was broken. "Yeah, you?"

"I feel badly in need of a bath," she admitted. "The Koan do not believe in basic hygiene, apparently."

It was pretty rank in here now. John stepped past her to where the first Koan lay sprawled against the rock wall. In life, the creature hadn't cared for itself well. The gray and silver splotched skin looked like it was molting, and the white hair was ragged and lank. There were white and silver spines through the hair and bristling from its ears, but John saw for the first time how human its facial features actually were, scrunched up in pain from the wounds in its chest. It looked fairly young, about Ford's age.

It wasn't wearing anything like clothing, but it had a cord around its neck with a small handheld data pad attached.

John picked it up, staring at it incredulously. The case looked like it had been scavenged from something else, like a puddlejumper remote or maybe a handheld sensor of some kind. An Ancient control crystal that was a little too big for the case had been crammed into it. The rest of the insides, even from John's limited experience, looked makeshift. Teyla recovered the life sign detector from where John had dropped it and held it out, showing him the screen. She said softly, "It does not even show us, now."

"Yeah. This is the jammer, all right. But it wasn't built by the Wraith." John felt cold, the adrenaline rush of the fight giving way to grim realization. It was just believable that the original Wraith sensor-jammers might be lying around here after ten thousand years, still functional. They had certainly gotten bitten in the ass by other lost pieces of Wraith technology that had lasted at least that long. That the Koan would know what the jammers were and remember them as a thing to take with them when they hunted humans was vaguely possible too. But that they could be living like this and figure out a way to build one from scratch, from scavenged Ancient technology? *I don't think so.*

John used his knife to cut the cord, then pushed to his feet, controlling a surge of homicidal fury. The immediate thing was that he no longer thought it was Corrigan, Boerne, and Kinjo who were in danger. He tucked the jammer into a vest pocket and said deliberately, "Let's go surprise somebody."

Rodney hurried back through the passages, checking the life sign detector to make sure Dorane was still down in the other room with Kavanagh and Kolesnikova.

Ford watched his approach from the gallery, brows drawing together. "What's up?"

Rodney motioned urgently for him to come closer and met him halfway up the stairs. "I think something's wrong. Dorane is lying to us about the timing."

Ford shook his head slightly. "What do you mean?"

Intent, Rodney explained, "This facility was powered by three ZPMs, with two now at maximum entropy and one at minimal power. From the readings I'm getting, the draining had to have occurred at least fifty years before the Ancients left Atlantis for Earth."

Ford stared. "That doesn't make sense. Why didn't they come here to look for survivors, then? Why couldn't he contact them through the Stargate?"

"My point exactly."

"Are you sure?" Ford demanded. He touched his radio headset, then grimaced, obviously recalling that Sheppard was out of reach.

"Of course I'm sure." Rodney gestured impatiently. "Look, I need to examine that stasis container. I want to see how long he was actually in that thing. I need you to keep an eye out and make sure I don't get caught at it."

Ford nodded, his mouth set in a grim line. "Yeah, let's do that."

Rodney started back down into the stasis chamber area, Ford behind him, moving quickly and quietly. This whole thing was making Rodney's skin creep. It would be nice if Dorane was confused, his memory a little scrambled by putting himself in and out of stasis. If the trauma of the repository's destruction had so unhinged him that he couldn't remember the exact sequence of events.

It would be nice. But according to Rodney's experience in the Pegasus Galaxy, things were never nice.

Rodney crossed the foyer into the stasis chamber lab. Behind him, Ford took up a position in the archway, where he could watch the passage to the communications room.

The stasis container had closed itself up again, looking like a glass coffin on a metal plinth, as if it was meant for a postmodern Snow White. Rodney knelt beside the control console at the foot end, tapping the pads, trying to get it to bring up a diagnostic. The container, like the ZPMs, was definitely Atlantean technology, no question about that. The controls were similar, and the displays used the Ancient language. But there was a haphazard quality to the way it was tied into the other systems and the power conduits, that weirdly awkward air flow system with the pipes. He recognized that quality from his own attempts to mesh Earth-built components with Ancient systems.

After several minutes of struggle and coaxing, he got the panel to run a diagnostic. He ran a finger down the crystalline display, muttering under his breath as he translated the Ancient figures, rapidly calculating the power outputs and shutdown sequences, translating the time markers into hours and minutes.

The answer was worse than he thought. "Three days." Rodney sat back on his heels, appalled. The container had been powered down a little more than three days ago, immediately after the MALP had come through the Stargate. "He knew we were here all along." The system was configured to automatically cycle down and release the occupant when an external sensor suite recorded a power surge from the direction of the Stargate. The diagnostic showed that it hadn't been powered up again until roughly six hours ago. *When I started picking up intermittent power signatures. The intermittent power signatures that lured us down here.*

Rodney pushed to his feet and headed for the door. *So if it's a trap, and obviously, it's a trap, why did he let Sheppard and Teyla go up to the surface?* He answered himself, *Obviously, he didn't.* Ford was still in the foyer, warily watching the doorways and stairwell. "Lieutenant," Rodney whispered harshly. "We need to go after the Major and Teyla. They—" The lights went out. "That wasn't a coincidence!" He swung his pack around, frantically digging for his flashlight.

The light on Ford's P-90 snapped on, and he said, "Listen."

Rodney froze. The silence seemed complete. He fumbled out the detector and showed Ford the screen. "There's nothing," he whispered. "Wait. Oh, no."

Ford's eyes widened as the screen suddenly came alive with blinking dots. Twenty, thirty, more, filling the level just above them. Ford swore and ran for the stairs.

His light flashed across the doorway, giving Rodney a

good view as the first Koan crowded in. The silver-mottled skins, the wild spiny hair glinted in the light. They spotted Ford and howled.

Ford halted on the steps and fired up through the doorway, driving the first surge back with a spray of three-shot bursts. "Get the others!" he shouted. "We need to fall back."

"Right!" Rodney dashed for the passage down to the com room, bumping off the rocky wall in the dark.

"Hey, there's—" He froze in the doorway. His flashlight revealed an empty room. Empty except for Kolesnikova, sprawled facedown on the floor. Rodney swore, jolting forward, dropping to his knees beside her. He grabbed her shoulders, rolling her over. "Irina—"

There was a stain on her chest just above her tac vest, dark against her blue uniform shirt. Her eyes were open. Rodney automatically felt for a pulse in her neck, even as part of his mind cataloged the fact that he was kneeling in a pool of blood, that it was minutes too late.

He choked down a sudden rush of nausea and shoved to his feet. "Oh, God," he breathed. Where the hell was Kavanagh?

Rodney turned back for the passage, shouting, "Ford!" over the staccato bursts of gunfire. He reached the foyer again and saw Ford braced against the railing, firing up at the Koan. In the muzzle flashes Rodney could see more of them crowding around the doorway, ducking in, forcing Ford to shoot to keep them back, pinning him down in the stairwell. Rodney tucked the flashlight under his arm and dragged out his sidearm, fumbling for the safety. "Ford, Kolesnikova's been killed! Something's— Someone's—" Distracted, Rodney stared as his light caught another figure, running across the dark chamber toward Ford. It was Kavanagh. "Kavanagh," he shouted, anger and relief that at least the bastard was still alive temporarily overriding fear. "Where the hell were you? What happened to—"

Ford threw a glance over his shoulder and spotted Kavanagh. He turned back to face the Koan, starting to back away from the stairs. "McKay, fall back to that second passage, try to—"

Kavanagh came up behind Ford and Rodney saw his arm lift. He didn't see the gun in Kavanagh's hand until he cracked Ford across the head with it. Rodney stared in shock, his mouth hanging open, as Ford jerked forward and fell across the steps. The Koan howled and poured through the upper doorway. Then Kavanagh, his face blank and preoccupied, swung toward Rodney, lifting the pistol, aiming it at him.

Rodney's brain lurched back into gear, and he clicked off his light, throwing himself sideways. The shot went off but missed him completely. Thinking, *Oh, no, oh, no, oh, no,* Rodney fired into the dark shapes of the Koan, scattering them, even as he scrambled for the open passage behind him. He pushed to his feet, fired two more shots, then bolted off into the dark, the Koan howling after him.

John half expected the door at the end of the passage to be locked, but it started to slide open when he touched the controls.

Confirming the bad feeling he had about this whole situation, he saw as it started to lift up that the room beyond was now dark. *Oh yeah,* John thought, *now I'm really pissed off.* He braced against one wall, Teyla against the other.

The door opened fully, and their lights revealed no movement. A few of the blue emergency lights were on, but none of the brighter overheads. John flicked the P-90's light off and eased out into the room cautiously, saying, low-voiced, "Teyla, I think somebody played a little trick on us."

"I do not understand this," she whispered harshly, following his lead. "Surely, even if he was lying about being an Ancestor, he would want to be rescued from this place."

"Well, you know, maybe he didn't." John checked the detector; the sensor-jammer had been jury-rigged, which meant there might only be one of them. He grimaced. "Oh, here we go." There were life signs, about twenty of them, in the direction of the area with the stasis chamber. Where they had left Rodney and the others. Coldly angry, John thought, *If he's touched one of them*— He handed off the detector to Teyla, then switched on the Koan's handy sensor-jammer. "Let's find him and ask him if he wants to be rescued."

John and Teyla found an alternate route through the maze of passages, coming out into the big room with the support pillars. The room was lit only by the blue lights, but John could easily see Dorane standing in the center. He was holding something that looked like an Ancient life sign detector, frowning at its screen. A couple of Koan stood near him, their silver-gray skins tinged blue by the light, the spines in their wild hair glittering. It looked as if they were waiting for orders. The blast door out into the corridor was open and more Koan hovered near it, with still more loitering out in the corridor. There was no sign of Rodney, Ford, or the others.

John glanced at Teyla, got a grim nod in response, and stepped out of cover into the room. "Hi. Somehow I get the idea you're not really an Ancient."

Dorane turned, startled.

"Put whatever that is down," John instructed, watching him narrowly. "Or I'll blow it out of your hand. And, you know, your hand'll have to go too."

Dorane stared at him for a moment, his face expressionless. He didn't make the mistake of underestimating John's sincerity and carefully lowered the device to the floor. As he straightened up, John thought incredulously, *Is he taller?* He must have been slumping a little earlier, making himself look less threatening. Dorane said lightly, "You used the jammer. How astute."

"Yeah, well, I catch on pretty quick when I'm attacked. What did you do with my people?"

Dorane folded his arms, and weirdly it reminded John of one of the older and calmer science team members explaining a theory. "There is nothing to fear. I locked them in the laboratory where my stasis container is."

"Okay." *He's lying,* John's instinct said. His worst fear added, *he's killed them.* He pushed the thought aside. The detector hadn't shown them, but then with all this shielding they might have been out of range. But if Dorane had locked McKay, Kavanagh, and Kolesnikova in a lab, of all places, with tools and power, John couldn't believe they would be in there for more than five minutes. And he knew damn well that Ford was carrying extra ordnance in his pack. John would reserve shooting bits off of Dorane for a last resort, though at the moment it was his first choice for getting accurate information. "Let's go get them out."

Dorane said easily, "Very well." He smiled. It wasn't the evil smile John had been half expecting. There was a quality to it he couldn't quite define. "This way."

John didn't move. "Tell your friends there to back up, right out through that doorway."

Dorane turned back to him, lifting a brow. "They aren't my friends, they are my people." He touched the iridescent shoulder of one of the Koan. It twitched away from him with a growl, edging back.

John's brows lifted. "What?"

"Oh, we were like you once," Dorane assured him. "Human, or so genetically similar that any difference was immaterial. We knew the Lantians, the people you call the Ancients, your honored ancestors. They shared their technology with us, in dribs and drabs, built the Stargates. And antagonized the Wraith into destroying us."

The last was said in almost the same even tone. Almost. "Antagonizing the Wraith isn't that hard to do," John felt compelled to point out. "Now tell them to leave, or I'll kill every one of them. This gun holds a lot of bullets. Their buddies in the tunnel found that out."

Dorane's expression turned a little colder, but the Koan, in response to some invisible signal, backed away, muttering uneasily among themselves. They moved out through

the doorway into the corridor, and when they were clear
John flicked a look at Teyla, a jerk of his head telling her
to seal the door. She moved over to it, sparing a hand from
her weapon to hit the controls. As the door slid closed, John
caught a glimpse of her in the light. She didn't look so good,
her face paling enough that her eyes seemed enormous. Her
bangs were matted with sweat, though it wasn't that warm.
He remembered she had been acting oddly right before the
Koan attack; *oh great, maybe there is an airborne disease
down here*. They had to find the others and get this over with
fast.

He told Dorane, "Now move."

Dorane turned reluctantly, starting across the chamber. He
said, "I was not lying when I said my people were attacked
by the Wraith. We tried to use biological and chemical weapons to fight them, but the Lantians would not help us. We
believed our biological weapons would only affect the Wraith;
we didn't realize they would affect us as well. Our weapons
drove the Wraith away—temporarily—but they also caused
terrible genetic changes in our own people." He paused to
look back at John. "I went to the Lantians to beg for help, and
they allowed me to stay with them for a time, working in their
laboratories. They pretended to help me."

"Pretended, yeah, uh huh, keep moving," John echoed
skeptically. He didn't get it. The Koan didn't act like any
kind of people, genetically altered or not; there was something wrong with their minds, not just their bodies.

Dorane's eyes narrowed. He was obviously angry that John
wasn't paying attention to his little story. "They betrayed me.
The attempts they made to stabilize the damage only made
the situation worse, and my people were destroyed."

John said pointedly, "They weren't gods, they were just
people. Technologically advanced people. They couldn't fix
everything or they would have destroyed the Wraith." He
squeezed off a three-shot burst, scarring the floor about two
inches from Dorane's feet. "Now keep moving, or the next

time I'll shoot your kneecaps, and drag you."

Dorane hadn't flinched, but his face had gone still. He turned, leading the way toward the stairwell on the far side of the room. He said, "The Lantians obviously gifted your people, their favored descendents, with the gene, but they withheld it from us." Dorane gestured like a man who was only being reasonable. "It would have helped us recover, but of course it would also have given us access to all their technology, all their secrets. I begged, but they refused to share it."

John pressed his lips together. He doubted Dorane was giving him an accurate account of what had happened. The Ancients probably had tried to help the Koan, but it could have been too late to do anything for them. The Ancients hadn't been able to stop the plague that had driven them to the Pegasus Galaxy in the first place, either. "But you've got the gene. We saw you activate the com system, or was that another trick?"

Dorane reached the stairwell, looking back at John with an almost noncommittal shrug. "They would not share it, so I created my own. I developed a drug— You would perhaps not understand the details."

"We call it a retrovirus." The big room was too dark to see much, but a door now closed off the archway into the stasis chamber. There was a trap here, John could practically taste it, but he couldn't see where it was coming from. Maybe more Koan hiding in the stasis lab? "Keep moving."

Dorane started down the stairs. "Yes. I knew your people must have an artificial way to give yourselves the gene. Even in crossbred human-Lantian populations it is rare. Of your companions who had it, I could tell you were the only one born with it. I could smell it on you." While John thought, *oh, that wasn't creepy. He sounds like a Goddamn Wraith*, Dorane continued, "The Lantians were so confident in their superiority that they let me do what I wished in their great city. I could go where I wanted, copy what I wanted. I stole the secret of a great many of their precious devices, completed my work on my alternate gene serum, and escaped back to my world. But it was too late. Most of my people were dead. I brought a group of survivors here to this planet, to where the Thesians were building this place to the Lantians' direction. Here I could continue my experiments and try to reverse the physical and mental damage the survivors had suffered."

They reached the bottom of the stairs. "It looks like you didn't do so great at that." John was enjoying pretending lack of interest in a sick kind of way, but he couldn't help asking, "What happened to the Thesians? Were they locked up in those little cells?"

"I needed a baseline human population to test my attempts to cure the other Koan. I told them I was a Lantian, that I had come to help them finish the repository and to use it to defeat the Wraith."

"Yeah. That works every time," John said. They had reached the doorway of the stasis lab. "Open the door."

"Of course it does. It certainly worked when the Lantians tried it on us," Dorane agreed. He faced John calmly. "I'll have to turn the power back on."

"I hope you can do it from here, for the sake of your knee-caps."

Dorane nodded toward the stairs. "There is a routing control over there, in the wall."

"Okay, you know the drill, do it with your mind."

Dorane snorted amusement. "It's not that kind of technology."

John said over his shoulder, "Teyla, see if you can get the power turned on. If that's a trick," he added to Dorane, "you're going to get really, really hurt."

"I didn't expect you back alive." Dorane shrugged slightly. "There was no time for more tricks."

John kept part of his attention on Teyla, as she moved around under the stairs searching for the control with the P-90's light. Dorane continued, "But the Lantians discovered me. They invaded through the Stargate, destroyed my defenses, took away all my subjects... They left me here, meaning this place to be my prison. Their last act was to leave an explosive device on the Stargate's dialing apparatus."

"They must have been really pissed off. Like me." Finding their repository turned into some kind of nightmare genetics lab and the people they had chosen as builders and custodians for it being used as guinea pigs, the Ancients must have gone completely berserk. Or maybe John was just projecting. Then he remembered the bomb craters outside, and thought maybe not.

"Here it is, Major," Teyla said, her voice cracking with effort. *Crap, something's wrong, I have got to get her out of here,* John thought. The overhead lights flickered and he heard a low-power hum.

Dorane put his hand on the door control, as if waiting for the power to come completely online. He said, "Supplies were very low, so I put myself and the remaining members of the Koan in the stasis containers I had used to secure subjects with particularly interesting results. I set my container to wake me periodically so I could continue the experiments. I did not mean to let the Lantians stop me." Dorane's face changed, a look of weary relief passing over his features. "Finally. Your companion is strong. Almost too strong."

The blow came from behind.

CHAPTER SIX

Plunging through the blue twilight corridors, Rodney estimated he had been on the run for about half an hour.
He wouldn't have lasted five minutes, but he had run into
another blast door and discovered that, while the lights were
out, the main power grid was still functioning. That gave him
some options. He had sealed the door behind him and, working quickly, flashlight clutched in his teeth, had reconnected
some cabling in the circuit panel to deliver a substantial shock
to the next person to touch the door. A Koan shriek muffled
by the thick metal was his reward as he bolted away.

Now, using the detector to trace power signatures, he made
his way rapidly through a maze of rock-walled passages.
About twenty yards ahead of the Koan, he found a maintenance crawlspace roughly carved out of the stone. He managed to cram himself into it and scrambled through and down
into another corridor on a lower level. The main lights were
still on, which meant that Dorane hadn't expected any of his
visitors to make it down here. Sitting back against the wall,
breathing hard, Rodney set the detector to map the power grid
around him, which should supply him with a rough idea of
the layout of rooms and passages in this area, and watched
the alternate screen for life signs.

It would be nice to know what the hell had just happened.
*Kavanagh is working with the Koan? I knew the man was a
jackass, but how the hell does that happen?* The whole thing
was a nightmare. And speaking of nightmares, if he was the
only survivor... Sheppard and Teyla had walked off into a
trap, Ford might or might not be alive, the radio was still dead
and he had no way to contact the others on the surface for
help. Rapidly calculating how much current it would take to
blow out the last ZPM in the power grid and wondering how

tough it would be to crack this area's computer system if he could find a working console, he absently thought, *Oh yes, dead man sitting here. Very dead. Dead, deader, deadest.*

Then he saw two other life signs appear on the edge of the detector's range, making their way in toward the signs still moving through the upper lab area. Rodney sat up straight, heart pounding with sudden hope. *Sheppard and Teyla.* The direction was right. Then all the life signs vanished.

They're dead? Rodney thought, incredulous and horrified. Then he grimaced at himself. Every life sign, even the ones that must be Koan, had disappeared simultaneously. *That was the apocryphal Wraith sensor-jammer Dorane mentioned, obviously.*

Rodney tried his radio again and snarled in irritation when all he could pick up was static. He had to get back up to Sheppard and Teyla, but the route he had taken down here passed right through the last known position of the highest concentration of Koan. He checked the readings the detector had managed to take before the jammer had cut in, hoping for more options. *Hmm, that's intriguing,* he thought, studying a high concentration of power signatures in this lower area. It just might be a lab or other work area. Labs meant tools, and weapons. His kind of weapons. Taking a deep breath, Rodney pushed to his feet.

John hit the floor face first, and everything after that was hazy and vague. He remembered being dragged up off the floor by Koan—he knew they were Koan from the smell, though he couldn't get his eyes open all the way. Then he was being carried and had a strange upside down view of a dim corridor.

He came to when he was dumped face down onto a cold stone surface. He rolled over in time to get slammed on his back by another Koan. He punched it, feeling bone crunch under his fist in a particularly satisfying way, and it staggered back. But as he tried to push himself up another jumped on

him, straddling him and pinning him down. He writhed and
shoved, getting a knee up into a vital spot and a hand on the
creature's throat. Its snarl turned into a choked gasp, its claws
digging painfully into his shoulders through the thin fabric of
his t-shirt. Then somebody else slammed John's head back
into the stone.

He didn't lose consciousness completely, but he was
woozy enough that he couldn't resist when the Koan moved
around, locking his wrists and ankles into manacles. When he
finally managed to fight past the throbbing in his head and
the scene came back into focus, Teyla was leaning over him.
There were two Koan standing behind her impatiently, as if
they were waiting for her. And she still had her P-90 slung
around her neck.

John blinked and squinted, for a moment thinking he was
having a head-injury-induced hallucination. *Something is
wrong with this picture.* Maybe it was him. "Teyla— What—"

She braced her hands on the stone thing he was lying on,
shuddered, winced, then choked out, "I am sorry, Major."

"Sorry for what?" John said. He knew he wasn't going
to like the answer. He felt weirdly pathetic, like they had
been dating and she was breaking up with him and he had
no idea why. His blurred vision was starting to clear, and he
saw that the chamber they were in was high-ceilinged and
round, almost like a large well. There were a couple of lights
high in the ceiling focused in on the lower part of the well,
leaving the top in half-shadow. There was a gallery up there
with metal railings; a gate led to a narrow spiral stairway that
curved down the wall to reach this lower level.

"I have to do what he says. He has something, a drug, it
affects the mind, it forces you to obey him." Teyla squeezed
her eyes shut for a moment. "He says you should understand
it. It works on humans the way the Ancestors' gene works on
their machines."

John stared. "Are you serious? Sorry, stupid question." He
tested the chains, putting his full strength, augmented by the

adrenaline now pumping freely through his body, against each one, but the links held firmly. They were solidly cemented into the block and probably would have held a Wraith, let alone him. He was missing his tac vest and belt but his shirt, pants, and boots were still present and accounted for, which made the situation marginally less terrifying. He could feel that his sidearm was gone, as well as his knives, probably including the little one that he kept for the can and bottle opener. "He just— What, you can hear him in your head?"

She gritted her teeth. "Yes. It's like nothing—" She shook her head violently. "I cannot make it stop. I cannot make myself stop."

John was getting a scary picture of what had happened. Teyla hadn't been ill up in the lab, she had been fighting off a drug she hadn't even known she had been given. "Teyla, you're strong, you're the strongest person I know, you can fight it."

She just took a sharp breath, her face strained with effort. "He gave it to Dr. Kavanagh, not long after we first arrived. Dr. Kavanagh did not know he had been infected, and was forced to pass it along to me. But it did not work on me as quickly as it should have. He has now given it to Ford also. It does not work well on those who have the gene or the gene therapy." For an instant, tight anger replaced the fear and frustration on her face. "He killed Dr. Kolesnikova, I saw her body. He says the Koan have killed Dr. McKay."

"No." John's gut went cold. *Rodney's dead. God, Kolesnikova should never have come here. I can't believe Rodney's dead.*

"He is going to use us to take the jumper back to Atlantis, he wants to—" Teyla gasped in pain and her brow furrowed with effort. "He says I have to give you this."

She lifted her hand. In it was a little box of black metal or plastic, hardly bigger than her palm. She turned it and as it caught the light he saw one side was all needles, like an old polio vaccination injector.

"By 'give' I guess you don't mean you're going to hand it to me." John's throat was dry. "Is that the mind-control drug thing?" He jerked involuntarily on the chains, feeling sweat break out all over his body; the thought of having Dorane in his head giving him orders he was helpless to resist...

"No." Teyla stared down at the device in her hand as if she was holding a venomous snake and was powerless to drop it. "This is the retrovirus he gave the Koan, and the Thesians, to make them like the Koan so he could experiment on them. Some of the Thesians also had the Lantian gene—he said this made them all go mad." She choked on the words, but couldn't seem to stop herself. "He thought since you believed so strongly in the Lantians' genetic superiority, you would benefit from the demonstration."

"Hey, I did not say I believed in the genetic superiority of anybody, that's stupid Nazi-talk from a bad movie, I said—" He couldn't remember what he had said. *She's really going to do this.* "Teyla, don't! Teyla, try to fight it!"

"I am trying!" He saw her arm tremble. Her face was set in harsh lines, her jaw clenched with effort. Then she slammed the injector down onto the underside of his bare arm, jerking it away almost immediately.

John yelled, more from surprise than pain. It had been too quick to hurt much; he craned his neck to see the neat square of red marks on his arm. The skin there tingled and burned, and he felt a sudden flush of heat through his triceps.

Teyla stepped back, staring horrified at the injector in her hand. She started to speak and her voice cracked. She managed to say, "He is leaving you here, with the Koan that are too far gone into madness to obey him well. They may release you and let you live, to join them. Or they might eat you. It is their choice." She turned away, nearly fell across the first steps of the stairway, then stumbled up.

"Teyla!" John yelled after her, but she didn't pause, didn't answer, didn't look back. She reached the top and disappeared into the shadows of the upper gallery.

He swore, wincing as he dropped his head back against the stone. The warmth was already fading from his arm, though he could still feel the sting of the needles. *Maybe Dorane was lying, maybe it was nothing*. He didn't feel any different, but he was still half-expecting to die of anaphylactic shock in the next few minutes.

John could hear more Koan up on the gallery, making those soft noises at each other that sounded like distorted speech. This place looked an awful lot like an operating theater or a room for experiments that you needed to watch but that you definitely didn't want to get too close to. Neither of which was a pleasant thought.

He took a deep breath. *Okay, think. Get yourself out of this*. The manacle on his right arm was just a little loose. John worked his wrist, gritting his teeth, through sharp pain to dull pain to numbness, but he couldn't drag his hand out of the manacle. *Hold it, now how do magicians do this? Oh, that's right, they swallow the keys first. Or dislocate a joint or something*. But there was another way. The manacle hadn't been machined very well, and one edge was a little sharper than the other. John ground his inner wrist against it, grimacing. It was a little like trying to cut yourself with a spork; a sharper edge would have hurt a lot less. But he only needed a little blood, just enough to lubricate his skin.

Finally he felt moisture on his wrist. He worked his hand around, getting slick wetness everywhere, then pulled with all his strength.

It hurt like crazy, but his hand popped out. "Ow. Ow, ow, ow," John hissed, fumbling at the other manacle. His fingers were almost too numb to be able to tell, but he couldn't find a release or even a lock. "Son of a bitch," he said wearily, letting his abused arm fall limp. The catch or whatever it was must be lower down to prevent just this kind of escape attempt. He was going to have to do the same damn thing to the other wrist, only that manacle didn't seem to have that extra few millimeters of room. He wasn't sure what he was going to do about the ankle chains if he still couldn't reach any kind of a release mechanism. But if he could get his boots off maybe—

A scraping sound made him look up toward the gallery. A Koan had opened the gate and stood on the narrow stairway. It had a bloodstained rag wrapped around one leg. John rolled his eyes in exasperation. "Oh, I bet you're the one I shot." It had to be the one he had wounded in the passage, when they had found the sensor-jammer. "That's what this situation needed," he said sourly.

It started down the narrow stair, limping badly on its wounded leg. It was growling softly to itself, sounding almost amused.

It reached the floor and moved closer to him, sniffing. John said reasonably, "Come on, I know there's a person in there somewhere. You don't want to hurt me. Didn't you hear what Dorane made Teyla do? I'm, you know, one of you now. Or whatever. This isn't working, is it?" He kept both arms limp; he wasn't sure it realized he had a hand free.

It circled the slab, passing close enough that he could see its eyes. They were yellow, the pupils dark ovals, and there was no awareness there. They were empty, like looking into the eyes of a shark, and that made its human features just that much more terrible. "I have a bad feeling there's nobody home in there." John felt a sick fear settle into his stomach. *He gave you something that's going to make you end up like that.* He shoved the thought aside. Maybe it had been a lie, just to torture Teyla and scare the hell out of him. *Well, it worked.*

The Koan reached the end of the slab and stood thoughtfully, long enough for John to wonder again if maybe he could talk to it. Then it lifted a hand and stabbed its claws into his thigh.

John swore through gritted teeth, reflexively jerking away from the pain and feeling the manacles grind into his flesh. "Oh, yeah, I get it," he said with a gasp. "I hurt you, you hurt me. We're even now. All's forgiven. Bye."

It pulled its claws free, and he felt blood well up. It moved up the slab to lean over him, one hand resting on his chest, the claws just snagging in the material of his shirt. John held his breath, waited until it started to press down. Then with his free hand, he punched it in the larynx.

It staggered back, clutching at its throat and making gagging noises. But John could tell he hadn't had the leverage to make it a killing blow. "Oh, crap," he muttered. The creature eyed him with pure hate, gasping for a breath. *Yeah, I've done it now, all right.*

The lights went out abruptly. Something clanged as it hit the metal floor of the gallery, and a brilliant white light exploded in the darkness. The Koan up there yelled in pain, and John winced away. A quick scatter of shots echoed off the stone while a flashlight beam waved wildly around. John twisted frantically, trying to see who it was. He could tell from the sound that whoever was shooting had a 9mm but—

His Koan buddy snarled angrily and flung itself toward the stairs. The flashlight beam swung toward it, catching it midway up. Another shot from the 9mm dropped it. It sprawled across the steps, twitched a few times, then went still. "Major Sheppard?" It was McKay's voice, coming from the gallery. "Are you all right?"

"Rodney!" John's throat went tight with relief. He should have known it; McKay was too smart to get killed. "Yeah, I'm fine, get down here!"

"Good, I didn't know—" More thumping and clanging and flashlight waving, as McKay must have been wrestling the gate open. He sounded harried and breathless and almost as relieved as John. "—how I was going—" There was a gasp as the gate gave way and muted thuds as he half-climbed, half-fell down the narrow steps "—drag you out of here if you weren't conscious." Then McKay was standing over him, waving a 9mm and a pocket flashlight. He shoved the pistol back into its holster and pointed the light around, demanding,

"Are you hurt?"

"Rodney, Rodney, not in the eyes," John said urgently, twisting his face away. His eyes still felt sunburned from the explosion of light up on the gallery.

"Sorry." McKay juggled the flashlight and something that had the low power hum of a laser cutting tool. The light flicked around to the manacles. "You're bleeding— Did that thing bite you?" he asked worriedly. "God knows what kind of diseases—"

"It clawed my leg a little, and that manacle was loose and I was using the blood to work my wrist—" With McKay, alive and well, standing over him apparently loaded down with weapons and tools, it now sounded kind of crazy. "I was trying to escape, okay? What did you do up there, what was that explosion?"

"Potassium perchlorate and aluminum powder. I found a biochem lab that still had some viable materials." McKay put the flashlight in John's free hand, positioning it so the beam would illuminate the other wrist manacle. "Hold that still. And don't move."

McKay cut through the manacle, and John sat up, then nearly reeled over as a wave of dizziness hit. He felt flushed and hot and had to take a deep breath to keep from throwing up.

McKay was too busy working on the ankle restraints to notice; he snapped, "Will you hold that light still? I don't think either of us wants any accidental amputations here."

John pushed himself up again, taking deep breaths to clear his head and trying to steady the light. It might be blood loss. He could see now that his wrist was bleeding a lot more than he had thought, to the extent where trying to free the other arm the same way might have been a big mistake. His last mistake. While McKay cut through the ankle chains John held the flashlight in his mouth so he could dig out a bandana to wrap around his wrist. His pockets were empty of anything else that might be useful. He said around the flashlight, "He took the others to the surface, to the jumper. They're going to Atlantis. We need to get up there."

"Yes, I thought it must be something like that." Sounding exasperated, McKay asked, "What the hell was up with Kavanagh? He attacked Ford."

John tied off the bandana and took the light out of his mouth, holding it out for McKay. His eyes still hurt, but considering the massive headache and the puncture wounds, it was the least of his problems. "Teyla said Dorane got Kavanagh with this mind-control drug. It works like the Ancient Technology Activation, but on people. Once you've been dosed with it, apparently you just do what he wants you to do, you can't stop yourself. He got Kavanagh with it when we first arrived, and Kavanagh passed it on to Teyla. The drug doesn't work too well if you have the Ancient gene or the therapy, so he couldn't get Kolesnikova or you or me. It didn't take right away on Teyla, probably because she's Athosian."

McKay's voice was grim. "The sick bastard killed Irina, did you know? I found her body."

"Yeah, Teyla told me." John took a sharp breath. One more civilian he hadn't been able to protect. *She shouldn't have been here, we never should have brought so many civilians, she should have been home in a lab discovering stuff.* "She had the ATA therapy, that was why he killed her."

McKay looked up, frowning. "I've got the ATA therapy."

"He told me you were dead too."

"Well, despite what you and Ford think, I'm a hell of a lot faster than Kavanagh at everything, including running in panic down dark corridors." McKay got the last chain cut away, and John hopped off the slab. He started to tell McKay to give him the pistol, but the dizziness hit again. John dropped to his knees, just barely able to keep himself from doing a face-plant on the stone floor.

"What's wrong?" McKay asked urgently, leaning over him, fumbling with the flashlight. "Did he shoot you? You should have mentioned it earlier. Rugged stoicism has its place in these situations, but—"

"Can you tell if I feel hot, if I have a fever?" John asked him. He felt like heat was radiating off him in waves. This wasn't from blood loss, and it wasn't from getting hit on the head.

McKay sat on his heels and put the back of his hand to John's forehead. "Yes, you're burning up. Are you sick? How did you get sick? This is lousy timing—"

"Rodney, just shut up and listen." John bit his lip. He had to admit it to himself; Dorane hadn't been lying about the injection. Whatever Teyla had given him, it was starting to take affect. Concussions didn't give you fevers. But saying it aloud was like giving in to it. "Dorane made Teyla give me a drug."

"What? Like the mind-control thing, whatever, that he gave the others—"

"No, no. She gave me what he's been giving the Koan. The drug he developed when he was experimenting on the humans who used to live here. It's like Beckett's retrovirus. It was because I had the Ancient gene, that I was born with it instead of needing the therapy like you guys. It's like he thought I was one of them, or something. And he really hates them."

In the glow of the flashlight, John saw McKay's mouth twist down. For a long moment McKay didn't say anything, then he let his breath out. "Right. I'll have to get into his data-base—hopefully he used the Ancient nomenclature—chances are he didn't take the time to destroy it. Or he couldn't bear to destroy it. Megalomaniacs are often unable to take those kinds of preventative measures." He pushed to his feet. "But how am I going to get you up those stairs? Maybe a safety rope—"

John glared up at him, frustrated. "Rodney, you don't understand—"

"Of course I understand!" Trying to shout quietly, McKay's voice cracked. "Who the hell do you think you're talking to? A nutjob looking for revenge on people who have been dead ten thousand years tried to turn you into a monster by giving you a drug that's going to wreck havoc with every cell in your body! And will you shut up while I'm trying to think? We need a plan here!"

"Okay, okay! Just calm down!" About the last thing John needed right now was to have to talk McKay down from a panic attack. But part of him knew that if McKay, of all people, had gone all sympathetic, it would have been that much worse. John would much rather have him acting normal, which meant yelling like a crazy man and making it all about him. "But you have to stop him from getting to Atlantis. Or warn them. When he dials the Stargate, you can use that communications suite to—"

"I tried that first, as soon as I could get back into that area. I thought I could call Boerne and the others for help," McKay said flatly. "That console hasn't worked in hundreds of years. The key control crystals are missing and the others are broken. There were only enough left to make a convincing display of blinky lights and noise when Kavanagh was pretending to use it. That's why he wouldn't let me near it."

"Oh. Crap." John pressed his hands to his eyes. The pounding in his head was just getting worse. "Look, just go. I'll catch up with you. Just—" John didn't remember what he was going to say after that, because the room swung around and then he fell over.

He wasn't really unconscious, just in a kind of waking delirium that made it really difficult to talk or stand or help while McKay dragged him up, shouldered his arm, and started hauling him up the stairs to the gallery. McKay had taken off his pack to do it, and John hadn't been able to tell him not to, which was even more annoying. He started to come back to his senses a little, mostly in self-defense, when McKay banged John's head against a metal support. He grabbed the railing to help steady McKay, who was muttering, "— find a stranded survivor in a stasis container in the middle of a bombed-out Ancient repository, you'd think he was an Ancient, right, but no, this is the Pegasus Galaxy, so he's a serial killer! And you, you obstinate product of the military industrial complex, expect me to leave you in this filthy pit, surrounded by decomposing genetically altered people, and dead people I might add, like something out of a Dr. Phibes movie—"

"That was Dr. Moreau," John told him, then the rest of that little speech registered. "Are you still bitching about me telling you to leave me? 'Cause nothing's changed, you're going to have to leave me."

"Can I not emphasize strongly enough the fact that you should shut up right now?"

"Hey, I'm still in command here." They staggered off the stairs onto the gallery level, and the way John felt at the moment, it made reaching Camp IV on Mount Everest seem like a walk in the park. His knees gave out, and McKay managed to lower him to the floor.

McKay leaned over him, breathing hard. "There may only be two of us left on this hellish planet, Major, and until we can make contact with the others or Atlantis again, we're an autonomous collective."

"Go get your pack," John ordered. His head hurt like crazy, and even the reflected glow from the flash light stung his eyes.

"Yes, yes, I know, I'm going!" McKay turned back for the stairs.

"And if we're an autonomous collective, how come you keep telling me to shut up?" John added, as McKay clattered down the steps. He tried to sit up, realized that was a mistake when his stomach lurched and his head swam, and eased back down again.

John watched the dark ceiling swing around until McKay reappeared, the 9mm in his holster, the pack slung over his shoulder, the flashlight stuffed into a pocket. John shoved himself up, grimacing, ignoring nausea and vertigo. McKay caught his arm as John flailed to his feet, saying, "We have to hurry, the Koan are coming back."

John squinted and saw McKay had the life sign detector in his free hand and it was blinking urgently. At least the Koan weren't using that damn jammer. He was willing to bet Dorane had taken that with him. "Right, let's go— Where?"

"Good question." Sounding a little desperate, McKay hauled him along the dark gallery, back into a narrow passage. "I have a vague idea but I haven't had a chance to—" they reached a metal door, round like a hatch, standing partly open, and McKay shoved at it "—test it."

"Good, I love it when we wing it."

The hatch opened into a landing overlooking a big shadowy room, with more of the swooping pipes overhead. There was a walkway along the wall just under the pipes and McKay helped John along it, then down a series of twisty rock-walled passages and through another hatch. He said in relief, "Good, these passages do connect, I wasn't certain." He added, "There's a control area with sensors and a security system through here that Dorane somehow neglected to point out when we first arrived." The sarcasm in McKay's voice was more biting than usual.

"How the hell did you find me?" John demanded. The hatch opened into a small control room with consoles, a holographic screen, and a couple of semi-circular bench seats with gray padding.

"Did I not just say sensors and security screens—" McKay looked down at him, then pressed his lips together. "Never mind."

"Oh, right." John sprawled on one of the benches while McKay bent over the largest station and tapped the touchpads. John closed his eyes, forced the dizziness down. "Can you find Dorane?"

"Yes, yes, yes, hold on. Let me check the Stargate... Oh."

"What?" John opened his eyes, saw McKay staring grimly at the flickering screen. He shoved himself upright, nearly lurching to the floor as he leaned forward to see.

It was a long-distance view of the Stargate, in color though fuzzy and pixilated as the system tried to enlarge the distant image. The 'gate held an active wormhole, and a puddlejumper hovered in front of it. Their puddlejumper. John swore.

McKay spread his hands helplessly, his face bleak. "There's nothing I can do. These are just sensors, cameras, there's no communications equipment. No weapons. Though if we had weapons what would we do? He's got our people in there."

John shook his head, sick. It wasn't McKay's fault. "He'll come back for the Koan, the ones that still follow his orders. After he gets control of our 'gate."

The tiny jumper on the screen vanished into the wormhole's event horizon.

Confusion reigned in the jumper bay for some time before Elizabeth Weir found herself facing their new guest. Lieutenant Ford and Private Kinjo had both been injured and taken off on gurneys, and Dr. Corrigan had seemed confused and probably needed to go to the medlab as well. She had gotten the most information out of Dr. Kavanagh, upset and barely coherent himself. He had told her that they had encountered a group of about fifty refugees from another world hiding in the ruins, that there had been a Wraith attack, and that Dr. Kolesnikova and Corporal Boerne had been killed. The Wraith had withdrawn temporarily but the Stargate was such a distance from the repository that the refugees were afraid to approach it in daylight. They had agreed to come out once night fell.

Boerne and Kolesnikova. Elizabeth felt it like a little stab in the heart. *Two more dead.* She had taken a sharp breath and asked, "Where are Major Sheppard and Rodney?" The medical team had cleared out of the back of the puddlejumper, and she could see now that no one else was aboard. "Who flew the jumper back?"

"It was Dorane," Kavanagh had said, already backing away from her, avoiding her eyes and her first question. "His people have the Ancient gene as well."

Now, facing Dorane and Teyla in the relative quiet of the jumper bay, with Zelenka, Sergeant Bates, and the Marine security detail gathered around her, she could finally ask the question again.

Dorane was saying, "I would ask you to send a gateship back for the rest of my people, but they feel they must wait until nightfall, when they can go to the Stargate under the cover of darkness."

"Yes, of course. Are Major Sheppard and Dr. McKay waiting with them?" Ignoring the tightness in her chest, Elizabeth tried to keep her eyes on their visitor, not Teyla. The other woman looked awful, her face drawn and ill, and the look in her eyes told Elizabeth she had seen something terrible. She knew Sheppard would have stayed behind to make sure the stranded refugees reached the Stargate safely, but would he have kept Rodney with him rather than Teyla?

Dorane looked startled and uncertain. "Did no one tell you?" He shook his head, spreading his hands regretfully. "I am sorry, but there was nothing we could do. In the Wraith attack— They are gone."

John was in that drifting state of consciousness again. He couldn't remember how long he had been here, or why it was happening. The heat came and went in cycles, as if he was staked out on a beach under the hottest sun imaginable, with only an occasional wave washing up high enough to give him some relief.

There were long periods where he was convinced that he had been taken by the Wraith.

Sometimes it was the Wraith from the downed supply ship, and it had him pinned to the floor of the jumper, sucking his life out slowly, trying to make him unlock the controls so it could go to Atlantis. Sometimes he was webbed up in one of those little cubbies, sick with fear and writhing uselessly against the sticky bonds, hearing familiar voices—Rodney, Teyla, Ford, Elizabeth, Kolesnikova, Zelenka, Stackhouse, Beckett, Halling, Jinto—calling frantically to each other somewhere in the darkness of the hive ship.

Fortunately for John's sanity, there were times he knew clearly that he was badly ill and that Rodney was trying to take care of him, making him sit up to drink water or just pouring it down his throat when he was so out of it he refused to drink. He remembered having several conversations where he kept asking questions and fading out when Rodney tried to answer him.

When John finally woke up, everything was still weirdly vague and dreamlike. He was lying on an uncomfortably hard floor in a small rock-walled room, and he couldn't remember much of the immediate past. He could see, because there was a small pocket flashlight balanced on its base, pointing upward so it mostly lit the little space. His head was propped on a pack which felt like it was stuffed with hammers. Large awkwardly-shaped hammers.

The fever was burning through him, making his own body feel distant and strange; his skin felt too tight, as if it had shrunk a little in the heat. He remembered that they had been moving around a lot, finding different places to hide. McKay had seen the Koan coming toward the security area on the detector, and they had had to run for it or, in John's case, hobble for it. They couldn't afford to be boxed in, for the Koan to trap them in a room and starve them out.

He shifted a little and winced. His leg was throbbing where the Koan had clawed him, and his wrist still hurt; McKay had had a small medical kit in his pack and had wanted to use most of the contents on him. John had argued him down to pouring antiseptic into the punctures and bandaging his wrist, and he had taken a couple of antibiotics. Other than that, there wasn't much else to be done. They had an epinephrine hypo McKay kept because he was allergic to just about everything;

it would come in handy if John went into respiratory arrest, but it wouldn't do a damn thing for his other problems.

Head swimming, he pushed himself up enough to see that there was a half-empty water bottle, a couple of power bars, and the medical kit stacked neatly within easy reach. There was no sign of McKay.

He left. Good, John thought, easing back down onto the hammer-stuffed pack. He remembered ordering Rodney to leave, several times. *You got your way. He followed your orders. You can lie here and die alone. Yay for you.* It didn't matter. John was history, and Rodney had to stop Dorane from reaching Atlantis.

But was it really a good idea to send an astrophysicist who was an average shot at best and had barely started to learn unarmed combat after a ten-thousand-year-old man who had dozens of genetically-altered Koan to back him up, a puddle-jumper, and who was holding a few of your friends as helpless mind-controlled hostages?

You know, if you sent Rodney off to die, you'll never know. You'll die and rot or turn into a Koan and spend your short life eating other Koan, because Dorane didn't leave any food. Or maybe the smart ones went off into the woods or learned how to fish in the ocean. He didn't see why they shouldn't.

Then John hazily remembered that they had seen the jumper go through the 'gate. Dorane would have to come back for the Koan, but that wouldn't take long. And they were stuck down here, trapped by the Koan Dorane hadn't wanted to take along. And even if they got up there, how could they stop them? McKay had said he only had one extra clip for the pistol. He tried to sit up again and something fell off his chest. He picked it up, realizing it was a folded square of paper.

It took him a while to get his eyes focused well enough to read it. It said, "Back soon," and was signed Dr. Rodney McKay, Ph.D., like John might have thought somebody else had left it. He crumpled the note and dropped back on the pack, groaning. "God, Rodney, don't get yourself killed."

CHAPTER SEVEN

The next time John drifted back to half-awareness, there was a ZPM next to the flashlight. *Was that there before?* he wondered vaguely. Maybe this was some sort of wish-fulfillment hallucination.

Then he was dreaming about being a kid again, about the time he had been attacked by fire ants. The little bastards crawled all over you, waiting to bite until they had swarmed over as much of your skin as they could reach. Then they sent a chemical signal and all bit at once, and the bites hurt like hell, like little pinpoints of acid in your flesh, and then itched and itched—

"Stop it, don't scratch," Rodney ordered, leaning over him and slapping at his hands.

"Don't hit," John told him, shoving his hands away and glaring. He was lying on the floor, in the little room he remembered, and there was the flashlight and the ZPM, apparently not a hallucination. The itching was real, too. He still felt too hot, but he was sweating now, as if the fever had broken. "What— what are—" He wiggled his fingers, surprised to see them in a pair of slightly oversized lab gloves from the medical kit. "Why am I wearing gloves?"

Rodney looked exhausted. "You were scratching at your skin, leaving marks, I was afraid you were going to hurt yourself," he explained. He brandished a water bottle. "Here, you need this."

John realized his throat was painfully dry. "Yeah." He struggled to sit up, accepted the bottle and took a cautious sip, not letting himself drink as much as he wanted. "This isn't all we have, is it?"

"We have enough for now." McKay nodded toward the pitiful little cache of supplies arranged next to the ZPM. There were now two more bottles.

John handed the water back. He eyed the non-hallucinatory ZPM. "That's a ZPM."

"Very good, Major." McKay was obviously too tired to give the sarcasm the usual bite. "When it was time for sunset on the surface, the Koan temporarily cleared out of Dorane's lab area. I went up there and tried to find any of our supplies. There wasn't much. I found Kolesnikova's pack, but her pistol and ammunition were gone. So I took the opportunity to poke around through Dorane's data storage, and take the ZPM. He had three! Three! But two were at maximum entropy, and that one is almost completely drained." He gave the ZPM a disgusted look, as if it was at fault for being a disappointment.

John still felt distanced from reality. "You went back there alone?" It seemed like a bad idea, even with the detector.

McKay glared at him. "Hello? You were unconscious."

"Okay, okay." John let it drop. He knew McKay had gone for the water because he needed it to keep John's fever down. "How long was I out?"

"About ten hours. It's dark up on the surface now, and most of the Koan are up there, so there isn't much we can do." McKay hesitated, shifting uncomfortably. "At first light, if you feel up to it, we'll have to get moving."

"Ten hours? I feel fine, I just..." John absently ran a hand through his hair and felt something prickle against his palm. *Huh?* He rubbed his head, baffled, then froze. He stared at McKay. "What do I look like?"

McKay didn't even blink. "I don't think we should discuss that right now. I think we need to talk about what we're going to do at dawn when the Koan come back down here. I've had good luck avoiding them using the detector, and—"

"Rodney..." John said slowly, with emphasis. McKay was way too calm, which meant it was really, really bad. He must have gone so far past panic he had come out on the other side. "What do I look like?"

McKay met his gaze, eyes narrowing in determination. "Major, Dorane has been in Atlantis for more than ten hours. Think about that."

John took a breath and looked away. Everybody in the expedition could be dead. *And the Athosians, damn it.* Would Dorane find them on the mainland? *Oh hell, of course he will. He'll show up in a jumper, with Teyla or somebody else he's controlling to smile and say he's an Ancestor and everything's hunky-dory, and they'll welcome him with open arms.* It made John's stomach try to turn.

His face must have shown his feelings because McKay abruptly broke down. "All right, fine! You have those little silver spiny things, like the Koan. They're on the outside of your ears and in your hair and eyebrows. It's not shocking or awful or even particularly unattractive. It's just a little odd. That's the only physical change I've noticed." McKay cocked his head, squinting. "I'm almost certain your ears were always that shape. Of course, if I see you every day and I can't tell, it's probably not a big issue." He added, "I was hoping the spines were sensory organs, and you'd be able to tell how the Koan communicate with Dorane, maybe figure out if they know where we are. Any luck on that?"

"Uh, no, I don't—" John shook his head helplessly. He touched his ear, felt the spines. They were unexpectedly soft, like thick coarse hair. He suppressed a shudder. His body suddenly felt weird and foreign, like an outsized boot he was knocking around in. "Rodney, I'm not just going to look funny here, there's mental changes too. They used to be just like us, and the Ancients apparently thought they could make the genetic changes stable, until Dorane messed with them more and drove them all nuts. I could go crazy and try to kill you, and you could be all Atlantis has left." He took a deep breath. "You've got to go."

McKay rolled his eyes, flung his hands up in irritation. "Will you stop saying that while I'm trying to think?" he snapped.

"I can't stop saying that, dammit! You're the only one left who can do something to stop Dorane. I'm a liability. You have to—"

"No, Major." McKay sounded bitterly angry. "I'm not leaving you to die here. I know what you think of me, but I'm not a coward, and I'm certainly not a quitter."

"Rodney, I don't think that!" John sputtered. "And will you stop trying to make this about you? I'm the one with the problem, and I'm being practical here! Before I go nuts, you have to—"

"Shut up or I'll—"

"Kill me?" John interposed. "Promises, promises."

"Oh, ha ha," McKay snarled. "Morbid humor, still not helping!"

John tried, "Hey, if you asked me to kill you I'd do it."

"No, you would not," Rodney snapped. "You wouldn't give up. You'd do something flashy and heroic and crazy, and you wouldn't give up until you saved my life or got yourself killed too. You don't think I know that? Now stop confusing the issue so we can decide what to do!"

John sat back, thwarted. He was also oddly touched, but maybe that was the fever talking. And it was probably incredibly stupid to sit here trying to convince McKay to kill him or leave him when they still needed a plan, whether John was sane enough to participate once it was time to implement it or not. "Okay, okay, fine. At dawn we go to the surface."

"Yes, exactly." Rodney threw him a suspicious glare. "Now, as I've been trying to say for the past five minutes, I've had good luck avoiding the Koan with the detector, so at dawn, if you've recovered enough to walk, that shouldn't be a problem. Then we have to get back to Atlantis."

"Well, yeah, that's kind of the plan's problem area." John rubbed his eyes. "Dorane took the damn jumper, and the Ancients blew up the DHD to keep him from using the 'gate." He looked up sharply as a solution occurred to him. "You can't build a new DHD, can you?"

"No, I can't, but thank you for the thought." McKay looked mollified by the suggestion. "But we don't need a DHD, we can dial that 'gate manually."

"That's right." John should have remembered that, but his head was intermittently aching, making it hard to think. There had been a few instances where SG teams had dialed 'gates manually; it was in the mission reports in the expedition's database. "We can shove the inner ring around like a giant rotary phone. All we need is a power source." He looked at the ZPM. "Which apparently we have."

"Exactly! The first Stargate experiments in the 1940s did it with a generator. And in fact, the Heliopolis in our galaxy had a broken DHD and the gate had to be dialed manually, using a lightning strike for power. We, however, don't need such extreme measures, since we have—" McKay gestured triumphantly "—a ZPM."

So that was why McKay had taken it, plunging the entire complex into darkness. He had probably wanted to conserve its resources, saving them for the 'gate. And hopefully for Atlantis, if they could get it there and deal with Dorane. "So we have a plan. Except that if Dorane's taken over the 'gate room—which he probably has by now—he's not going to open the force shield for us."

"Yes, the plan has flaws," Rodney admitted.

"The plan's flaws could end up turning us into impact events." If they tried to go through the 'gate to Atlantis with the force shield up, it would be suicide. When the Genii had tried to invade the city, John had killed around fifty-five of them by managing to raise the shield while they were in transit through the wormhole. He hadn't had any other choice, and seeing the city that was the only chance of protecting his people from the Wraith about to be invaded had made it an easy decision. He shifted uncomfortably on the hard floor. The itching had mostly stopped, but now he was having weird aches in his hands and arms. "But we can go to another world, some place we have a trading agreement with, then dial Atlantis from there and try to bluff our way in—"

McKay grimaced unhappily. "We can try. But I suspect that the Ancients did more than just blow up the DHD. If they wanted to keep Dorane here, the logical thing to do is to alter the gate's control crystal so it couldn't dial anywhere except Atlantis. They could still 'gate back and forth through it using the jumpers, but Dorane would have no choice but to stay here or dial Atlantis and walk into the force shield." He gave a little shrug. "It could also explain why he wasn't too worried about finding me, or making sure you were dead. If the only way off this planet is the 'gate, and the 'gate will only connect to Atlantis, a place which he would shortly control, there's not much point in hanging around here eliminating pesky survivors. We'll have to test it, but—"

"But you're right, that is logical." John let out his breath wearily. He started to run a hand through his hair and dropped it abruptly when he encountered the spines. Something else occurred to him, and he said, "You know, that holo projector, set off by itself in that room like it is— I bet it was a memorial to the Thesians, the people who died here, that Dorane killed. Whoever they were, the Ancients picked them to help build this place. Their meeting hall, their United Nations of the Pegasus Galaxy. They must have been pretty special people."

McKay's mouth twisted downward. "And Dorane probably developed his control drugs so the Ancients could show up here to check on things, see it all looked normal from the outside, and not have any reason to question anyone's word that everything was fine."

John grimaced in agreement. It would be the same way on Atlantis with the Athosians and any 'gate teams who had been out during Dorane's arrival. Everything would look fine until it was too late.

They sat there for a time in glum silence. John shook his head, shifting with a wince. His arms were aching right down to his fingertips. To distract himself, he said, "We'll need to go back up through that main shaft. That could be tricky."

"The one Kavanagh 'discovered'?" McKay's expression was sour. "The Koan probably don't use it. It didn't look as if it had been opened in years, and I don't think they could fake that."

John nodded. "We can duck in somewhere out of sight until the detector shows it's clear up on the surface—and hope Dorane didn't leave them another jammer." It wasn't so much a plan as a statement of intent, but it was what they had at the moment. "We need to— Oh, crap—" An intense pain seized John's hands, as if he had thrust both into a wood chipper. He doubled over, tucking them under his arms, trying to curl into a fetal ball against the agony.

After an endless moment the pain receded, and John managed to gasp a breath. His eyes were watering and he was trembling and Rodney was hovering over him repeating, "What happened? What happened? What happened?"

"Just...shut up for a minute. I'll tell you when I know." His stunned brain was starting to process sensation again. Biting his lip, he wiggled his fingers tentatively. *Oh, yeah, it's worse*. He pushed himself upright, Rodney gripping his shoulder when he nearly swayed over. John leaned back against the wall and took a deep breath. *Might as well get it over with*. He pulled the first glove off.

McKay made a garbled noise, then coughed and managed to say, "Well, that was... Not entirely unexpected."

John had claws. Short and curved and silvery-gray, they protruded from his fingertips, formed out of what had been his fingernails. He flexed his fingers and they slid back into their nearly invisible sheaths. He knew the Koan had claws, but somehow, whatever Rodney said, he hadn't expected this. He pulled off the other glove to examine that set, wondering what else he should be expecting.

Rodney was staring, fascinated. "That's so—" He reached out, carefully pressed John's fingertip and a half-inch of claw slid out. "It's very like a cat's claws. I wonder—"

"Hey, stop that." Indignant, John yanked his hand back. "That feels weird."

"It looks pretty weird, too," Rodney admitted readily.

John took a deep breath. It had been a really, really long day, and he thought his and Rodney's relationship could benefit from a time-out just at the moment. He used his forearm to rub the sweat off his face. "I don't want to talk about this anymore. Look, you need to get some sleep before dawn. Give me the pistol and I'll watch the detector."

McKay sat up straight, eyeing him narrowly. "No."

"Huh?" John stared at him, then pressed his lips together. Even though it proved his argument, it still pissed him off, which ought be a sign of approaching insanity, only it actually felt pretty normal. "Oh, a minute ago, everything's fine, and now my claws grew out, so you don't want me to have our only weapon. Doesn't that prove my point?"

"No, it does not. Nothing proves your point, because your point is stupid and defeatist. Note that I said stupid first before defeatist, because that's the salient feature of your wholly ridiculous point." Rodney unclipped his holstered sidearm and held it in his lap, staring at it. Then he said, "You have to give me your word you won't shoot yourself."

"What? Oh." John had forgotten about Dr. Gall. A young guy, a super genius like Rodney, with his life mostly sucked out of him by a Wraith, he had put a bullet in his own head so Rodney wouldn't have to stay with him in the downed Wraith ship. So Rodney could go help John. John looked at the ceiling, around at the stained walls, uncomfortable. Would he use a gun on himself? He didn't think so, but then Gall probably hadn't planned on suicide before the Wraith had taken him, either. Feeling incredibly awkward, he finally said, stiffly, "I give you my word I won't shoot myself."

Rodney looked at him for such a long moment that John turned shy and picked up the life sign detector, fiddling with it to make sure he could still make the buttons work. It was a little strange working with the claws when they kept coming out unexpectedly. It was like having extended fingertips with no feeling.

Finally Rodney put the pistol on the floor next to John. He shifted over to pick up the flashlight, saying, "I'm going to turn this off to save the batteries. We only have two flash-lights and no spares."

"Good idea." John left the gun where it was. He just hoped Rodney wouldn't have reason to regret asking him for that promise.

In his work area in one of Atlantis' large airy rooms, Radek Zelenka sat in front of three laptops, trying desperately to concentrate on any one of the five diagnostics and two data analyses he had in progress. He had once liked this room very much, but now the bright sunlight visible through the softly colored window panels seemed like a mockery. He hadn't been able to eat lunch, and his ration of the terrible coffee from the pot in the main lab bay sat in his stomach like a pool of motor oil. He couldn't stop thinking about the news Teyla and the others had returned with.

Boerne the Marine he had not known well, just enough to speak to casually in the mess hall, or when someone played a DVD in the evening. Irina Kolesnikova he had worked with over several projects, and his heart hurt for her.

But the worst part was that there was a good chance Rodney and Sheppard were still alive, terribly alive, sealed up in a Wraith hive ship to be drained at their captors' leisure.

Radek winced and rubbed his eyes, trying to banish that image. It was one thing for friends to be killed in a war, to grieve and to know that they were at least safe from further pain and terror. To know they might be suffering for days yet was quite another.

He set his jaw, turned to yet another laptop and brought up the connection to one of the Ancient data readers. He had pulled the damaged memory core out of the pillar and had been trying to reconstruct the scattered fragments of data. If he could concentrate on nothing else, he could at least submerge himself in the intricate and elegant patterns of the Ancients' data matrix.

Sometime later Radek sat back, frowning. "That is very odd."

At the nearest table, Ling was paging through reports, frowning in concentration. She glanced up, blinking. "What's odd?"

Radek shook his head slowly. He had been able to pull together and decipher one section of the damaged core, the one containing the 'gate address to the repository. "The gate on Dorane's world was altered so only the Atlantis 'gate could connect to it."

Ling pushed her hair back, her mind still obviously on her own analysis. "By who? The Wraith?"

"No, no. By the Ancients." *It was supposed to be a meeting place. Why would they alter...* Radek could think of a lot of reasons why the Ancients might think that was a good idea. None of them were good reasons.

At the briefing earlier, Elizabeth and Bates had outlined the plan to gate back to the repository after night fell on the planet, taking two puddlejumpers to escort Dorane's people to the Stargate. *They should be leaving soon—* Zelenka checked his watch. He pushed to his feet, found his headset on the desk and put it on. "Dr. Weir, I need to speak with you immediately."

No answer.

"Dr. Weir?"

Faint static. A sinking feeling settled in Radek's stomach that had nothing to do with the bad coffee. But she might simply be taking a personal moment. He tried again, "Dr. Grodin? Peter, are you there?"

No answer. Ling and the two other technical assistants in the lab were now watching him worriedly. He tried, "Sergeant Bates, come in please."

No answer. If the head of city security was not answering— There was no reason to panic, but Radek found himself pausing to tell the others, "Get your laptops, emergency gear. Just in case. I have a funny feeling. Humor me." He had barely finished speaking before they were up and scrambling to stuff computers and equipment in carrying cases. Radek tried the radio again. "Carson, can you hear me?"

"Yes, Radek." The answer from the medical lab was gratifyingly quick. Radek had never been so glad to hear Beckett's voice, except possibly for the time he had gotten his leg stuck in a faulty transporter door out on the southwest pier. "What's up?"

"Carson, I can't raise the operations tower. Or Bates."

Radek heard Carson say to someone in the background, "Katrien, love, see if you can reach anyone in the operations tower." There were muffled voices for a few moments. Then Carson's voice said sharply, "Radek, you'd better get yourself down here. We can't raise them either."

"We'll be with you in a moment." Radek cut the connection. His lab staff were gathered around him now, clutching emergency packs and laptops, watching him anxiously. "It's probably nothing," Radek said, opening a compartment in the table and taking out the holstered pistol that lay inside. "But we'll pick up the others on this level on the way."

They were halfway down the hall when the lights went out.

John was stretched out on his side, his eyes on the softly glowing screen of the life sign detector, watching the Koan move around on this level. McKay had been so tired he had fallen asleep almost before he lay down. The holstered 9mm still lay between them, and John had left it there, just checking to make sure it was loaded.

After a time he realized the fever was completely gone, leaving him with a dry mouth and probably a good case of dehydration, but blessedly cool. Except for McKay's soft breathing, it was very quiet, and John kept imagining that he could hear the detector making a soft, almost inaudible humming noise. Listening to it, he tried to decide if it was really there and he had just never heard it before, because he had never used a detector in a place this quiet. Then he started imagining that the ZPM was making soft little whispery noises to itself, and that was just weird.

John was deeply glad when McKay's watch alarm beeped.

Beside him, McKay groaned, batted at his watch until he got the alarm turned off, and sat up, moving like an old man.

John asked him, "Hey, you okay?" McKay usually woke up instantly. John hadn't noticed it earlier, but he was pale and bleary-eyed, like a drunk on a bender. It might be the lack of actual food; they hadn't had anything except the power bars since yesterday.

"Yes, yes, I'm fine." Yawning, McKay scrubbed at his eyes, took the detector away from John, and peered at the screen. "I dreamed Atlantis was attacked by a hive ship, and Samantha Carter showed up with SG-1 and rescued us. It was a little humiliating, but under the circumstances I was willing to cope with that."

In the past couple months, John had mostly dreamed about killing or getting killed. He meant to make a joke, to ask if Colonel Carter had brought beer with her and what was she wearing, but instead what came out was, "That's not going to happen, Rodney."

"I know." McKay sighed and fumbled for the flashlight tucked into his vest pocket.

That was when John realized something else had changed. It had happened so slowly during the last couple of hours that he hadn't noticed. "Hey, don't turn on the light just yet."

McKay had finally managed to get the flashlight out of his pocket and right side up. "What?" He squinted at John in the darkness, then went still. "Did something else happen? I mean, while I was asleep, did...something change?"

"No, not like that! Oh, wait." John realized he had better check and make sure. He did a quick personal inventory, as well as he could without a mirror. *No, spiny things still the same size, claws as normal, nothing else obvious.* "No, it's just that I can see in the dark, really well. Better than really well. Like—" He picked up a power bar from their tiny stack of supplies. The ambient light from the detector's screen was enough to light the whole room for him. "I can read the writing on this wrapper. Jeez, these things are mostly preservatives."

"Oh. That's good, though. That'll come in handy." Rodney rubbed his face, obviously still trying to wake himself up. "Not the preservatives, the seeing in the dark thing."

McKay stuffed everything in his pack, and John turned his back so he could use the light to make sure they hadn't left anything behind. John took the 9mm and put the remaining extra clip in his pocket. They couldn't afford to meet many Koan on the way.

John slung Rodney's pack over his shoulder, so Rodney could carry the ZPM. John didn't ask what happened if you dropped one of those things. He guessed that either it would be impressively shock-resistant and nothing would happen, or the resulting explosion would be so violent they wouldn't be in any position to care.

There was nothing in the upper levels of Dorane's lab except a few dead Koan. John, his eyes squeezed nearly shut, held the flashlight while Rodney got the sealed blast doors open. The life sign detector assured them there was nothing waiting outside, but as the doors slid away, John covered the growing opening with the pistol.

The corridor looked empty, and John stepped out cautiously, making sure there were no Koan equipped with a new sensor-jammer crouched in hiding. He signaled for Rodney to follow him, realized Rodney couldn't see jack in the dark space, and whispered, "Come on."

McKay groped his way out into the corridor, the ZPM tucked firmly under his arm, and John grabbed his free hand and guided it to the pack strap on his shoulder. "Hold on to that. Let's go."

"Right." Rodney sounded uncertain, and John didn't blame him; he wouldn't have wanted to be blind in this darkness.

Holding the detector across the 9mm, John led the way back through the maze of passages. "Can you see in color?" Rodney asked at one point.

"No. It's like normal night vision, just a lot better."

"Huh. It's probably something to do with an increase in the rhodopsin in your eyes. That's the chemical in the rod cells in the retina." He hesitated. "If the flashlight bothers you, what about daylight?"

"Crap," John muttered. He hadn't thought of that. If the Koan avoided the surface because they couldn't see in bright light— A nocturnal lifestyle and incredible night vision might even be considered a trait helpful in surviving the Wraith. But John wasn't willing to trade it for permanent day-blindness. "We'll deal with it when we get up there."

The detector picked up life signs in the corridor leading to the nearest stairwell, so John took another route to the upper level. Since the ZPM was with them rather than powering the repository's systems, the blue emergency lights were out. John looked around, squinting, trying to get his bearings again. They were near one of the monitoring bays for a cell area; he thought the surface shaft was only a couple hundred yards to the south. He heard a voice whisper and flinched, then realized it was the damn ZPM again. He thought about telling Rodney about it, but he just couldn't make himself admit it aloud.

Rodney had recaptured the detector, clutching it to the ZPM. "We were wrong about the Koan ignoring the big surface shaft. I'm getting a large concentration of life signs right around it."

John grimaced. "There's got to be alternate ways to get up there." He frowned up at the rocky ceiling, thinking over the layout of the control area not too far above their heads. "Hold it. Right before Kavanagh started acting funny—"

"Oh, and that would be when? 1986?" McKay snorted.

"Recently acting funny. He was out of visual contact in the control area, remember, when his headset went dead?"

"Yes. Yes, you think Dorane was up there with a sensor-jammer, waiting to get one of us alone." Rodney pivoted, using the detector to check the corridor. "That's in this direction."

The ZPM whispered again, and before John could stop himself, he snapped, "Will you shut up?"

His attention on the detector, Rodney said, unperturbed, "You have to wait until I'm talking before you can say that. That's the way it works. I thought you got that about us."

"I wasn't talking to you, I— Never mind."

Finally, using the map from Rodney's PDA, they found a passage leading to a room in about the right spot. John shielded his eyes while McKay investigated the walls with the flashlight, until McKay finally said, "Hah, here it is. The panel is set right into this wall, so you wouldn't find it unless you already had a suspicion it was here." McKay turned the light off so John could help him wedge the panel open. They had found a small one or two person elevator, the metal walls etched with abstract designs. "That must be what lured Kavanagh off alone." McKay's tone was deeply self-satisfied at solving that small mystery. "There would have been a brief power signature from the elevator, and Kavanagh followed it into the room. After Dorane gave him the drug, he ordered him to forget it ever happened."

"We're going to have to climb the shaft." John felt around the ceiling, searching for a catch for a trapdoor.

"If this is part of the original Atlantean design, and from the decoration and its position in the building I suspect it is, there should be—" McKay clicked his flashlight on, and John recoiled with a curse. "Sorry. Access ladder." There was bumping as McKay opened the sliding panel in the elevator's side. "Here we go."

The detector still showed several dozen Koan moving

around on the ground level somewhere above their heads, and by Rodney's watch it was about twenty minutes until dawn. Chafing at the delay, John searched around nearby and found a cubby with a grille over it that might have been part of the upper level's air system at one time. It was far enough away from the small surface shaft that, if the Koan came down that way, they would go unnoticed.

They crouched inside the narrow space, John putting Rodney behind him so he could face the grille, the 9mm in his lap. Rodney propped the detector up behind him, so he could see the screen, but John's body would block any light from it and keep it from giving away their position. Then he broke out the last of their supplies: a bottle of water and one crushed power bar.

"You can have it," John told him. "I'm not hungry." They had split a couple of the bars earlier, before Rodney had gone to sleep, and John had spent some time forcing himself not to throw up since it would have been a waste of their failing resources. He didn't want to do that again, and he knew Rodney needed the food more than he did.

"Take the water," Rodney urged him, bopping him in the back with the bottle until he took it. "You're probably still dehydrated." John heard him inhaling the candy and licking the wrapper. Then Rodney added, "If we can't get that 'gate dialed, in just over four hours I'll be dying of a hypoglycemic coma and you'll be stuck here alone."

"Uh huh," John answered absently. Rodney had been predicting new and increasingly horrific ways for them to die since he had first stepped through the Stargate into Atlantis. "Where do you want me to bury you?"

"Oh, I don't know." From his voice, Rodney was giving this serious consideration. "Not in the ruins. Down by the beach, maybe? I think that would be nice."

Listening to the detailed plans for the funeral that John was apparently going to hold in his copious spare time after Rodney died later that day was better than listening to unintelligible whispers from the ZPM. John choked about half the water down, made Rodney drink the rest, and by that time the detector showed the Koan life signs moving back down below the surface.

When the detector and John's instinct said it was clear, they found their way back to the little elevator, went through the side panel, and started up the ladder. John reached the intensely dusty cubby at the top, sitting on the edge while below him McKay climbed awkwardly, the ZPM clutched under one arm. A little daylight leaked through from a sliding panel that no longer fit properly, enough to tell him that they were on the surface. Then he froze, listening. He could hear voices. Shrill voices, like people in pain, murmuring in a language he couldn't understand. "What the hell is that?"

"What the hell is what?" McKay said from below, breathless with the effort of the climb. "Would you please consider giving me a hand with this thing?"

John braced his leg across the opening and reached down to help, just as McKay's hand slipped. John caught his arm with one hand, grabbed the ZPM that was slipping out of his grip with the other.

As John deposited the ZPM safely on the floor, McKay got a better grip on the ladder and pulled himself up. "Okay, that was scary, but I have to admit you really do have some tactile control with those things."

"What?" John stared at him. McKay was thoughtfully rubbing his arm just below the sleeve of his shirt, and John realized that he had grabbed him with his claws out. But the skin wasn't broken, just dented. He was more worried about the voices. "Don't you hear that?" he demanded.

"Hear what?" McKay looked at him for a long moment, though it must be hard for him to see in the near darkness. "Major, it's quiet out there."

John swallowed in a dry throat. *Oh, this isn't good.* At least these voices drowned out the whispering ZPM. "Seriously?"

"Seriously." McKay was regarding him worriedly. "What

do you hear?"

"Just people...screaming, and...things. And the ZPM's been talking to me." Knowing you were going to go crazy was one thing; having it actually happening right this moment was really another.

McKay nodded slowly. "Okay." His mouth twisted, and he rubbed his forehead. "Okay. Okay. I have to stop saying okay. Let's just...try to get out of this closet."

John helped him push the panels apart, squeezing his eyes shut. With his eyes closed, the voices were worse, coming together in a growing swell of shrill sound. But trying to open his eyes was like being stabbed in the head. As McKay stepped out of the shaft, John followed him, but he kept a hand pressed over his eyes. "I can't see out here."

"It's barely dawn." He heard Rodney's steps on the gritty floor, pacing back and forth nervously, nearly drowned out by the rising noise. "Wait, wait. I'm going to go see if I can find something you can use."

John sank down beside the wall, barely hearing him over the voices. *This is not going to work,* he thought, resting his aching head in his hands. He fumbled the bloody bandana out of his pocket and got it tied around his forehead, the dark fabric blocking out some of the piercing light. He could live with not being able to see if he could just shut that noise out of his brain. Just for one minute. Just for one second.

John wasn't sure how long Rodney was gone. It took all his concentration just to keep still, not to start screaming himself. Finally over the cacophony he heard, "Major! Major, here, I found a pair of sunglasses."

It still took John moments to realize what they were when McKay put them in his hand. He squeezed his eyes shut and pushed the bandana up far enough to fumble the glasses on. He opened his eyes cautiously. He could see. It was bright, achingly bright, but the glasses helped. Now he just needed ear plugs. Mental ear plugs. Or a lobotomy. He could really go for one of those at the moment. He pushed unsteadily to his feet.

"Those are Boerne's." Something in McKay's voice made John focus on him. McKay looked sick. "I found him. What was left of him, near where we camped last night. It must have been the Koan. His clothes were nearby, and those were in the pocket. Just him, not Corrigan or— God, what's his name? The kid, the Asian Marine kid—"

"Kinjo," John supplied automatically. Rodney's voice was very far away and John could barely understand him over the roar of sound.

"Right, they weren't there. Dorane must have taken him and Corrigan. They didn't have the gene or the therapy, did they? Just Boerne."

"Rodney, I can't— I have to go." The voices were rising into a crescendo and John was terrified of what would happen for the finale. He might be crazy, but he didn't want to hurt Rodney.

"Major, don't! I can help you." Rodney reached for his arm and John stepped sideways away from him, moving so fast Rodney flinched.

"You have to get out of here. I can't—" Waves of sound were crashing in his head with hurricane intensity, drowning out his thoughts. John held on just long enough to dump the pack off his shoulder, stooping to set the pistol on top of it. Then he ran.

CHAPTER EIGHT

"How did they take the operations tower so quickly?" Carson Beckett asked in frustration. It was really a rhetorical question. They were losing Atlantis, and there was nothing he could do but look over Radek Zelenka's shoulder and go mad with worry.

There were only three casualties in the medlab so far: two botanists with minor injuries who had managed to escape their lab moments before the alien what's-its had arrived, and a badly wounded Marine. Sergeant Bates had dragged him through the corridor access doors just before Radek had sealed off this section. Dr. Sayyar was tending to him, leaving Carson with nothing to do but fret. They had all heard the shooting and the calls for help before the radios had gone dead, and Carson knew there must be wounded all through the upper levels of the operations tower; they just couldn't bloody get to them. *First Rodney, Sheppard, Irina, and Boerne are killed,* Carson thought, sickened. They had barely begun to reel from that disaster. *Now we're inches from losing the whole city.*

Zelenka looked up from the laptop to gesture helplessly. "The aliens must have come back on the jumpers sent to rescue supposed refugees, but I do not understand how they took over our systems so quickly. It's as if they had all our security codes."

Carson nodded bleakly. Zelenka had set up his equipment in the back research bay, and Carson wasn't certain what he was doing, but it was keeping the invaders out of the medlab's section. The other scientists were ransacking the medlab's emergency stores, trying to put together things they could use for weapons, booby traps to protect the corridor. Besides Bates, only two other members of the expedition's small military contingent had made it here; they were Marines who had been patrolling the edge of the city's secure area and had barely made it to the lab before Radek had had to seal the corridor. Carson was badly afraid that the others were lying dead in the 'gate room, where the attack had begun. "Security codes," he said, mostly to himself. "You don't think this Dorane got them out of Rodney or Sheppard somehow?" He didn't feel particularly hopeful; it might mean the story about the Wraith was so much rubbish, but it didn't mean that Dorane hadn't killed both men.

Radek winced, but before he could answer, the Atlantean com system clicked on and Carson heard a woman's voice saying, "—try it now, it should be through to the medlab—"

Startled and hopeful, Radek said, "Dr. Simpson, is that you?"

But it was Elizabeth's voice that replied, "This is Weir—"

Carson asked urgently, "Elizabeth, are you all right?"

Then Bates pushed in from the other bay, cutting through the confusion to demand, "Dr. Weir, what's your situation?"

Elizabeth's voice was rushed but calm. "I'm in the small science meeting room below the operations level, with Simpson and some of the operations staff. Simpson's managed to keep them from getting the door open." She took a sharp breath. "It was Dorane. Sending the jumpers back to the repository was a trap. And he's done something to our people. Ford, Teyla, Kavanagh, and the two jumper crews who came back with the aliens are obeying him like robots, like they were under some kind of mental control. They captured the 'gate room before we even knew the aliens were here. I don't know how he's—"

The com cut off. "Dr. Weir!" Bates shouted. There was no response.

"My God," Radek muttered into the sudden silence, sounding horrified. "That explains the codes. If he is controlling our people..."

Bates' face could have been carved from stone. He turned

to Carson, asking, "Do you know what would cause that?"

"Son, I don't have a bloody clue." He wondered if the man could handle this. He had briefly wondered the same thing about Sheppard, until the Major had taken a team to a hive ship and brought all their missing people back, except for Colonel Sumner and one of the Athosians. After that, Carson hadn't wondered. And he knew Bates could be something of a bastard, but no one in his right mind would want Sheppard's job, and Bates certainly didn't look as if he wanted it now. He explained, "I need data, something to work with. If we could get one of the affected people down here—"

"That's not an option at the moment, Doctor," Bates snapped. One of the Marines called for him and he walked away toward the main part of the lab.

"He is afraid," Zelenka murmured, turning back to the laptop. "It is bad enough that Dorane could take hostages. If he can send our own people to fight us..."

"Aye," Carson answered, not wanting to hear the rest of it aloud. "It scares me, too."

John came back to himself leaning against the rough warm trunk of a tree, at the edge of the forest that lay past the Stargate's platform. Breathing hard, almost sobbing, he realized he couldn't hear anything except the rush of the surf. *That... was freaky*, he thought, cautiously glad he could think at all. He pushed off from the tree, his legs still shaky from adrenaline overload, the puncture wounds from the Koan throbbing painfully. Dry leaves crackled under his boots, reassuringly normal. The breeze was sweet and cool, and birds were singing somewhere in the forest, the song a strange mix of familiar and exotic. He could see the ocean through the scattered trees, where the land curved around to embrace the bay. It wasn't long after dawn. *I'm running around blind—literally if I lose these glasses—on an alien world. That's incredibly stupid.*

Without that cacophony in his head, he could think now. *I*

didn't imagine that. It was there. It had been as real as a punch in the gut. As a whole lot of punches in the gut. He looked back toward the dead city, the dark shape of the repository looming over it. It had been like a mental broadcast that only he—and the Koan?—could hear.

Dorane had said he had developed his own altered version of the ATA gene. And on their first night here McKay had talked about a theory, that the people who had taken over the repository after the Ancients had tried to imitate the Ancient Technology Activation, and that the differences in their version of whatever field it broadcast was what was making the people with the gene and the ATA therapy feel so uneasy.

Rodney was right again, damn him. Then, *Crap, I left him alone.*

Cursing himself and Dorane and this planet and life in general in the Pegasus Galaxy under his breath, John started back inland, moving along the edge of the forest toward the Stargate.

He moved quietly by habit, walking in the short yellow grass, sticking to the shadow of the trees. After a couple of hundred yards, he felt a tingling in the back of his neck and knew there was a Koan nearby. *Oh great, I can sense them. Rodney was right about that, too*, John growled mentally, turning back under the shadow of the trees. He didn't have time for this.

He circled around, then saw a shape ahead, crouched at the base of a tree.

It was facing away from him, looking toward the city, a slight figure in a rough sleeveless tunic. It was also wearing a hooded wrap, a fold of fabric pulled forward to shield its face, and its hair was long and silver-gray, collected in a neat braid that hung down its back. And there was something else on its face, too. Fascinated, John stepped forward and a dry twig shifted under his boot.

The figure shot to its feet in alarm, causing John to leap backward from pure adrenaline. It was a Koan; he could see the silvery mottling on its bare arms and chest, the spines on its ears as its hood fell back. It was wearing a pair of primitive goggles, the lenses tinted dark. Instead of attacking him it scrambled back in confusion and bolted away through the trees.

Well, that was different, John thought, staring after it.

He studied the ground, kicking aside dead leaves and twigs, and something rolled free. Slowly, John picked it up.

It was a wooden tube, with a braided cord strap for carrying, with little decorative bands inset with bits of polished rock or shell. He turned it over, looked down one of the open ends and realized he was holding a telescope. The lens was colored with some kind of amber pigment. John peered through it, found it too dark, and had to cautiously lift up his sunglasses to see through it. Turning toward the city, he could see the repository's main entrance from here, though he couldn't make out much detail.

He lowered the telescope, looking off into the quiet forest. He didn't need Corrigan to tell him a species composed entirely of animalistic psychopaths didn't figure out how to grind lenses or make eye protection against the daylight.

So they aren't all crazy. Over the years some of the Koan must have escaped Dorane's influence, traveled away from the ruined city, reinvented some kind of life for themselves. And Dorane had said the Ancients had tried to stabilize the Koan's genetic changes. Maybe they had succeeded, and it had just taken a few generations or so to show up. And Dorane had been too bent on revenge by that point to notice, or care. John looked back at the city. *If the ones still inside hear those voices, that noise, all the time...* No wonder they were nuts.

John found a branch at about eye level and hung the telescope on it, so the guy could find it if he came back. He searched himself for something else to leave and came up with a power bar wrapper he had shoved in his pocket by habit. He attached it to the branch next to the telescope. It wasn't much of a way of conveying "I come in peace, sorry I scared the crap out of you" but it was all he had. He could, at least, say it to McKay.

John found Rodney trudging doggedly across the plain between the city and the Stargate, the pack slung over his shoulders, carrying the ZPM. His shirt was stained with sweat and his face red from exertion. He knew Rodney wasn't in that bad a shape; he must have chased John most of the way through the city before having to give up. As John jogged toward him Rodney stopped, waiting for him to approach, regarding him hopefully. Reaching him, John said, "Sorry. Had a moment back there. Want me to carry that?"

"Yes." Rodney handed the ZPM over with a gasp of relief.

John hefted the ZPM against his chest. It felt inert, like a kitchen appliance, and not like a subspace power source that when fully charged made a nuclear bomb look like a popgun. It whispered to him again, but this time, without Dorane's dying technology screaming in his head, he understood it. It was speaking in something that was more like musical notes than words, but he knew it was saying that it was at minimal capacity, and needed maintenance. It was a reassuringly ordinary thing for a ZPM to say, if you thought about it.

They walked for a few moments, and John cleared his throat. "I think I know why the Koan are crazy. It's got something to do with Dorane trying to create his own version of the ATA gene. Even with everything broken and powered down, something in that equipment in there is still broadcasting, and once he gives you his Koan gene retrovirus, it gets louder and louder until it's screaming in your head. You were right, that was probably what was making us feel so weird when we first got here. Why we thought the place was creepy. Why I kept smelling rot and dead things when nobody else did."

McKay nodded, wiping his forehead off on his arm. He took it all in like they were sitting around in a lab or conference room talking about how the puddlejumper's propulsion system worked. "Because of the gene and the ATA therapy, we were subliminally conscious of it but couldn't sense it well enough to be more than minimally affected."

"Right. It didn't really hit me until we got to the surface. Once I got far enough away from it, I could think again." John shrugged awkwardly. "And I saw another Koan out there. He was watching the city and ran off when he saw me. So some of them must have escaped over time, and, you know, got over it. They probably saw the jumper land and they've been watching us from a distance ever since."

"Sensible of them." McKay took a deep breath. "All that aside, I had an idea. If we find the 'gate is actually locked against any destination except Atlantis, we can transmit a message with the MALP. If you can convince Dorane that you want to join him, he may open the shield for us. Then when we get there, you can shoot him. We'll still have to do something about all the Koan, but if he's not there to control them, it should be a little easier."

John lifted his brows. It wasn't exactly the best plan ever, but they didn't have a lot of options. "Okay, so he figures I'm due for a psychotic break around about now and believes me. But suppose he doesn't care how his experiment on me turned out. He's got plenty of Koan already; what do I tell him I have that he might want?"

Rodney smiled, a weird combination of his normal smug expression and a look of resignation and terror. "Me."

Any stairs or ramp that had led up to the Stargate platform had been a casualty of the bombing, and the scramble up the resulting pile of rock and rubble was not made any easier by the ZPM. John and McKay reached the top without dropping it or breaking their own necks. The MALP still sat to one side of the platform, coated with a layer of blown sand but otherwise unharmed.

McKay went immediately to the hole in the platform where

the DHD had been. He poked around at the remains of it for a few moments, then sat back, shaking his head. "I was right, this DHD wasn't destroyed by an energy weapon, there was some sort of internal overload. Which means that maniac was out here trying to get around whatever control inhibition the Ancients placed on the crystals and blew the damn thing himself."

John chewed his lip, thinking about it. "He would have still tried to dial manually. Maybe he tried it a lot."

McKay had followed his thought. He snorted. "You think he killed two ZPMs manually dialing a 'gate? It's impossible. It takes comparatively little power to initiate a 'gate, which is probably a safety feature to keep travelers from being stranded. The outside power source isn't creating the wormhole, it's just unlocking the inner ring and then locking in the chevrons for the address. He would have to dial..." McKay frowned.

John lifted his brows. "Over and over again for ten thousand years? In between stasis chamber naps?"

"And I thought I was obsessive-compulsive," McKay muttered, diving back into the hole. "I find the fact that he must have been unsuccessful all this time mildly terrifying."

John wasn't thrilled with it either. "Maybe he wasn't unsuccessful. Maybe he went there after the Ancients left for Earth. Which means—" He hesitated, not liking where this was going. "It's not the city he wants, it's us. He wants to keep experimenting." He took a frustrated breath, looking out over the bright plain. "Why didn't the Ancients just kill him? All these tricks with the 'gate, it's like they wanted him to squirm around trying to escape."

"Or as if they wanted something from him," McKay said quietly. "They didn't touch his inner sanctum lab complex. Or they searched it, didn't find what they wanted, and left it intact hoping the answer was just hidden too well. That they could force him to reveal it eventually."

Antidotes, John thought. For the Thesians, for whoever

else Dorane had managed to infect. He didn't want to say it aloud; he didn't want to sound that hopeful—as if it would tempt the universe to conspire against him.

McKay was quiet for a moment, then he said, "You look like an alien biker," and started working again. He poked and prodded at the DHD's remnants, dug tools out of his pack, and muttered to himself. The day was getting hot, the sun reflecting off the stone platform, and the brightness was giving John yet another headache. Then McKay connected in the ZPM, and John felt a sudden shiver travel down his back. It was not an unpleasant sensation.

He stared up at the Stargate, which still looked like an inert hunk of naquadah, but something in John's head told him it was now powered up, ready to be dialed. "You did it," he said, just as McKay sat back from the ragged hole in the paving and said, "I did it."

"What?" they both said at the same time. John waved for McKay to shut up. "I felt it. Like it was an Ancient gene thing. Except I've never felt a 'gate before. And ZPMs have never talked to me."

"I actually didn't think you had been holding out on us all this time, Major." McKay stared at the Stargate, then at John. "Maybe that's what the spines are for. Maybe they're meant to enhance reception of Dorane's alternate mental technology activation, and they also function that way for the real ATA."

John caught himself trying to roll his eyes back to see the spines in his brows. "Like antennae?" It did make a sort of sense.

McKay rubbed sweat and dust off his face with his shirtsleeve. "Can you dial the 'gate mentally, by any chance? Because that damn thing looks heavy."

"Let's see." John concentrated on the first symbol for Atlantis, then for a few other destinations he had memorized. Nothing. The inner ring just sat there, making a deep metallic purring noise that John could feel in his back teeth. He felt like it was staring accusingly at him. Or possibly laughing. "Guess not."

"Of course." McKay pushed to his feet, stumbled, and John stood, giving him a hand up. "That would be too easy."

They decided to test the theory that all destinations except Atlantis had been locked out to keep Dorane here. If they could dial another destination, that meant they could use Plan A, which was to try to dial into Atlantis from another 'gate address, and trick Dorane into letting them in by pretending to be traders or something else unspecified that they hadn't quite figured out yet. "Let's try the Hoffans," McKay suggested, leaning tiredly on the gate. "They were nice people. Hopefully a few of them are still alive."

"It's worth a shot," John agreed. The Hoffans put a high value on fighting the Wraith with science, and were advanced enough to understand genetics. If any of them were still around, they would probably be willing to give them the benefit of the doubt and listen to McKay's explanations, instead of shooting the freaky alien creature who had just come through their 'gate (i.e. John) on sight.

They wrestled with the 'gate's inner ring. It was heavy, like pushing a loaded truck up a hill. But while it would rotate all around, it stubbornly refused to lock in the first symbol in the Hoffans' gate address, no matter how hard they both shoved at it, or how hard John mentally begged it. John swore. "It's going to have to be Plan B."

McKay stepped back, eyeing the 'gate with weary disgust. "You know what you're going to say?"

John had no idea what he was going to say. He thought he would be better winging it. "I can sound crazy and desperate, how's that?"

"Crazy and desperate is standard operating procedure." McKay went to his pack, rooted around in it for a moment, and pulled out something that looked like a little PDA, but John could tell it was Ancient technology. It buzzed with a low note, a minor key compared to the bass orchestra of the

Stargate, but much friendlier. "Major, I'm going to put this in the MALP. I assume if this goes hideously wrong, we'll both be searched and I don't want Dorane to find it."

"Okay." John blinked, distracted, as the little device sang that it had lots of data but was ready for more. "Uh... What is it?"

"A download from Dorane's database. He thought he had it adequately protected, but let's say his system security skills don't match his Frankensteinian expertise in biochemistry. The Ancients must have been able to get this data too, so I don't know how useful it might be, but it's still worth saving." Rodney tucked it into one of the MALP's code-locked compartments. The metal muted the little device's song, and it settled into quiet. McKay dusted his hands off on his pants. "Now, this has got to look good. We need some stage dressing. I have to look like your prisoner." Covered with a sticky combination of sweat, dust, and sand, and turning red from incipient sunburn, McKay already looked like he had been dragged to the Stargate by the ankle. He patted his pockets and handed over the 9mm to John. "You should tie me up," he added, looking absently around. "Better use my belt. There's some cable in the MALP's compartment, but we'll need that to hang ourselves if this doesn't work."

John went to the MALP to start powering up the transmitter, making sure it was ready to send as soon as they got the last chevron locked. "Right. How about a chorus of *Always Look on the Bright Side of Life?*"

"Maybe later."

Having McKay's hands awkwardly tied with the belt made pushing the inner ring more difficult, but the symbols for Atlantis' address each locked without hesitation when the ring slid into place. They hastily scrambled out of the way as the last chevron encoded.

The wormhole whooshed into existence with a blast of ozone and a bass fugue John could feel through his whole body as he bolted around to the MALP. The jumpers' instant response to him was like coming home, but he wasn't comfortable with this intimate a relationship with a Stargate, let alone random data pads and ZPMs. He reached for the transmitter and froze. He felt something building in the DHD's ruined base, heard a weird little scatter of dissonant notes. Then it cut off abruptly. He realized what it was and swore in frustration. "Rodney, I think the 'gate just ate the ZPM."

Rodney stepped to the DHD's pit, staring down into it. He moaned a little, sounding as if he was deeply in pain. "I think the Ancients might have anticipated that Dorane might try to dial manually. Obviously, they wanted to keep that to a minimum, so they not only doctored the crystal, they booby-trapped the DHD to eat any directly connected power source."

"Yeah. I guess it didn't take him long to use up those two ZPMs after all." And that meant they only had this one chance to convince Dorane to let them in. "Here we go." He keyed on the transmitter. "Sheppard to Atlantis."

The radio crackled and static filled the little screen. The moment stretched and John had time to wonder what he would say if Peter Grodin answered as though everything was normal. The moment stretched longer, and every muscle in his body tensed as he felt the sudden conviction that no one was going to answer, that he was talking to a dead city, as dead as the ruins behind him. Then Dorane's voice said, "Now this is unexpected."

"Unexpected is right," John said, having no problem making his voice sound rough and on edge. His imagination presented him with a picture of Dorane standing at the 'gate control console on the gallery, surrounded by dead operations staff. "The Koan didn't eat me, though not from lack of trying. How's that invasion of Atlantis going?"

"It surprises me that you were able to dial the Stargate." Standing next to John, Rodney mouthed the words *no, really.* "Why did you bother?"

"My guess is it's not going so well there. I figure you

didn't realize how many changes we'd made, how many of the Ancient components had failed, how jury-rigged everything was." Dorane would have been expecting Atlantis as it was before the Ancients left, not consoles with laptops tied into their systems and naquadah power generators.

No answer. *He wouldn't be talking at all if he wasn't at least curious,* John reminded himself. He said, "I have something that could make the transition a little easier for you."

"And that would be?"

"McKay. The Koan didn't eat him either. He knows more about how our equipment meshes with the Ancients' than anybody else there." *If he's got Zelenka under his control, this is so not going to work.*

Another long silence, while John's nerves grated. He forced himself not to speak, to pretend he was the one holding all the cards. Then Dorane said, "Better than Kavanagh?"

Beside him Rodney rolled his eyes in disgust. John said, "Kavanagh's a specialist; McKay knows the whole city. He set up the new power grid, the new 'gate protocols." McKay was motioning with his bound hands, encouraging John to continue. "Everything."

"And he will agree to help me, to buy your freedom from my old prison?"

"Well, he won't agree, but I'm sure you can convince him otherwise. He doesn't have a choice."

Dorane still didn't sound that interested. "You would turn against your own people to assist me?"

John took what he figured was their last chance. "Maybe you ought to turn on the visual and take a look."

McKay, now hovering behind John and hopping from foot to foot, apparently decided he should be unconscious, and threw himself down on the platform, sprawling half on his side, bound hands stuck out obviously in front of him. He raised inquiring brows at John, who nodded and gave him a thumb's up. McKay was right, it did look convincing. The video crackled into life, and McKay slumped over,

eyes closed. The MALP's camera swiveled toward them, but
John was more interested in the image fuzzily forming on
the screen. It was the 'gate control gallery, Dorane standing
over the dialing console, frowning thoughtfully at something
beyond the edge of the screen. The MALP's telemetry and
video went through a laptop, and John wondered if Dorane
realized the little thingy to the side was a camera, that the
system had been set to send video at the same time it received
it. *As soon as we step through, I can get him from the 'gate
platform.* His chest tightened at the thought that this plan just
might work. Knowing where Dorane was standing in the large
'gate room was going to shave seconds off his time.

Someone else moved in the video's background, and John
saw it was Peter Grodin. He was sitting down and someone
was covering him with a P-90. Grodin craned his neck to see
the laptop's screen, his expression confused and incredulous.
Then Dorane said, "Take off the eye protection."

John gritted his teeth, feeling like somebody's science
exhibit, and pulled off the glasses and the bandana. The light
stung his eyes, and he shaded them with a hand, flexing his
fingers to extend the claws.

Dorane said nothing. Afraid he was losing his audience,
John added, "Yeah, it worked. You think my own people
would take me back after this? I'm not human anymore! If
they got their hands on me, I'd spend the rest of my life locked
up in a lab, as somebody's pet experiment, cut to pieces while
they took tissue samples and made things out of my blood!"
He put the glasses back on, unable to stand the glare, and saw
Peter looked shocked, utterly boggled, and a little offended,
as if he couldn't believe John would really think that. John
started playing to him, finding it easier than trying to convince Dorane. He twisted his face into his best impression
of Jack Nicholson playing an ax murderer, and added on a
note of rising hysteria, "And they never trusted me in the first
place! I'm only the military commander because I shot Colonel Sumner! He never even wanted me on the expedition, I'm

only here because I had the gene and O'Neill forced him to take me!" He paused for breath. His throat was dry and it made his voice so rough he barely recognized it.

Grodin's expression now clearly said, 'Fine, Sheppard's turned into an alien and gone barking, that's just lovely.'

Behind John, Rodney groaned, obviously wanting in on the drama. John pretended to kick him, his boot connecting with Rodney's ribs though not nearly as hard as it would look. He hissed a heartfelt, "Will you shut up!"

John saw Dorane turn his head, and heard him ask someone, "Who was this Sumner?"

A voice, so dull and lifeless that John couldn't recognize it, answered, "The military commander of the expedition."

John took a deep breath. Dorane had obviously been using his control drug. Dorane asked, "Did your friend Sheppard truly kill him?"

"That's what we were told. He said...it was because a Wraith was killing Sumner, he was dying."

Whoever it was was speaking literally, as if he was under hypnosis, but the effect of it was to make the incident sound less like a mercy killing and more like a murder. Feeling this just might work, John snarled, "Hey! Are you going to drop the force shield, or should I just kill McKay?" The Stargate's bass harmonic was turning impatient as it counted down its thirty-eight minute window. He shouted, "Come on, the Stargate's getting pissed off!"

Dorane looked into the video monitor for another long moment. Then he smiled. "I'll drop the shield. Come through."

John cut the transmission, made sure the light on the MALP's camera was out. "We're clear."

McKay shoved himself into a sitting position and glared at him. "Ow," he said pointedly.

"That didn't hurt." John gave him an arm up. "I could see Grodin in the monitor. He looked okay, and I think he bought the act."

"Who knew Peter was that big an idiot." McKay took a deep breath. "It occurs to me that if you don't take Dorane out in the first minute, I'm going to be tortured to death and you're going to be dissected, and everybody else will still die."

"Yeah, Plan B sucks, but considering that Plan C was hanging ourselves—" The Stargate informed John that the shield on the receiving gate was down and they were clear for entry, so go already. He picked up the 9mm and made sure it was ready, then grabbed McKay's arm. They stepped through the wormhole.

CHAPTER NINE

After the heat of the plain, the cool air of Atlantis was a mild shock. They walked into a 'gate room that was lit only by low-level emergency lights and the wormhole's watery blue glow, the late afternoon sun muted by the colored window insets. The Stargate was playing a loud surrealist concert in John's head, and he hadn't stepped into a darkened 'gate room since they had first found Atlantis resting on the bottom of its alien ocean, just before the city had come alive to welcome him and the others who had the Ancient gene. The large space would be oppressively dim to normal human eyes, but John could see and recognize the figures standing on the gallery level.

There were a dozen or more Koan up there, as well as Ford, Benson, Kinjo, Parker, and Yamato, all with P-90s, all of whom must be under Dorane's control. That really wasn't good. But Dorane still stood beside the dialing console, and he couldn't control anybody if he was dead. John pulled off the sunglasses, meaning to disguise the motion of raising the pistol; he stopped just in time.

Though he couldn't see it, there was a little harmonic of active Ancient technology, announcing its presence right in the center of Dorane's chest. *Oh, crap,* John thought, sick, his hand tightening on the pistol's grip. *Apparently Plan B was worse than we thought.* He kept the pistol at his side.

Managing to talk without moving his lips, Rodney said, "Why aren't you shooting him?"

Teeth gritted, John replied the same way. "Because he's wearing a personal shield."

"Oh, God," Rodney said aloud.

"Shut up," John snarled at him, making it loud enough to hear up in the gallery. All they had between them and being shot by their own people was convincing Dorane. And John had just recalled that McKay, like most people with minimal filtering between brain and mouth, was kind of a lousy liar. "Seriously," he added, hoping McKay got it. McKay looked righteously offended, so John could only hope he had.

John heard the Stargate make a low bass groan right before it shut down. The wormhole popped out of existence, plunging the 'gate room into another level of shadow. In its absence John could hear whispers and echoes in the crystals and conduits, murmurs under the floor, in the walls, stretching up into the sealed jumper bay above the room. It didn't hurt, it wasn't intrusive, but it made his skin crawl like a constant low-level electric charge. In a way, it was a relief. If Atlantis' ATA had sounded anything like the repository's screaming and dissonance, John would have been out of his head before he got ten feet away from the Stargate. But still, he had the feeling this wasn't right. *I really, really don't think the ATA gene is supposed to work this way.*

Dorane was coming down the steps from the gallery, dressed now in a loose gray jacket and pants. It might just be John's altered eyesight, but he looked different. The flesh around his eyes was sunken and his cheeks were hollow, as if he had aged another decade in the past day. It might be some kind of delayed effect of the stasis container.

John could see Peter Grodin up at the dialing console, watching anxiously. It was Ford who was covering Grodin with a P-90, and that was just weird. Ford's face was blank, his eyes on Grodin. He hadn't looked down at the Stargate, at John and McKay standing on the embarkation floor. It suddenly occurred to John that they had been assuming the people who were infected with the mind control would get over it, either with help or on their own, and they had no guarantee of that. The empty expression on Ford's face made John wonder what it did to your mind, your brain, if there was permanent damage.

Dorane stopped at the base of the stairs, watching them

with that thoughtful absence of emotion. Carson Beckett probably felt more in common with his lab mice than Dorane did with his experimental subjects; he certainly treated them better. "I'm surprised you trusted me to open the force shield," Dorane said. He made no signal, but several Koan followed him down from the gallery, moving fluidly in the half-light. Most of them were armed now with pistols or P-90s. John wondered what their learning curve was, how many of them had accidentally or on purpose shot each other so far.

"I didn't have to trust you," John told him, "The Stargate said it was open." Dorane must know John could hear the bastard version of the ATA gene that the repository was saturated with; John just wasn't sure if he knew about the side effect on the real ATA gene. And it was easier to sound crazy if he could just stick with the truth and not have to make things up.

Dorane's gaze flicked to the Stargate, but he didn't argue. He said, "Then demonstrate trust by giving up your weapon."

John could see from here that the personal shield, a small crystal device that rested on the chest, was concealed by a fold of Dorane's jacket. If John hadn't had the new sensitivity to the Ancient technology, he wouldn't have known it was there and would have blown what little cover they had. *So giving me a clear shot at him was a test*. Maybe Dorane really did need them here for some reason, which seemed to indicate they might survive longer than the five minutes that was John's original estimate. He grabbed McKay's arm, dragging him forward, while McKay helped by saying, "Ow," a lot and trying to look more beat up than he actually was.

The Koan shifted forward, blocking the way, their dark eyes alert and steady. They looked far less twitchy, and somehow even more dangerous here than they had in the tunnels under the repository. John would have thought being removed from the place might have made them less susceptible to Dorane's control, but it just seemed to have solidified it.

John said, "Hi, guys. Miss me?" He ejected the clip and laid both it and the 9mm on the floor. It wasn't like the gun was going to do them any good anyway. The shield made Dorane invulnerable, creating an impervious body-hugging force field. He must have brought it with him; they had only found one in Atlantis, which had initialized to McKay so no one else could use it. Then the Darkness creature had sucked the energy out of it when McKay was trying to get it out through the 'gate, and the shield had never worked since.

Dorane's expression was impenetrable. "Search them."

John submitted to being awkwardly patted down by the Koan, though the one doing him growled the entire time, making it clear it would much rather be disemboweling him. When they stepped back, empty-handed, Dorane said, "Very good," and didn't order anybody to shoot. He turned away, starting back up the steps to the control gallery. The Koan gestured with their weapons and John and McKay followed.

Seeing Dorane in control of their 'gate room was painful in a way John hadn't expected. He had never been part of the SGC; this was a Pegasus Galaxy thing, where access to a Stargate was to be protected at all cost, at any cost. Wraith might come through the 'gates, but mostly they came from the air, and controlling your 'gate meant survival.

McKay asked tightly, "What did you do with the rest of the people who were stationed in this area?"

It was the question John had been trying to think of a way to ask without wrecking his act. Dorane glanced back with mild interest. "They are being held in a secure room on the level below. Your leader Weir was very sympathetic to my people's plight, and obligingly sent two gateships back for them. Teyla and Kinjo accompanied them, and by the time they landed to pick up the Koan, the majority of each crew, besides the pilots, of course, were mine."

The pilots would have had the Ancient gene or the ATA therapy. John hoped they were both still alive. "And so you're moving in permanently?" he asked. He threw a look at Ford where he stood like a statue on the gallery, guarding Grodin.

Dorane laughed. "Of course not. Without full power, this city is ridiculously vulnerable to the Wraith. It's fit only for scavengers, now."

"Tell us something we don't know," John said, giving Rodney, whose mouth was open, a chance to think twice and shut it.

Dorane reached the gallery and stopped to look directly at McKay. Private Benson came to stand at his side, his expression dull-eyed and blank. Dorane said, "Some of your people have managed to fortify one of the levels lower down in this section. The doors are sealed, the transporters refuse access, and I can't convince the city systems to give me control."

That's a relief. John was betting it was the area around the medical lab, which was in one of the most defensible sections of the city's center and a designated point of retreat if the operations tower became compromised. Which meant, if they were lucky, Dorane hadn't found and killed Beckett, who was the strongest natural Ancient gene carrier next to John. He doubted Dorane had managed to trap the entire expedition. If the group holding the medlab had been able to raise any kind of alarm, there were probably people who had escaped to go to ground in the remote parts of the city. But even if they couldn't be found, they were still trapped. There was no way off Atlantis other than the Stargate or a jumper, and the mainland was too far away to reach except by air. Hopefully Dorane hadn't had time to send anybody there to mess with the Athosians yet.

Dorane was still eyeing McKay with thoughtful deliberation. Rodney said grimly, "I don't know yet if anyone has told you about my various allergies, but if you use any of your freakish retroviruses on me, I'll probably just fall over dead." He managed to sound as though he was sort of looking forward to it.

Dorane countered, "But it might just make for a more interesting—if brief—experiment."

John shook his head and stared at the ceiling. *See, this is why I told you to shut up, Rodney.* McKay did a little uncomfortable twitch, but lifted his chin and snapped, "Would it be more or less brief than getting shot?"

Dorane didn't bother to answer that one. "Are you willing to help remove the naquadah generators for transport back to the repository in exchange for your life—for the moment? Dr. Kavanagh has explained how the generators are tied in to the original power systems, but he admits that they are dangerous devices, and that as you installed them, you are better qualified to remove them."

The naquadah generators? John thought, eyes narrowing. *He's serious—he really is going back there.* McKay looked as if he had been asked to remove his own kidney with a spoon, but he said, "Oh right, as if I have any choice."

Dorane inclined his head, apparently taking that for acceptance. "If you complete that successfully, perhaps I will need you for a longer time."

"You've been here before, after the Ancients left," John said, interrupting whatever McKay was about to reply. "Why didn't you take the ZPMs? You could have gotten through the 'gate with at least two of them without collapsing the city shields."

"I had no need for them at that point. I had given up." Dorane's eyes fixed on John. He said, with an eerie lack of inflection, "Your people have given me new hope." His expression shifted and he almost smiled. "And you seem to have done an excellent job of reviving the city of your forebears. Except of course for the essential defensive elements. I'm certain the Lantians would be delighted that their children have made such good use of their legacy. And that those children will be of such help to me."

It wasn't comforting to know that their speculation had been correct; Dorane didn't want the city, he wanted the people in it. John said, "Yeah, it's too bad they aren't here to see it. Of course if they were, they'd probably be killing you right about now. Too bad they didn't take care of that earlier." He showed his teeth in something that wasn't a smile. He could feel McKay glaring at him, but he was supposed to be crazy, so he didn't think a lot of hostility was out of place.

"I'm sure they felt their punishment was effective." Dorane turned, starting down the gallery, telling John, "Come with me."

John followed, Benson trailing behind him, obviously as insurance he didn't change his mind.

McKay started to follow, but a Koan blocked his way. John glanced back over his shoulder, keeping his expression non-committal. McKay managed to glare and look frightened at the same time. John didn't like the idea of being separated either, but he didn't see any way to prevent it.

Dorane led the way down to the conference room. The embossed panels were already open, allowing access into the room where the walls were all soft metallics, with squares of copper, lapis, and turquoise. When Dorane walked in and sat down at the table, John had that sudden feeling of violation you got when your house was robbed, that 'unwelcome strangers touching your stuff' feeling. This was the room where they had briefings, yelled at each other, made plans, worried about overdue 'gate teams.

Laroque, one of the operations staff who worked with Grodin, was seated at the table already, an open laptop in front of her. The dead expression on her face told John that she had been given the control drug. She had a bruise on her cheek, and her dark hair had been pulled out of its usually scrupulously neat bun, as if someone had grabbed her by it. It provided John with an image of what might have happened on the control gallery, and he had to stop in the doorway and quell a violently homicidal impulse. Benson had a P-90 aimed at his back, and it wasn't like the personal shield would let him rip Dorane's throat out anyway.

Dorane regarded him for a moment with that chill calm, then gestured to another chair. As John dropped into it Dorane said, "There is another small pocket of resistance. They have not sealed themselves off as well as the others, but they are trapped, so there is not much point in attempting to extract them, at least for the moment. I have jammed your communication devices and had the Lantian com system taken offline, but I can speak to them through this technology." He glanced at Laroque, and she used the laptop's keyboard to call up a program.

John just had time to realize that the laptop must be set up for video conferencing when the screen flickered to a view of another room. Elizabeth was leaning on a table, turning her head to face the video feed. He heard a rustle as someone else moved just out of the camera's range. It gave John an instant to brace himself. Elizabeth saw him and straightened. "John!" Then, staring, she asked uncertainly, "John?"

He didn't answer her, on impulse slumping in the chair and avoiding her eyes like a sulky teenager. He knew he might not be able to resist trying to give her a signal of some kind, and Dorane would be watching for that. It was probably one of the reasons that he wanted this little confrontation.

"Your Major Sheppard is helping me now," Dorane told her. He didn't gloat, he just said it calmly, as though they were at a staff meeting talking about reassignments.

John could feel Elizabeth's eyes boring into the side of his head. The laptop's microphone picked up other people moving in the room, a startled murmur. John slumped a little further in the chair. He hoped she had Bates with her, and at least a couple of men from the Marine security detail. He realized his claws were out; there had to be some sort of impulse-control mechanism there that he just hadn't mastered yet. She asked quietly, "What did you do to him?"

Dorane gestured, as if the answer was obvious. "Just a successful experiment."

John slanted a look at her in time to see her expression harden. Behind her he could see blue-gray wall panels with silver trim, but that didn't narrow it down enough to tell him which room it was. She asked, "Is Dr. McKay alive as well?"

"As long as he is useful." Dorane leaned forward, sounding reasonable. "This can all be solved in a very simple way. You have something I want. If you give it to me, I will leave you in peace."

John didn't think there was any way Elizabeth would buy it, but just in case he looked at Dorane, brows lifted in incredulous amusement. He considered bursting into laughter but decided he should hold onto that until later.

Elizabeth smiled thinly, making it clear she was humoring Dorane. "And what would that be?"

"The memory core of the display chamber you found recently. Your people spoke to me of it, that you managed to make it play a portion of the display, and found the 'gate address for the athenaeum there. I have been to the chamber, but the memory has been removed."

"I don't know anything about that." Elizabeth eyed him. "Why do you want it?"

Good question, John thought, keeping the surprise off his face. He wouldn't have guessed that the display held any information that Dorane didn't already have.

"It contains data that is useless to you, but important to me. I've tried to retrieve it before. After the Lantians departed, I had to destroy two subspace power sources in order to make my crippled dialing device work, to come here searching for it. I found the display, but I thought it damaged beyond hope."

Elizabeth's brows drew together, and John knew she didn't understand. He didn't either. *He came to the city just to look for the display, and when he found it was broken he didn't trash the place, didn't go anywhere else through the 'gate, he just gave up and went home. Okay, that...doesn't make sense.* Elizabeth asked, "If you've come here before, why didn't you escape through our Stargate to another world? You could've taken a jumper—"

Dorane spread his hands. "Woman, escape from what? I have always been exactly where I wanted to be. I would not stay in this city for any reason; its atmosphere is inimical to me. I need to stay at my athenaeum." He showed faint exasperation. "Now the only reason to remove the memory core was to try to read the damaged portion. Tell me which of your people would do that."

Zelenka, John thought. He must have removed the core after they left, to keep working on it in case there were maps or structural information that they could have used. Elizabeth said, "I have no idea. No one was assigned to work on that."

"I hate waste, but I will begin killing your people if I do not get a satisfactory answer." Dorane regarded her steadily.

Dorane must have already asked the personnel he had under his control, who would have had no choice but to answer. But unless Zelenka had mentioned it to some of the other scientists and techs, they might not realize he had been with John and McKay when they found the thing. *Except Ford. Ford knows Zelenka's the most likely candidate. And Ford knows I know.* John said, "I bet I can guess who has it."

Dorane shifted, lifting his brows. "And?"

"And it's Dr. Zelenka, but you already know that from questioning the others." He tilted his head toward Benson. "I'm guessing what you really want to know is where he is."

From the screen, Elizabeth said sharply, "John, don't—"

Dorane motioned to Laroque, and she cut the video. He turned to face John directly.

John said, "He's down in the medlab, keeping you out of the computer system." Elizabeth wouldn't have been as worried if Zelenka was holed up with her. "You've cut off access to Atlantis' com system and you're jamming our radio traffic, so they won't know about me. I can get in there and talk them into giving me the memory core."

Dorane lifted his brows. "I thought you said that they would no longer trust you, or consider you one of them, after your transformation?"

Crap. John hesitated for a half a heartbeat, then remembered just in time that he was supposed to be crazy and crazy people believed contradictory things all the time; he shouldn't be trying to come up with an elaborate rationalization here. He made himself look confused, and gave Dorane his best 'I said what?' expression.

It worked. Dorane's eyes went hooded. "Very well. I suppose it will be quicker than waiting until they starve." He leaned back in his chair. "The Koan will follow you to the first obstructed passage."

On the control gallery, the Koan guards, who seemed more in charge here than the Atlantis personnel Dorane had under his control, let Peter Grodin untie Rodney's hands. Squinting in the dim light, Rodney eyed him suspiciously. Kavanagh had behaved normally, or at least in a Kavanagh-like fashion, for a long period after being infected. "Why didn't he give you the control drug?"

Grodin threw a grim look at Ford. "He wanted someone to operate the equipment up here. As far as I can tell, he can't allow an infected individual enough initiative to perform any kind of complicated task without losing control over them. Unfortunately, 'stand here and shoot anyone who disobeys orders' isn't a complicated task."

"Well, that's just fantastic." Rodney sat down at one of the locked stations, rubbing his eyes. It explained why Dorane needed Rodney to disconnect the naquadah generators. He hadn't maintained that strict control over Kavanagh initially, but the first order he must have given was for Kavanagh to forget anything out of the ordinary had happened. That kind of loose control wouldn't work on people who were dismantling Atlantis' power grid.

Grodin said quietly, "He tried to initialize some of the other consoles, the ones we haven't been able to make work, but he couldn't. Is—"

One of the Koan came and stood over them, glaring suspiciously, but after that Grodin kept trying to catch Rodney's eye, until Rodney turned and gave him the 'oh my God, will you stop that' glare. Ford, his head still bandaged from the blow Kavanagh had given him, stood nearby watching them completely without expression, like some alien pod-person replica of the real man. Rodney had no idea whether Ford would be compelled to volunteer information to Dorane or not, but he didn't want to take the chance.

"McKay," Grodin whispered.

"Not now," Rodney said through gritted teeth.

Grodin persisted, "Sergeant Stackhouse's team has been on that three-day trading mission to the Enarians. They're due back later tonight—"

Rodney interrupted, "He'll order you to open the force field. You won't have to kill them." *Though if we don't get out of this, they may not thank you for that later.*

"How do you—"

"He doesn't want them dead. That's what, six more bodies for his experiment? Markham's with them, so that's one more Ancient gene carrier to torture."

Grodin hesitated, watching Rodney uncertainly. "What did he do to Sheppard?"

"What did it look like?" Rodney snapped. He was desperately afraid of giving something away, and starting to have flashbacks to the Genii and Kolya's occupation of the city. Not to mention the sour stomach and a pounding in his left temple that signaled the incipient arrival of a headache from hell.

He finally saw Sheppard and Dorane emerge from the conference room, the Koan and Benson following. The tight pain between Rodney's shoulderblades eased just a little. He realized he had been waiting for the sound of gunfire.

Sheppard swept the gallery with one tight glance, giving nothing away, then went down toward the center stairwell without glancing back, the two Koan following him like well-trained attack dogs at heel.

Rodney swallowed in a dry throat, craning his neck until

Sheppard was out of sight. *Great, great, great. I have no clue what we're doing.* Or if Sheppard had a clue what they were doing. In the shadows of the gallery it was impossible to tell if he looked any worse. In the bright sunlight before stepping through the 'gate, he had already looked drawn and obviously ill. Sheppard had always seemed as if he was nothing but bone and muscle, but in the last few hours Rodney was willing to swear the man had actually lost weight.

"You are concerned for him?" Dorane asked, and Rodney realized with a start that he had been watching him. Dorane strolled down the gallery toward him. "He betrayed you."

"Well, you know, that would really be your fault, wouldn't it?" Rodney snapped, swiveling around to face him. "And can we just get back to threatening me? Because frankly I'm not comfortable discussing my personal relationships with you, considering how you're planning to kill everyone I know."

Dorane dismissed that with a slight shrug. "It will be interesting to see how long he survives."

Rodney hesitated, knowing he shouldn't fall for the bait but unable to stop himself. "What do you mean?"

Dorane watched Rodney, his eyes opaque. "The Lantian-descended Thesians I tested that particular strain on only lived for one or two days. But I understand that your people also have some degree of genetic variation from the prototypal Lantian stock, so that estimate may be unrealistic." His voice hardened. "Now, let's get started on your naquadah generators."

Rodney stared at him, trying to tell if that was the truth or just another sick little lie. It was depressing enough to be the truth. His jaw set, he stood up. Dorane would be gauging the time by the rotation of the repository's planet, and by that measure it had already been a full day since Sheppard was infected.

They didn't have much time.

John took the central stairs down, ignoring the two Koan for now. Despite this minor victory, he couldn't shake the feeling that Plan B was still circling the drain. The problem was that Dorane really, really liked playing with people, and he had a tremendous amount of experience at it. John could too readily imagine that Dorane was playing both him and McKay, making them think they were fooling him.

But he obviously wanted that memory core very badly, badly enough to risk letting John run loose around the city to get it.

They had speculated that all the Ancients' tinkering with the Stargate had been a cat and mouse game to force Dorane to give up something. *If all he gave up was information... what's the point in getting it back?* But if there was something else there, something the Ancients might have recorded on the core that Dorane needed, or at least thought he needed, maybe to keep his experiments going... Since he now had a new pool of human DNA to meddle with, he would be all the more anxious to get it.

John paused on the next landing, getting a view down the corridor. There was a room down there that was used for big meetings and science team conferences. It had one door and had always looked as if it would be relatively easy to secure. And yes, there were at least six Koan and four dead-eyed Marines stationed outside it. That had to be where Dorane was keeping the rest of the operations staff and the other expedition members he had managed to capture.

John eyed the corridor, considering it. Dorane had basically tried to hand them a scenario where John would have to kill half the Marines to save the rest of the expedition. But John had no plans to take him up on that one. Though it was really starting to worry him that he hadn't seen Teyla yet. He had expected to find her guarding the prisoners.

The Koan growled, and John moved on.

The lights were dimmed through every section they passed, the green bubble pillars motionless and silent. A few levels down in an open foyer, another group of Koan were gathered around the sealed door to the medlab corridor. They growled, glaring at John, but apparently they had gotten the word to let him through. He pushed past them, pretending to ignore the claws and bared teeth and the inexpertly held guns. As he reached the door, it slid open without waiting for him to touch the control, invitingly undefended. It revealed the long corridor that accessed most of the labs and work areas on this level, the walls decorated with copper bands enclosing squares of soft metallic grays and blues. The Koan hung back uneasily.

The half-light was like daylight to John's altered eyes, and he could see there were six dead Koan scattered at various points down the hallway. It was probably lucky that Dorane was using the Koan for cannon fodder so far, obviously meaning to save expedition personnel for experiments.

John took a long step forward and, without glancing back, said, "Bye, guys," and told the door to close.

It slid shut, leaving the Koan on the other side.

He studied the corridor again, making out a wet area about midway along, and something further down that looked like a car battery that had been blasted to bits with gunfire. John would bet that the car battery object was a decoy; this corridor had been booby-trapped by desperate and frightened men and women, some of whom had been able to build atomic bombs by the time they were twelve. There was no way he was going down there, not even in rubber-soled boots.

Maybe that was the game Dorane was playing; he had sent John down here to be accidentally killed by his own people.

John turned left instead, taking the side corridor toward the outer ring of this section. He knew it would be easier to get to the medlab from the level above through some access passages in the floors, but he didn't want the Koan to twig to that. Dorane obviously didn't know about it, or he would have tried it by now.

Even though Dorane had lived here with the Ancients for a time, they had probably never had to send people to crawl around in the floors replacing fried crystal conduit, with

Kavanagh and Simpson debating the right procedure and giving contradictory instructions via headset radio, with the added attractions of McKay berating them between bouts of claustrophobia and Miko having to be retrieved from where her pants had gotten caught on a support brace. The Ancients probably had robots or genetically-trained sea monkeys or something to do those little jobs for them.

The next doorway was quarantine-sealed and stubbornly refused to respond to the wall console or ATA coaxing, but John fiddled the crystals the way McKay had shown him. As the door started to slide open, John got the sunglasses on, wincing. Even though the sky was starting to redden into sunset, the glare off the water was still bright enough to blind him.

Outside, his back to Atlantica's endless sea and the cool evening breeze ruffling his hair, John sized up the expanse of city wall looming above him. There were tiny little ledges and arching girders that formed a decorative roof over all the balconies. The open platform he thought he had remembered was there, up one level and over to the side. It was the 'over to the side part' that was going to be tricky. It would have been crazy to try this without the claws; they would give him just enough extra purchase to make it possible. Sort of possible.

John stepped up on the railing, balancing easily. A long way down, waves washed up against the platforms and supports at the tower's foot. He knew his own weight and the approximate distance down, so it was hard not to automatically calculate the velocity he would reach by the time he hit the base. *Right. Here goes.* He caught a handhold in the decorative embossing, and wedged a boot into the junction where the girder met the wall, and hauled himself up.

CHAPTER TEN

Rodney really, really didn't see a way out of this. Watched carefully by the Koan, he was forced to follow Dorane, two Marines, and Ford to the naquadah generator that powered the lower center section of the city, including the medlab. Rodney had tried to steer Dorane toward one of the generators for the other sections, but Dorane hadn't gone for that.

Part of him was wondering how much of the system Zelenka had trashed while sealing off the medlab. As Rodney knew very well, there was nothing like the threat of certain death to inspire speed and creativity. Between the damage Dorane and the Koan had caused, and the damage Zelenka and the others had done trying to stop them, it would probably take a month to repair everything. If they got out of this alive. Rodney groaned mentally, wishing an insane repair schedule was his only problem.

If the power was completely cut, the doors on the medlab level could be pried open manually. Rodney knew that was where Dorane had sent a large number of the Koan and several of the expedition's military personnel that he had under his control, ready to move in.

In the lead, Ford took the last turn in the corridor, reaching the doorway to the generator room. A cardboard sign with the words 'stay out' and a badly-drawn skull and crossbones had been stuck on the wall next to it with sticky tape. At the time Rodney had thought the symbolism was a nice touch; now it was all too appropriate. Even if some of the expedition members escaped into the unexplored sections and managed to evade Dorane, how were they going to survive with the city a dead powerless hulk? And Rodney didn't suppose Dorane would be stupid enough to leave any jumpers behind.

The door slid open to reveal a dimly-lit five-sided room

with antique gold walls and burnished copper trim, colors that suggested an upscale restaurant more than they did a main access point to the city's power grid. Unless you were Ancient, apparently. There were three other sealed doors, all corridor accesses, and the naquadah generator sat near the center. It was small for something so powerful, positioned on a low pallet and connected into Atlantis' system through the access points in the floor and wall panels. Dorane eyed it with an expression Rodney could only interpret as skepticism, asking Kavanagh, "Is that it?"

"Yes," Kavanagh said, as bland as if they were discussing the weather. "That's the generator."

Rodney eyed him sharply. He told Dorane, "You shouldn't have killed Kolesnikova. She knew more about naquadah power generation than Kavanagh could ever learn."

"I could control Kavanagh," Dorane replied easily, as if it was nothing. "She had your gene retrovirus."

Rodney had wondered if Dorane had ordered Kavanagh to kill Irina. But that sounded as if he had done it himself.

Rodney remembered thinking once that it was bizarrely unfair that Sheppard and Carson and the others had come by the gene naturally, just because they had promiscuous ancestors who must have been lining up at the proverbial dock the day the Ancients had landed on Earth. And it had been a huge relief when the ATA therapy had worked for Rodney. Now it was going to get all of them killed in a horrible way, and that was just typical.

"You know why we're here. Prepare it for transport." Dorane looked at Kavanagh. "Bring the tools. Make sure he uses only the correct ones needed for the job at hand."

Rodney looked down at the generator, grimacing. He had put so much work into getting these things to mesh with the city's more advanced systems; taking it out was really going to hurt. At least he could do it slowly and blame the low emergency lighting. "I assume you want it intact, and not in burnt-out pieces, so it's going to take some time since I can barely see what I'm doing."

"That can be remedied," Dorane told him, his expression bland.

Rodney threw him a wary look, not sure if he meant a flashlight or a little genetic adjustment. Except for the lights on the P-90s, which the men weren't using because of the Koan, nobody seemed to be carrying a flashlight. He said stiffly, "I'll make do."

Kavanagh brought a tool case over and opened it. Rodney glared at him, but Kavanagh's normally annoying face was blank, just like the Marines and Ford. Rodney selected the screwdriver needed to get the generator's panels open, holding it out to Kavanagh for inspection. Kavanagh nodded, and Rodney sneered, saying, "I'm not quite insane enough to blow this thing up with me standing over it." *Not yet, anyway.* If they got to the fifth generator and Sheppard still hadn't shown up, Rodney knew he might rethink that position. For all he knew, Dorane's genetic tampering had finally run its course and Sheppard was already lying dead in one of the corridors.

Dorane watched him get the panels off the generator's access points, and it made the back of Rodney's neck sweat. He flinched when Dorane said suddenly, "I am only just realizing how apt my earlier comment was about the city being fit only for scavengers. Your technology is cobbled together from many different sources, is it not? You weren't lying about coming here from another galaxy."

I'm only just realizing how apt my earlier comment was about you being a serial killer. Rodney said flatly, "No, we weren't lying." Dorane seemed to know the Ancient systems fairly well, but it was the interfaces with Earth-based computers and technology that baffled him. Considering how much of it was a hybrid mix of Terran, Goa'uld, Asgard, and Ancient, it probably wasn't surprising that Dorane didn't understand it. *Or us.*

"You did not know of the Wraith, when you came here to

loot Atlantis? I suppose your Lantian ancestors did not bother to pass along the story of their defeat."

Rodney set his jaw, barely managing to stifle his first knee-jerk reply. He knew Dorane wanted him to assert the expedition's right to the city, based on Earth's inheritance from the Ancients. *Guess what? You're the only person with an ATA gene handy, and he wants an excuse to torture you.* He said only, "We didn't know."

Dorane continued to watch him from what Rodney thought was way too close a distance, but didn't reply. Rodney tried to focus his attention on the delicate maze of circuitry inside the generator's connection panel and ignore the lingering painful death that was in his immediate future.

In his more optimistic moments, of which there were few, Rodney had imagined what things would be like if they ended up staying here forever, or at least all lived long enough to die of natural causes. Somehow in that scenario, Sheppard had still been here too, though God knew after years of crash landings, head injuries, and Wraith stunner attacks he would probably have even more impulse-control issues than... *Of course,* Rodney thought with a sudden surge of hope. He leaned down over the connecting conduit to conceal his expression. Now he knew what the plan was.

He just hoped Sheppard was still alive to carry it out.

The climb was an intense few minutes, but John was able to make the other balcony without dying. From there he went to the corridor just above the one that approached the medlab from the outer wing of the city, then found the correct floor access panel. He pried it open and crawled through the floor to find the ceiling panel that would open inside the quarantine-sealed area, on the opposite side of the medlab from the booby-trapped corridor of death that led from the center stair shaft.

The floor space was just as cramped as he remembered it, and much warmer. *Not to mention airless,* he thought, wriggling past the layers of conduit. When they had had people working down here, McKay had managed to deflect the return air for the circulating system through this passage, and John hadn't realized what a difference it made. It was also much noisier this time, with the sounds from the ATA growing into a painfully incessant clamor. By the time he reached the ceiling panel, John was gritting his teeth and having unpleasant flashbacks to the repository.

He hung upside down out of the ceiling for a moment, just glad to be able to take a full breath, checking the copper-colored floor for suspicious objects and substances. He had been hoping this corridor would be clear, that Beckett's group had planned to retreat down it if the medlab was compromised. Not seeing anything indicative of traps, he unfolded himself out of the narrow panel and dropped to the floor. The door to the rear area of the medlab area was around the next corner, and it was sealed tight.

John listened at it for a moment and heard muffled voices. He pounded on the door and called, "Hey, can anybody hear me in there? It's Sheppard."

After a moment he heard, "Major Sheppard?" It was Beckett's voice, incredulous and so relieved John could barely understand him through the slurring vowels. "Radek, get over here and open this thing, it's Sheppard!"

"Wait, wait," John said hastily. *This could be awkward.* "Guys, listen to me. When you open the door, I want you to remember that it's me. Don't freak out and most importantly, don't shoot me. Okay?"

There was silence from the other side of the door. John could practically feel Zelenka and Beckett exchanging a look. Then Zelenka's voice said, warily, "Okay."

The door slid open, revealing one of the main medlab bays. It was as dimly lit as the rest of Atlantis, with storage cases and wire-framed supply racks standing against the soft copper and silver metallic walls. Then Beckett cautiously peered around one side of the door. He stared, blinked, and said,

"Oh, dear."

"What?" Zelenka peered around the other side of the door, holding a 9mm. His eyes widened, and he gasped, "*Kurva drát!*" He grabbed John by the front of his shirt and dragged him into the room.

John hit the wall console to seal the door again, and Zelenka stepped back, staring at him, gesturing helplessly. "What— What—?"

"What—?" Beckett echoed, then took John's wrist, turning his hand over so the claws were visible. "Holy crap. What in the hell did they do to you, boy?"

Covering the door were Ramirez and Audley, members of Bates' security detail, both carrying P-90s. Ramirez managed to keep his face blank, but Audley looked like he was having one of those Pegasus Galaxy moments where you had to keep doing your job but all you really wanted was a little time to freak out. John sympathized; he had been having one for the past day and a half. John said, "Dorane did this. It's a genetic retrovirus mutation thing. Rodney thinks—"

"Rodney's alive too?" Beckett demanded.

"Oh yeah, Rodney's fine. Sort of. He—" In the center section of the medical area where the diagnostic tables and beds were, he caught sight of Dr. Biro and several of the other medical personnel, as well as Dr. Sharpe, Miko, and a dozen or so others from the science team. Everybody was staring at John in consternation. Then a familiar figure shouldered a way through the crowd and John forgot about anything else. "Bates, what the hell are you doing here?" he demanded, furious. "Who's with Elizabeth?"

Bates had had his mouth open, probably to say something about how John should be held at gunpoint until they could find out why he looked like that, but John's irate question derailed that completely. "I don't know, Major," he said, his jaw set. "When they took the 'gate room, I was down on this level and I got cut off." He hadn't been patrolling or getting ready to go off world, so the only weapon he had was his sidearm.

"Oh, that's just fantastic!" John pressed the heel of his hand to his forehead, trying for calm. "So she's up there holding off a bunch of Koan and our guys with what, three techs and a laptop?"

Bates controlled a wince. "Dr. Simpson is with her—"

Simpson was another expert on Ancient technology, and she must be the one keeping the door sealed against Dorane. But that didn't make John feel any better. "Oh good, Elizabeth is being defended by another one of the *civilians* we're supposed to be *protecting*. Does something seem wrong with that picture, Bates? It's children, scientists, and diplomats first, did you not get the memo on that?"

Zelenka gestured impatiently. "Shout at Bates later! Tell us what happened now! Where is Rodney?"

John took a deep breath, forcing himself to calm down. Coming unglued at Bates didn't help, though it had made John feel better for about a minute. Bates' dark face was suffused with anger, Ramirez looked guilty, and Audley looked relieved, but then John had probably seemed a lot more like his normal self yelling at Bates than he had when he had first come into the room. "Rodney's with Dorane. The only way we could get back here from the repository was for me to pretend this retrovirus worked better on me than Dorane thought it would, that I wanted to help him take over the city."

Zelenka put his pistol down on a shelf to rub his eyes under his glasses. His face set grimly, Beckett explained, "When the bastard first got here, he told us you were both gone, that you'd been taken by Wraith. We thought— Well, you know what we thought."

Zelenka looked up, his eyes hard. "It was very affecting story, lots of detail. Rodney trapped by the Wraith and you going after him, only to be caught yourself."

"Later, when everything went to hell, we figured he had killed you both," Beckett added. "And just what is he up to? What has he done to Ford and Kavanagh and the others?"

John explained, "He used a drug, something that works on people like the ATA works on Ancient tech. Or at least that's what he said; he lies a lot. Teyla said he was in her head, and she had to do what he told her, and we don't think Kavanagh even knew he was infected until Dorane started giving him orders. It doesn't work so well on people who have the Ancient gene or the ATA therapy—that's why he killed Kolesnikova and Boerne." John flexed the set of claws Beckett was still examining, adding grimly, "I got the special."

Beckett swore. "I knew that damn gene would cause no end of trouble."

His face drawn, Zelenka shook his head. "That is... interesting problem. Interesting in the 'oh God' way." He gestured vaguely. "Does Rodney have little silver things too?"

"No, Rodney's normal—well, he's Rodney."

Beckett shook his head, his incredulous expression turning thoughtful. He took John's chin and turned his head so he could look at his ear. "What are these spines for? Antennae?"

John pulled away. "I have no idea, except it makes the Ancient technology seem a lot more interactive." Deciding it would be quicker to demonstrate than to try to explain, he nodded to a set of utilitarian metal shelves, incongruous against the smooth copper Atlantean wall panel. "That box there, on the bottom. In it there's five of those little portable medical scanners. No, wait, there's six. One...has a cracked control crystal." He had almost said "one says it has a cracked control crystal" but he didn't want to look that deranged, at least not in front of Bates.

Beckett and Zelenka stared at him. Zelenka muttered, "God, this would happen in middle of emergency."

"Oh yeah, it would have been so much fun if this happened without the invasion of the city and the whole helpless mind-controlled slaves bit." John conquered his irritation and continued, "Look, you guys have to figure out a way to stop the mind-control, because I'm stumped." He turned to Bates.

From what John could figure, they had one asset that Dorane wouldn't know about. "He's got a group of our people locked in that meeting room at the end of the south hall on the lower operations level. I need you to take Audley and Ramirez and get the Wraith stunners out of the armory, then take out the men guarding the door and get our people the hell out of there. I'll show you where the floor access is so you can get out of the medlab corridor without alerting the Koan. After that you're on your own; I have to go back to Dorane before he gets any more suspicious than he already is." It was there that the plan got really vague again, but he wasn't going to mention that aloud.

Bates nodded sharply, his expression of concentrated suspicion changing briefly to relief. The Wraith used the stunners to render their prey helpless for capture and feeding; with the four stunners the expedition had managed to acquire, Bates and the others could take out the controlled Marines without harming them, and it would be quicker and far more efficient than trying to use tasers. It would still be risky, as the men under Dorane's control would be shooting to kill, but it was the best chance they had to get out of this without a bloodbath. Bates said, "Then we take back the 'gate room."

"That's right." By that point Bates would have help from the personnel liberated from the Koan, and the 'gate room was a straight shot right up the tower. Cutting off Dorane's access to the Stargate would probably make him freaky and desperate as well as incredibly dangerous, but this was the only way they could play it. "They're holding Grodin and Laroque in there, and there might be some others, so don't give them time to shoot anybody. Grodin was the only one I saw who hadn't been given the control drug. Then come after Dorane. We should be at one of the naquadah generator stations—he's having McKay take them out for transport back to his planet. Don't waste any shots on Dorane, he's wearing a personal shield."

Bates' expression took on a new level of grim. Ramirez

asked quickly, "Sir? Personal shield?"

"That Ancient thing Dr. McKay was wearing the time I shot him and threw him off the control gallery," John told him.

"Yes, sir." Ramirez nodded his comprehension, then realized the implications. "Uh oh."

"Yeah." It had been funny when they were playing 'Captain Invulnerable' with McKay; now it was anything but. *And if the Ancients were going to make those damn things, why so few? Why not one for everybody?* Sometimes the Ancients were just annoying. John wasn't thrilled with the people who hadn't bothered to flush the plague-spreading nanites and the Darkness creature before leaving the city, either. "By the time you get there, I'll think of a way to take care of Dorane."

John could see Bates suppressing a comment on that piece of optimism. Instead he said, "What about Eliza—" He corrected himself stiffly. "Dr. Weir?"

John shook his head, though it ate at him to make this decision. "He can't get into that room, so he can't hold them hostage; we can get them out after we take out Dorane."

John could tell Bates saw the sense in that, though he didn't like it either. As Bates took Audley and Ramirez aside to work out a plan of attack for the level the prisoners were on, John turned to Beckett and Zelenka again. "Look, Dorane's going to send the Koan in here, probably when he has Rodney take out the generator for this section of the city. You need to get everybody out, get them to the lower levels, split up and hide. It's not Atlantis he's really after. He wants us, to experiment on."

Beckett grimaced. "I thought it might be something like that. We'll pack the emergency supplies and go as soon as we can."

"Oh, and he wants the memory core from that pillar thing— that's why he let me come down here." John asked Zelenka, "Do you have that?"

Zelenka nodded. "Yes, I took it out to work on further, and

it came with me when we evacuated the labs. There's information there he wants?"

"Yeah. I have no idea what, but— Can you make a copy of a part that's really damaged, something he won't be able to read? I just need something I can hand him, something that'll seem convincing."

Zelenka was already moving toward an array of laptops set up on the work tables at the back of the bay. "Yes, yes, we can do this."

Beckett rubbed his forehead wearily. "This mind-control can't be a completely organic process. If he really based this on the ATA gene, it just doesn't work that way. There has to be a technological component somewhere."

"I haven't seen him use—" John frowned. He had seen Dorane with something, when he and Teyla had caught him with the Koan. "Oh, crap. I thought he was using a life sign detector. But that was when McKay was hiding in the area; if Dorane had had a detector, he would've been able to send the Koan right to him." That was why Dorane had put the thing down and walked away from it so readily. If John had had the chance to follow through on his threat to shoot Dorane's hand off with the device in it, this whole thing would have been over in that moment. *There's a lesson in that,* he told himself grimly.

Zelenka had returned and was listening thoughtfully, tapping a memory stick against his chin. "We think life sign detector works by sensing a degree of electrical activity in nervous system—that is why it doesn't show the presence of hibernating Wraith." He lifted his brows. "If he has altered a unit so it also broadcasts to these infected individuals and can perhaps set it to inhibit any activity that is not directly provoked by some certain cue, such as his voice— But this is all hypothetical."

"Could you jam the hypothetical signal from the hypothetical thing?" John asked, not hopefully.

Zelenka shook his head, grimacing. "I doubt it, certainly

not in limited time before he decides to order our friends to kill us. We still have not isolated the exact element the Ancient technology uses to interact with the ATA gene, and that is happening all around us, all the time." He handed the memory stick to John. "Here is partial copy of the damaged portion of the core. It's nothing useful, but as you said, it may keep him busy for a few moments."

"Right, thanks." John pocketed the little device, still thinking about the mind control. "The control box isn't going to be Ancient tech, it's going to be something with Dorane's version of the gene. If we're lucky."

Beckett frowned. "You can hear that also?"

"It's what made the Koan crazy. That repository sounds like...I can't describe what it sounds like." The constant whisper of alien noise was getting pretty loud in here now, with all the Ancient medical equipment that Beckett had managed to activate stored in this area, the devices he had figured out well enough to use safely and those he hadn't. "I should be able to tell if he has it on him or hidden somewhere else. Maybe Atlantis' ATA just drowned out whatever noise it was making."

Beckett took a sharp breath. "We have to get our hands on that device, because there's no telling how long it would take to create a counteragent to the biological side." He lifted his brows. "Unless you could get me blood samples from a variety of victims—"

"Blood samples. Right." John nodded earnestly. "Want me to pick up anything else while I'm out? Some groceries, your dry cleaning—"

Beckett took his arm. "I can at least take a sample from you right now."

"Look, I don't have a lot of time—"

"If you'd be still for two seconds I'll have it done," Beckett told him briskly, steering him toward a chair. Dr. Biro already had a drawer open in the nearest storage cabinet, scrambling for a hypo and collection vials. "And if I could take a sample of one of those spines—"

"Uh, no." John sat down reluctantly, leaning away from Beckett. "What if they're attached to my brain or something?"

"Well, then we'd best find that out, shouldn't we?"

John ended up successfully resisting having a spine ripped out of his skull, but Beckett stood over him with one of the Ancient medical scanning devices while Biro took the blood sample. It took her a couple of minutes to get it, since John's veins apparently heard her coming and tried to hide. "You're badly dehydrated, Major," she told him, her expression severe.

"And you know, that's really the least of my problems right now," John said, and then had to convince her that he barely had time for the bottle of water she forced on him and that an IV was out of the question.

Beckett was still studying the Ancient diagnostic scanner, a faint professional frown creasing his brow. John started to ask something and saw Beckett's face change, caught the unguarded moment when the scanner showed Beckett something he must have suspected but had been hoping not to see. *Well, crap,* John thought, cold settling in the pit of his stomach. The ATA was getting louder and more intrusive; it wasn't just his imagination, or that there was less ambient noise here to drown it out, or that there was so much active Ancient technology in the medlab. Something was changing in his body and brain chemistry again, and from Beckett's expression, it wasn't good.

Beckett cleared his throat; his professional mask was back in place, but the lines on his face were etched a little deeper. "Major Sheppard, I need to talk to you in private."

"Carson, I don't have time, and I don't want to know," John said. Dr. Biro had finished with the blood sample, and he pulled away from her automatic attempt to put a bandage over the puncture; without one it was just one more bloody scratch on his arm and he didn't want anything to draw

Dorane's attention to it. Watching Beckett worriedly, Biro barely noticed. Though she hadn't seen the scanner, she must have caught the same implication from Beckett's expression. "Not unless it's going to happen in the next five minutes."

Beckett winced. He said, "I haven't even looked at your blood sample yet. We don't know—"

John avoided his eyes. *Okay, that means I've got more than five minutes.* He didn't want sympathy right now. Actually he did want it, a lot of it, he just didn't have time for it. And he wasn't sure he wanted it from the two people who, in a best case scenario, would be doing his autopsy. He shoved to his feet, suppressing the urge to ask them not to put him in the same freezer as the parts that were left of Steve the Wraith. "I've got to get back up there. Make sure Zelenka keeps that memory core safe. It's the only thing Dorane seems to want more than us."

As the others scrambled to gather emergency gear, Beckett followed as John led Bates, Audley, and Ramirez to the floor access panel that would take them down to the section below where they could reach the armory. It would be easier and faster for John to go back that way instead of going up and out again.

Waiting impatiently for Audley to pry up the panel, John felt something change in the direction of the central stairwell. It was that same weird tickly feeling in the back of his brain that had warned him about the Koan in the forest. He could tell there were a lot of them, and he could tell they were close but not too close, somewhere towards the inner portion of this section. He said, "There's some Koan nearby; they're probably gathering at the stairwell access to the main medlab corridor. Dorane must be getting ready to cut the power to this section." He looked up to find all of them staring at him a little warily, except for Beckett, who looked like he was making mental notes. John told him, "Remember, let them take the medlab, just get everybody out through here and further down into the city."

Beckett nodded sharply. "Right. Don't worry about us." He shook his head suddenly, running a hand through his hair in frustration. "Look, just don't— Don't give up. Give me a chance to fight this. I'll have my headset on. As soon as you can call us back, do it."

That was the sympathy thing again. John just nodded, and followed the others down into the access.

When John strolled up the central stairs, he found the large group of Koan waiting at the door to the medlab corridor. "So where have you guys been?" John asked them. "I was looking all over the place for you." He was starting to feel warm, though he wasn't sweating. He knew it was him; he could tell the circulation system in this section was still running, drawing in cool outside air.

Before leading him to Dorane, the Koan searched him again, making him glad for resisting the temptation to take a side trip with Bates to the armory for some grenades. Explosives were one thing that might be effective against the personal shield, since they didn't have to work against the body inside the forcefield, just the structural integrity of whatever building that person was standing in. But despite the difficulty of smuggling any kind of weapon into the same room with Dorane, the man would be too close to the naquadah generators, and the naquadah generators were too close to the operations tower and the Stargate, which was made from naquadah, and from what John understood, that could add up to losing a much larger chunk of the city than he was willing to part with. But if it came down to it... He would rather lie down in an open field on a Wraith planet with a 'get it here' sign than let Dorane take any people back to the repository. And John didn't think Dorane was the type to cut his losses and make a run for the Stargate before the last possible moment. If he couldn't take the expedition members back with him, he would kill as many as he could.

The door to the generator room was open, and the Koan led

John inside. Dorane was standing with several Koan, Ford, and two Marines. Dorane looked even worse than he had in the 'gate room; his eyes were yellow and bloodshot and his skin was gray. Maybe when he said the atmosphere of Atlantis was inimical to him, he hadn't been exaggerating.

McKay, crouched on the floor beside the generator, looked up warily. He was surrounded by open access panels and disconnected crystal conduit. Kavanagh, his expression blank, stood nearby holding a toolkit. "I'm back," John announced unnecessarily. He was listening hard for a faint thread of discord among Atlantis' whispery harmonics, and the ATA was relatively quiet in here. The naquadah generator was Earth manufacture, not Ancient, and the only other tech he could hear was the door control panels and Dorane's personal shield. *So where the hell is he keeping this thing?* It had to be nearby. Even if it didn't have to be physically close to work, John figured Dorane was too cautious to let it out of his control. *Unless he has it on him somewhere, and the shield is just so loud it's covering up any noise from the control device.*

"You didn't go to the sealed area through the main corridor," Dorane said, watching him carefully.

"Well, no, since I'd be dead if I had. I knew another way in." John lifted a brow. "Isn't that what you were counting on?"

Dorane didn't bother to answer. "But you found the memory core."

John fished the stick out of his pocket and held it out. McKay stared, winced, and ducked behind the generator. John knew the stick probably didn't hold a tenth of what the actual Ancient core held, but Dorane wouldn't know that. He just hoped it didn't occur to the man to ask Kavanagh.

Dorane's expression was impossible to read. He didn't reach out to take the stick. "What is that?"

"It's a data storage device for our computers," John told him. "I couldn't get the core itself."

Dorane looked at Kavanagh, who put the toolkit down and

came forward. Kavanagh took the memory stick from John, glanced at it briefly, and held it out to Dorane, saying, "That's correct, it's a data storage device."

John knew Dorane was still wearing the personal shield. *But he really doesn't trust me, and it obviously occurred to him that I might hand him something that would blow up or even short out the shield.* Too bad John didn't have anything like that. But Dorane obviously knew nothing about their technology; maybe he had seen just enough to realize there were elements of it he didn't understand.

Dorane finally took the stick from Kavanagh, his lips thin with distaste. "And I assume this will only display on one of your devices. Which one of you will have to operate for me."

John shrugged, as if he didn't care. "I guess." He took a couple of distracted paces to the left, so his back was to the Koan, Kavanagh, Ford, and the others.

Dorane watched him, eyes narrowing. "Surely you know."

"He doesn't know," McKay sneered, looking up from where he was crouched beside the generator. He had obviously reached the overly aggressive stage of his blood sugar crash. "He can barely check his email."

Dorane turned to regard him, probably with a great deal of skepticism. Rodney glared up at him, and John took the opportunity to mouth the words 'big distraction, soon.'

Rodney twitched in alarm, but he looked so flustered and annoyed, it would have been hard for someone who didn't know him to tell. He told Dorane, "You'll need a laptop to read it. That's one of the computers in the silver cases."

Dorane turned back toward Kavanagh, who said, "Yes, that's true." Something in the way Dorane was holding the memory stick suggested a great deal of frustration. Whatever was on the memory core, Dorane didn't want anyone else to see it, apparently not even one of the people he had under control.

John made an idle circuit of the room, still listening hard

for the control device. He was fairly certain now it wasn't on Dorane, but surely it was nearby. If it was up in the 'gate room... No, it had to be closer than that. *If it isn't, we may be seriously screwed.* But would Dorane just stick it on a shelf somewhere and leave it? The naquadah generators were spaced out widely over the center portion of the city; did this thing have the kind of range that it could... *Or he gave it to someone else to carry.*

"Is there one of these laptops nearby?" Dorane was asking Kavanagh.

Kavanagh shook his head; his attention was on Dorane and not what Rodney was doing with the generator. "I don't know. They would be in the 'gate room, the labs, the living quarters and offices—"

John wandered past Kavanagh, the two Marines, Ford, and caught the first hint of a tiny disruption in the ATA's ongoing cacophony. It wasn't insistent enough to be coming from one of them. The nearest Koan growled nervously as John went to the wall and leaned back against it. Dorane, still questioning Kavanagh about nearby labs, threw him a cold look, but he obviously wasn't much interested in however John wanted to occupy his last moments. John closed his eyes, tipped his head back against the metal, and tried to shut everything else out.

And there it was, somewhere on the other side of this wall, a thread of discordant sound, moving away. *Yeah, he gave it to someone who's been following him around the city. And I bet I know who.*

CHAPTER ELEVEN

John opened his eyes to see McKay crouched by the genera-tor, fiddling with the last connection, watching him anx-iously. *And here we go.* John lifted a brow, giving him a 'what are you waiting for' look.

McKay glared at him, then took a filament-thin loop of clear cable out of the floor access and did something with it inside the generator's panel.

John felt the shudder travel through the wall before he heard the explosion. The abrupt blast came from the south, from the outer part of this section, and it wasn't at all distant. *Oh, crap,* John thought, aghast, *what the hell did he do?*

His expression of stunned dismay bought them an extra few seconds as Dorane looked first at him, then at McKay, who was staring at the generator as if he had never seen it before. "What was that?" Dorane demanded.

Still looking at the generator, Rodney shook his head, as if really baffled. Then he grimaced in relief and said, "Oh, there it goes." He shoved himself back just as silvery sparks foun-tained from the access, shooting up toward the ceiling.

Even under low power, the ATA didn't so much switch on as burst to life inside the walls. John was suddenly aware of circuits threaded in the metal behind him, felt something whoosh through piping as if the room was drawing a breath; he knew exactly what was about to happen. Ducking around the bewildered Koan, he winced away from the sparking gen-erator. The emergency lights flickered, a wailing Atlantean klaxon sounded, and all four doors shot open. John slammed Ford out of his way, feeling the first blast of something that wasn't air. McKay was on his feet and John tackled him, send-ing them both out the nearest door and into the corridor. They landed hard and John thought *close, close, come on, close* at the door. Somebody got off a burst from a P-90 and bullets bounced off the silver wall panel right above their heads, just before the door slid shut.

Rodney was glaring up at him. "Oh fine, you just broke half my ribs."

John rolled off him, asking, "What about Ford and the others?" He shoved unsteadily to his feet, dragging McKay with him. He had gotten a lungful of the gas released by the emergency system and his throat felt raw. He could hear Koan howling and pounding on the door behind them, but it refused to budge.

McKay was red-faced and breathing hard, and he had to steady himself against the wall. But he said, "They're fine. The system will sense that there's no fire and flush the room with outside air."

That was a relief, at least. "God, Rodney, I said 'diversion' not 'blow up half the city!'" John started down the corridor, coughing. "And what was that stuff, halon?"

McKay hurried after him. "It's similar. And I'm fairly confident that the Ancients wouldn't use a fire suppressant that was poisonous to humans. That sparking was just a harmless light show, and the explosion was just the grounding station in this wing—"

"Oh, was that all? A harmless naquadah light show? And don't we need that station for grounding electricity?" John took the next corridor intersection. The lights were a little dimmer, and he couldn't sense any Koan moving towards them. But he could hear the control device heading rapidly away from the direction of the blast, trying to get back to Dorane, looking for a way around the sealed doors now blocking the direct path.

McKay waved his hands like John was being unreasonable. "That wasn't actually naquadah, that was just electricity, and this section can do fine without a discharger—for a while, unless there's a storm, or a buildup of static— Anyway, I created a small power surge in the generator that started a feedback loop between it and the grounding station. With Dorane shutting down most of the city systems, I wasn't sure the fire-control was still online. It probably helped that your Ancient gene panicked and set off the protocols." Rodney stopped at a wall console at the end of the corridor and tapped a rapid sequence into it. "Now that the fire-control is active I can tell it to block access to the generator room, which should seal off all the doors in this section."

"Dorane will have to get the doors to open individually." John was starting to feel a little better about the whole 'let's blow important and dangerous stuff up as a distraction' plan.

"So will we, but I'll be faster at it than he is." McKay finished keying in the sequence and the panel beeped quietly, displaying a series of Ancient characters. "Right, that should do it."

"Good. Now come on." John started down the corridor to the outer portion of the wing. The device was moving fast and he didn't want to lose it.

McKay jogged to catch up with him, but protested, "Why are we going this way? We should go—"

"Beckett and Zelenka thought Dorane had to have some kind of device that's helping him control our people. I think I saw him with it back at the repository, I just didn't know what it was. It's using his version of the ATA, and I can hear where it is." John barely paused at the next intersection, knowing his quarry was already about two corridors ahead. The emergency lighting was growing dimmer; this roundabout route took them into a part of the wing that had been damaged in the flooding just before the city rose from the sea bottom. The ATA was just a low background whisper, blending with the distant sound of the sea outside the walls, making the sour thread of the controller device much easier to follow. "Any reason he'd give it to someone else to carry?"

McKay gestured erratically. "Lots of reasons. That personal shield might interfere with any device emitting a signal. Or the device might interfere with the shield. We have no idea how compatible his version of the gene is with the real thing, and those shields are highly attuned to whoever's wearing them." He added in exasperation, "And just where is everybody? Didn't you go down there to get the Wraith stunners—"

"Yes. Bates is getting our people out of—"

"What about me? Us? We need to be rescued too!"

"You need to wait your turn, Rodney." The air was getting dank, and it was laced with the odor of stale seawater. Somewhere off in the dark corridors there were doors that were permanently sealed, deep shafts jammed with sand and sea wrack, rooms full of strange equipment that no longer operated. John knew this section fairly well; they weren't far from the passage out to the grounding station McKay had blown up. He didn't think Teyla had been through here before, and the way she kept trying to take direct routes suggested that Dorane was giving her instructions instead of simply commanding her to return to him and letting her find her own way. Hopefully that was because she was still trying to resist him.

McKay caught John's arm, saying, "About the waiting thing." He sounded worried and deeply uncomfortable. "That drug Dorane gave you, he said— He's probably lying, but he said—"

John pulled free and kept walking. "Rodney, I know, Beckett scanned me. And if Dorane said how long it would be, don't tell me, all right? I don't want to be looking at a clock while I'm doing this."

"Wait, wait!" Rodney caught up, staring at him incredulously. "Carson knows about this and he didn't do anything?"

"Like what? He didn't have any time."

"I can't believe that! He's supposed to be so damn brilliant and he just let you walk out of there—"

"Rodney, for God's sake, shut up about it!" After a short curve the corridor opened into a walkway over a larger chamber. "And shut up, period. You want her to hear you?" The few working emergency lights made the big space look as if it was etched in black and silver, and John could see it was empty. He paused before stepping out onto the walkway, trying to get his bearings. Teyla was past this point, down and to the right somewhere in the other corridor that led off the lower level of this room.

"Who? I don't even know what we're doing!" McKay whispered furiously.

"We're looking for Teyla." John thought he had said that already, but even in panic mode, McKay wouldn't have forgotten or misheard a piece of information as vital as that. It scared John the way nothing else had so far; they didn't have much time to pull this off, and he couldn't afford to lose his concentration. He started across the walkway, not wanting McKay to notice the moment of uncertainty. "I think Dorane gave her the device."

Fortunately, McKay had too many other things to panic about to notice. "How are we going to get it away from her? You don't even have a gun."

"That part's a little fuzzy," John admitted.

"Oh, God. This is a woman who puts on a dress to beat the crap out of you in that stupid stick fighting, and now you're dying, how are you going to—"

"Rodney, can we go, I don't know, maybe a minute without you reminding me that I'm dying? And you really need to shut up." John found the stairway down to the lower level of the room and started down it. He stopped abruptly and McKay bumped into him from behind. "She's coming back." There were two doors in that lower corridor that he distinctly remembered were wedged open, the metal around them buckled when the pressure from the sea had hit this section. After that he thought the corridor led back into the powered portion of the wing, but the fire-control must have blocked her path again.

John turned, and McKay scrambled back up the stairs.

John pushed him in the direction of the sheltered corridor access, and McKay hurried back along the walkway in the dark. He stopped at the doorway, flattening himself against the wall, and John crouched down where he was, at the head of the stairs, trying to fold in on himself and blend in with the darkness and the silvery material of the walkway.

He felt ridiculously exposed, and it was hard to remember that for Teyla and McKay, the emergency lighting was barely existent and the room was almost as dark as a moonless night. An instant later he heard her footsteps, the light tread of her boots on the metal. She wasn't bothering to be quiet; Dorane probably hadn't thought to give that order.

John stopped breathing when he heard her come up through the doorway below. She started up the stairs, and he grimaced. He had been hoping she would cross the room on the lower level and he could drop down on her from above.

She reached the top of the stairs and started to turn back toward the corridor access. John launched himself at her the same instant she must have sensed his presence. She was turning toward him, lifting her P-90 when he slammed into her. They hit the walkway, John on top, flattening the gun to her chest. The device was right there pressed between them, in the lower right hand pocket of her tac vest, the bastardized ATA sending a jolt of pain right through John's head. He felt her fingers scrabbling for the P-90's trigger and used his claws to rip through the cord holding it around her neck. He jerked it out of her grasp and lifted up just enough to fling it off the balcony.

She took advantage of the moment to roll them both, knocking him sideways into the railing and trying to shove him under the lower rail. Sinking his claws into her tac vest kept him from going off the walkway, and he got the heel of his hand under her chin and pushed her back. Then it was a mad scramble, with Teyla trying to do as much damage as possible and tear herself away, and John trying to hold on and get to the controller. Then he twisted in the wrong direction to duck a blow to the throat, and she tried to plant a knee in his groin. John writhed desperately to avoid it, but managed to keep one hand hooked in her vest. She clawed the pistol out of her holster, but John went for the device instead, ripping it out of her pocket. She cried out, shrill and pain-filled, and dropped the pistol, grabbing for the device.

Then McKay yanked it out of John's hand, slamming it against the walkway to get the case open and ripping the crystals out.

Teyla froze, gave a heartfelt gasp of relief, and collapsed on top of John. He slumped, letting his head fall back, taking a deep breath.

"Are you okay?" McKay asked, hovering anxiously over them. "Is she okay? Teyla?"

Teyla was a warm weight, limp and utterly still. "I think she's out." John rolled her off, McKay catching her and helping him ease her down onto the walkway. John pushed himself up on one elbow and felt for the pulse in her neck; it was strong, and she seemed to be breathing normally. He just hoped she wasn't in a coma, that they hadn't just given everybody under the influence of the control drug brain damage.

McKay nodded, relieved. "If this means everybody he gave that drug to just collapsed, then all we have is the Koan to worry about." He winced. "And I said that like it was a happy thought."

"It is a happy thought. The Koan we can shoot." John pushed himself up, grabbing the railing and leaning on it until he could stand up straight again. He found the pistol on the walkway, checked the clip and put the safety on, then tucked it into the back of his belt. He reached down for Teyla. "Help me with her. Dorane knows her last position and we need to get out of here.

"Right." But as McKay took her other arm, Teyla twitched and opened her eyes. McKay grimaced and muttered, "Uh oh," but her expression was bewildered and frightened.

John leaned over her, brushing the tangled hair out of her

eyes. He was just relieved she was conscious. "Teyla, it's us, Sheppard and McKay. We've got to get you moving, all right?"

After a moment, she nodded in relief and recognition, and they got her up off the walkway and sort of walking between them, though she had difficulty getting her legs to move. From the hard grip she had on his shoulder and the collar of McKay's shirt, John thought she was glad to see them.

They got her off the walkway and into the corridor, John steering them away from the area near the generator room and in toward the center section of the city. He wanted desperately to know what was going on in the operations tower, to find out if Bates had released the prisoners yet and how close he was to— John halted suddenly, making Teyla and McKay stumble. In the floor below his feet, radiating out of the walls, he felt the ATA rushing back to life and awareness, a dull roar of sound that started at the center of the city and spiraled outward. It scared the hell out of him for an instant and he couldn't think what was causing it, if the city was about to blow up, sink into the ocean, or lift off the planet. Then the emergency lights flickered and the swell of sound dropped a little, settling into what something told him was a normal level. "I hope that's what I think it is," he said under his breath, waiting tensely for confirmation.

Watching him anxiously, McKay demanded, "Oh God, what now?"

The tenor of the ATA changed and John knew lights were coming on in other sections. "We're getting full power back." With his free hand, he dug the sunglasses out of his pocket just before the corridor lights brightened to full strength. He kept his eyes squeezed shut until he could get the glasses on. "Hopefully that means Bates took back the 'gate room and Grodin's restarting our systems."

"Finally," McKay said in relief. "If we have the com back and our radio traffic isn't jammed—"

Teyla dug her fingers into John's shoulder. "Major," she

managed to say, her voice weak and uncertain. "I remember— He brought something with him, in the jumper. Another device..."

"Crap." John exchanged an incredulous look with McKay. "Another controller?"

"No, a weapon." She was struggling to get the words out, her face sheened with sweat. "He said...it would prevent Atlantis from being occupied again."

McKay looked simultaneously frightened and outraged. "A bomb? We scanned for that, the repository didn't have any munitions or explosive materials left, certainly nothing big enough to do more than—" He stopped suddenly, eyes widening. "Unless it's a—"

"A biological weapon," John finished, dragging them both into motion again. Teyla was still wearing a headset, probably because Dorane had never bothered to tell her to take it off. John took it, getting it over his ear while McKay found the base unit in the pocket of her tac vest and switched it on. "Which jumper, Teyla?"

"Five, the one...we used to bring the Koan."

The radio crackled with static and John said, "Bates, come in, this is Sheppard. What's your position?"

"This is Bates. We've retaken the 'gate room and—"

"Bates, I need you to seal off the jumper bay. We have a possible bioweapon in Jumper Five—"

John gave Bates the short version of the situation and got an acknowledgement, the radio cutting off to the sound of Bates yelling for Ramirez.

"Oh, God." McKay was muttering under his breath, running through a list of everything horrible that could be in a biological bomb. "Dorane has to know about the city's quarantine protocols—"

"Yeah. He's either got a way to turn them off or he's got something that the city can't stop that way." John knew which one he was betting on. And he felt like he should have expected this. *Dorane knew how many of us there were, he knows how big Atlantis is, that there was no way he could round up all of us. And he knew we were just that dangerous.* The bioweapon could have been insurance, making certain there would be no survivors left to free prisoners in the repository or to build bombs to lob through the 'gate. Or it could just render everybody helpless for collection by the Koan.

Two corridor turns further, they came to the first working transporter, the colored crystal doors sliding obediently open as soon as they came within range. They got Teyla inside, and the destination console with its map of the active transporters opened for John with a roar of white noise. He realized he hadn't heard the ATA as music for a long time, even as weird alien not-quite-music. He hit the location for the transporter in the operations tower, nearest the 'gate room.

The trip took less than a heartbeat, but the transporter and everything else dissolved into an intense burst of agony. As the doors opened John pitched out and rolled around on the floor, clutching his head, holding in a scream. Finally the pain faded enough that he realized McKay was kneeling beside him, snarling at someone, "It's killing him, what the hell do you think?"

"Rodney, shut up," John grated out. He could taste blood at the back of his throat. He told himself, *your brain isn't actually leaking out of your ears; it just feels like it.* He managed to get his eyes open and the bright light stabbed through his head; he didn't remember losing the sunglasses.

He didn't know why this was a shock; he had known it was getting progressively worse, that it wasn't going to stop, that he was going to get more and more sensitive to the ATA until it finally killed him. Somehow part of him just hadn't believed it until now. *Going through the 'gate would probably make my head explode.* Not that that was going to be a problem. He heard Rodney order someone to find Beckett, and John managed to say evenly, "Tell them we need the hazmat gear up here now."

"And a medical team," Rodney added, and then in frustration, "Why the hell didn't you say that would happen? We didn't have to use the transporter—"

Assuming this was directed at him, John interrupted, "I didn't know that would happen!" Somebody put the glasses back in his hand, and he managed to get them on and get his eyes open again.

McKay was kneeling on one side of him, Bates on the other. Bates had one of the Wraith stunners slung across his back, the curved alien shape of the weapon contrasting oddly with the business-like P-90 clipped around his neck. Past them John could see some of the operations staff who must have been released from the level below, all of them startled and battered and generally traumatized. Peter Grodin was supporting Teyla, both watching anxiously. John managed to focus on Bates. "Did you secure the jumper bay?"

"Negative, sir. There were armed Koan guarding the entrance when we arrived. They're inside the bay doorway, and we can't get a clear shot at them." Bates actually looked a little rattled, possibly from watching John writhe around on the floor, and for once he had forgotten to make 'sir' sound like an insult. But Bates was really the very last person John wanted sympathy from.

"Dorane beat us here," Rodney added, his mouth twisted grimly. "He must have made a run for the jumper bay as soon as he realized we had the controller device."

"Great." John gripped McKay's arm and struggled to his feet, trying to make it look like McKay wasn't actually holding him up. His head was throbbing, almost drowning out the hurricane-like rise and fall of the ATA. "We've got control back, right? Can you open the bay doors above the 'gate room?"

McKay looked blank. "Probably. Why? Wouldn't that—"

John turned to Bates. "Get some stun grenades and a launcher up here." That would take out the Koan but wouldn't harm the jumpers or set off the energy drones they were armed with.

Bates turned half away, tapping his radio. Rodney finished, "Never mind, I got it."

John put his back against the wall, trying to ignore the still-growing buzz of the ATA and his throbbing head. At least he had been able to borrow a tac vest and a P-90 from an unconscious Marine. Braced against the corridor wall opposite him, Bates watched him narrowly. Keeping his voice low, he asked John, "You sure you're up for this?"

They were in position in the jumper bay's access corridor, which was a lousy place to have to attack. There was a jog in the passage right as it turned into the bay, forming a small foyer, and the Koan could just stand in there and shoot anybody who made that last turn into the bay. John just said dryly, "That's a really stupid question."

He was working off pure adrenaline and a burning desire to kill Dorane. Waiting for the grenades to be brought from the armory, he hadn't even been able to sit down for fear he wouldn't be able to get up again. He had already told the others that, if the bioweapon was still in the jumper, he would go in for it alone. At least he hadn't had to explain why this was best, since Rodney had told everybody on the control gallery that John was dying. It was one small relief that Elizabeth had called in, reporting that the Koan had withdrawn when the controlled Marines guarding their room had collapsed. On John's instructions, Bates had told her to stay in the lower levels with the others until they dealt with the bioweapon. John hadn't wanted to speak to her himself, because he was desperately trying to avoid having the 'by the way, this is probably it for me' conversation with anyone.

Over the radio, John could hear the low-voiced discussions in the 'gate room as Ramirez got the launcher set up. He whispered into his headset, "What's your status?"

"Ready, sir." With the transporters back online it had only taken a few minutes to get the stun grenades, but the medlab was still scrambling to organize hazmat and biohazard gear.

John had put Ramirez in the 'gate room with the launcher, and himself, Bates, Audley, and the only other Marines still mobile enough to hold a gun in the jumper bay's access corridor. Most of the military personnel were still unconscious from the control drug or the stunners; Teyla, who had had some level of resistance to it that the others hadn't, was the only one on her feet, and she was still unsteady enough that John had made her stay down on the control gallery. Many of the others had been injured in the first Koan attack, and one man, Masterson, had been killed. "McKay, what about you?"

"Ready." McKay sounded tense. "I can override from down here if he tries to stop it from one of the jumper consoles."

John caught Bates' eye, got a nod in reply, and said, "Ramirez, as soon as you get a clear shot, fire. McKay, open the doors."

There wasn't a rumble in the floor; the Ancient technology worked too smoothly for that. But over the radio John could hear the faint hum of the doors retracting, hooting cries of alarm and surprise from the Koan.

There were distant clunks as the grenades hit, then a reverberation, muffled by the bay doors. John counted six seconds, gave Bates the signal, and ducked around the corner. The door slid open for him, and they moved into the bay, spreading out.

The big space was dark and would have been quiet except for the piercingly loud roar of the ATA in John's head. A chemical haze and an acrid scent from the grenades hung heavily in the air. Koan sprawled around the edges of the retracted floor, some moaning in pain, others lying limply. The jumpers were stacked unharmed in their vertical launch racks, all still powered-down. John couldn't see Dorane or hear his shield, but it might be blending in with the ATA's din.

Jumper Five was in a rack on the second level, innocuous and inert like the others, and John started toward it. Three

Koan suddenly popped up from behind a jumper across the bay, firing wildly. Bates and the others went for cover, returning fire, but John was closer to Five, and he was pretty sure the Koan's aim was lousy.

He ducked behind Jumper Two and climbed up the steps to the narrow walkway. Five's rear hatch was down and he bolted for it, slamming himself inside. He hit the floor, covering the interior with the P-90.

It was dark and John was still wearing the sunglasses, but he could just make out Dorane sitting on the floor in the cockpit doorway. He was holding a small black box. There was something different about the shape of his head, something odd about the way he was hunched there, but John could see the dim aquamarine glow of the personal shield on his chest, and hear his breathing.

There was still firing outside, but John's radio crackled and Bates' voice said, "Major, did you get it?"

"Negative, stay back," John ordered sharply. "He's in here with it."

He heard Bates cursing and McKay telling someone, "That's it, we're dead."

Dorane still hadn't said anything, hadn't moved, and that was making every nerve in John's body twitch in individual alarm. He flicked off the sunglasses.

Dorane just watched him, eyes gleaming faintly in the dimness. He had long silver spines threaded through his gray hair now, running all down the sides of his face and neck. The hand that rested on the little box had large hooked silver claws, twisted and useless.

John managed to say evenly, "Wow. You're a little different."

Dorane tilted his head. "The transformation occurs whenever I leave my athenaeum for more than a few hours. It's inhibited by the field I use to activate my version of the Ancient gene. It prevents me from staying in this city, from traveling to any other world." His voice was different, deeper, a little raspy. "I told you, all my people were affected by our biological weapons."

"Yeah, you told me," John agreed. Dorane's physical changes were so exaggerated he looked like a caricature of the other Koan. "But I wasn't listening to that part." *He hasn't set that thing off yet.* Because he wanted to bargain? Or because it was a timed release? "What's in the box?"

Dorane's claws tightened on the black container. "It's a very small explosive, only meant to release a substance into the air."

And McKay's right again; we're dead. But John was getting more sensitive to the ATA by the minute; maybe it was getting more sensitive to him. And if he could get this jumper out of the bay and through the Stargate...

Automated launch sequence, John thought at the jumper. Through the port above Dorane's head, he saw Jumper One's interior lights flash as it powered up. *No, no, not you, this one. Five.* Next to One, Three shuddered a little, as if its drive might have tried to activate and failed. *Oh, crap. Keep talking.* "That's disappointing, because I really didn't want you to have the satisfaction of killing me. But you already did, didn't you? Did you think I didn't know that?"

"I suspected it." Dorane had his back to the port and couldn't see what was happening in the jumper racks. "I didn't expect you to be able to function this well in spite of it. But it means nothing. You claim a Lantian heritage, but even with the gene, you're all just cattle for the Wraith."

"Thanks, but we already knew that." The firing outside had stopped, and through his headset John could hear Bates breathing heavily and McKay having a tense and mostly unintelligible conversation with Grodin. "Why don't you just head for the Stargate? You can probably make it." *Launch, you little bastard,* he thought, trying to focus on Five's unresponsive console. The ATA was just one omnipresent roar, and he couldn't sort out any individual signal from the jumpers. Across the bay, Three's interior lights flashed as it powered up. *Damn it*. He flew One and Three the most; Five had been Boerne's jumper. It made sense that the little ships would attune themselves to a regular pilot.

"I fear I have lingered here too long already," Dorane said. He sounded serene, as if the prospect of destroying Atlantis and its inhabitants had put him into a weird state of peaceful satisfaction. "Once my condition is triggered by leaving the athenaeum, it advances swiftly. I am dying, even as you are."

"You know, I really wish the Ancients had done a better job of getting rid of you." John didn't think Five was responding to him at all; the low ambient light in the jumper seemed to be getting even dimmer. Maybe he could get One to launch a drone, to blow Five up. It would probably take out this wall of the operations tower, but surely the heat would be enough to destroy whatever was in the box. He hoped. Into the radio, he said, "Bates, fall back to the corridor and close the blast door."

"That won't do any good," Dorane told him, still eerily calm. He added, "The Lantians didn't want to get rid of me. They wanted to punish me."

"Oh yeah, that was so unreasonable of them." *Why hasn't he opened it yet?* John thought. Then he looked at Dorane's hands again. Those hooked claws were too big to be retractable. "You can't open that container."

Dorane smiled, his teeth gleaming in the fading light. "Don't excite yourself, it's on a timed release. I really did think of every possibility, including the one that I might be incapable of opening it when the time came."

It didn't sound like a lie. The ATA was pressing painfully in on John's head, and something was changing inside the jumper, but he couldn't tell what it was. "And I'm guessing I won't just be able to seal the jumper's hatch."

"It will react rapidly with oxygen, becoming corrosive. The ship's shielding won't hold it in for long."

Shielding, John thought. It was still getting darker in here.

Darker because the aquamarine glow of the personal shield device was fading. The shield needed an Ancient gene to work, but Dorane's genetics were changing as the retrovirus altered his body; the shield must be losing its connection to him. When the shield shut down, the little device would fall off Dorane's chest. John shifted the P-90 to go for a headshot; he couldn't afford to hit the explosive.

Dorane blinked suddenly, staring at John. He must have felt the shield giving way or read it off John's expression. Before the glow faded and the shield device fell, he was moving, moving fast. John managed to fire one burst, then he was slammed back onto the jumper floor, Dorane clawing for his throat.

John grabbed his wrists, barely holding him off, thinking, *He's really fast, and he's really strong.* He knew he had hit Dorane in the chest, but the bullets weren't even slowing him down. And the explosive still lay on the floor in the jumper's cockpit. He yelled desperately, "Jumper Five, now would be a good time! Launch!"

This time, responding to his urgency, Five's interior lights flashed on and the console powered up.

Dorane tried to tear away from him, but John dug in with his own claws and held on. He pushed and rolled, and they tumbled backward out of the hatch.

They hit the ramp, then the walkway, and rolled off, slamming into the bay floor. John landed on top, which probably saved him a broken back, but he was winded and dazed.

Above his head, Five slid out of its rack and glided out to hover over the jumper bay's launch door, open to the 'gate room directly below. It stopped, and John realized the ramp was still open, that the safeties weren't going to let the jumper drop into launch position. He shouted, "Ramp close, come on, ramp close!"

Dorane threw him off, pushed to his feet, and bolted for the open ramp. It slid shut, sealing itself for launch with a faint puff of air. Dorane tried to stop on the bare edge of the drop, arms flung up. Then he fell.

John heard the thump and the startled shouts from below. *Crap, that might not be enough to kill him.* The man wasn't human anymore. Then, still on automatic, the jumper dropped into the 'gate room to take its launch position.

From below, John heard someone exclaim in horror. *Yeah,* he thought, *that probably did it.* The jumper would hover a few feet off the embarkation floor, but the forcefield it was using to support itself... John rolled over and shoved himself up, took a couple of staggering steps to the edge of the opening, leaning out and craning his neck to see. Bates ran up to stand beside him.

Squinting against the glare of the brighter light in the 'gate room, John saw McKay, Peter Grodin, and several others standing on the gallery steps, staring at the jumper floating in front of the 'gate. There was a spreading stain leaking out from under it as it still hovered serenely, waiting for a destination. John fumbled for his headset, but Dorane had torn it off in the fight. He told Bates, "Tell McKay to find a destination—a planet with no atmosphere."

Bates relayed it, and McKay hurried back to lean over the dialing console. It only took him a few moments to pull an address out of the database, but John was watching the jumper's port. He saw a bright flash from inside.

Bates swore. "The shielding—"

Watching intently, John shook his head. "He said it was corrosive." He hadn't said how fast it was. If they just had a minute for the 'gate to dial... He noticed he and Bates were both dripping blood onto the bay floor, Bates from a bullet wound in the arm, and John from the long scratches Dorane's claws had left on his shoulders.

Then McKay turned to the dialing console and started to hit the symbols, and John felt like something was squeezing his skull from the inside. For a horrified moment, he thought it was the bioweapon, that it had eaten its way through the jumper. Then he realized it was the 'gate. *Uh oh.* He thought the automated sequence would take care of it, but just in case, he thought at the jumper, *launch. When the wormhole opens, launch.*

Then the wormhole initiated with a blast of glassy blue energy, the jumper surged forward, and the world turned to white-hot pain.

CHAPTER TWELVE

John had a last moment of awareness, enough to realize he was lying on the jumper bay floor. The light was blinding, but he knew it was Rodney and Teyla who were leaning over him, and he thought it was Carson Beckett standing next to his head, yelling orders at someone. He grabbed Rodney's arm and tried to ask about the jumper, but he couldn't get the words out.

Rodney must have understood anyway. "It's gone, it went through the 'gate," he said, his voice thick and barely recognizable. Then he looked up at Beckett and shouted, "My God, Carson, will you get off your fat ass and do something!"

John decided that was a good time to let go.

John really expected to be dead, but being dead felt a lot like being in the hospital. Antiseptic odors, tubes and needles in places that tubes and needles should not be, too-bright lights, quiet serious voices with intermittent flurries of frantic activity and arguing. At some point he knew it was McKay standing over him, snapping his fingers at somebody and demanding to see John's chart, and Beckett telling him, "I would like to remind you, Rodney, that you are not a medical doctor." Teyla's anxious face leaning over him, then Ford's, then a distinct memory of Elizabeth, sitting nearby, her feet propped up on a stool while she read from a laptop.

He remembered all that as he came to gradually in the half-lit gloom of a medical bay. He was lying on his side on one of the narrow beds in the recovery area, a blanket tangled around his waist. He had loose gauzy bandages on his hands, and his left arm was secured to a rail with a light band, but that was probably to keep him from dislodging the several IVs that were stuck in it. Except for that, he felt mostly okay;

the intrusive tubes were thankfully gone, though there was a lingering ache in his throat. He had had a bath at some point and was wearing clean surgical scrubs. He could see into the next bay, where a couple of the medical techs and Dr. Beckett were working at a table spread with open notebooks, data pads, coffee cups, and laptops.

And it was quiet. John went still, listening intently. No whispers, no alien sound that his brain tried to interpret as music, no white noise. Everything he could hear was homey and familiar: the distant crash of waves washing against the city's platforms, clicking keys as someone typed, hums and beeps from medical equipment both Ancient and Earth-built. The only voices came from further away in the medlab, and were human. He felt his ear cautiously, then ran a hand through his hair. No spines.

John cleared his throat and said, "Beckett?"

Beckett looked up, brows lifted, then said something to one of the techs as he pushed his chair back. He came over to stand beside John's bed, pulling a portable scanner out of the pocket of his lab coat. "Ah, Major. Are we coherent today?"

"Is that a trick question?" He squinted up at Beckett. "How long have I been out?"

"Six days," Beckett said, seeming surprised and pleased. Apparently asking if John was coherent hadn't been a joke. Beckett set the scanner aside and took out a small pocket flashlight. "Hold still a moment and let me check your eyes."

Expecting to hear that it had been a day or so at most, John was too floored to try to avoid the light. But it was a relief when it just stung a little and didn't make him want to punch Beckett and throw himself off the bed. Beckett confirmed it, picking up the chart and making a note. "Very good. I think your eyes are quite back to normal."

"How is everybody?" John didn't need to ask if he was still dying; he knew what Beckett looked like when people were dying, and this wasn't it. "Teyla and Ford, everybody who had the mind-control drug—"

"Everyone who was given the drug has completely recovered," Beckett assured him. "And poor Masterson was the only death from the fighting. There were a number of injuries from the fighting, but everyone's doing fine now."

John pushed himself up a little more. "Hey, I can't hear the ATA anymore. Does that mean...?"

Carson pushed him back down again. "Yes, all physical symptoms are gone. You had us worried for a bit there. We got you on life support just as your body was in the process of shutting down. But that memory core of Zelenka's had a good deal of information on the various genetic treatments and how to tweak them back to normal for humans and for the Ancients. They did have to pop back to the planet to pick up that download Rodney took from the bastard's database to figure out exactly what you were given, but once we had that, I was able to start reversing the process."

John let his head drop back on the pillow. He wasn't as stiff and sore as he should be, though he could tell he really needed to shave. "I don't feel like I've been unconscious for a week."

"Oh, you haven't been unconscious for the past few days," Beckett said, making some more notes. "We were able to get you up and walking around. But the Ancient genetic treatments had a bit of a side effect in humans that apparently made you extremely, shall we say, loopy, so I doubt you remember any of that."

"Okay. That's...weird." He tentatively flexed his hands, feeling a little residual soreness. "So what happened with the claws? Did they just fall out during all this?"

"Oh, that. No, that took a wee spot of surgery." John frowned. Beckett tended to pull out the 'wee' bit when he was flustered or trying to be reassuring. It was always only a 'wee' seizure, a 'wee' dose of radiation, a 'wee' chunk of shrapnel in your abdomen. Beckett continued briskly, "But don't worry about it. I did it when I first initiated the other treatments, so your nails would have time to start growing back before you recovered."

"Oh." John suspected he was glad he didn't remember that. And he kept thinking of things he wanted to know more about. "Did Zelenka figure out what was on the memory core that Dorane was so desperate to get?"

"It was his cure, Major." Beckett's face turned grim. "Apparently the Ancients needed antidotes for the victims rescued from the repository, and they needed them fast. So they infected the bastard with a few altered strains of his own retrovirus. It was triggered by the altered version of the ATA that he created, or the absence of it. He couldn't leave the repository for more than a day or so without the full effect setting in, and killing him." Beckett lifted his brows. "They made a deal with him that if he produced the information they needed, they would give him the specifics of what they had done to him, so he could develop his own cure. He fulfilled his part of the bargain, but they were still trying to decide what to do with him as a permanent solution. There's no more information on the core. Rodney suspects they were fully occupied by the Wraith at that point and just let nature take its course at the repository. But the recording did have the specifics for the strains of the retrovirus they used."

He did say it was a punishment, John thought, considering it. "I would have just shot him," he said finally.

"I'm not a violent man, but it would have saved a lot of trouble," Beckett admitted.

John had more questions, but Beckett distracted him with an examination that involved multiple scanners, the Ancient MRI machine, and questions about how it felt to be poked in various places. John ended up falling asleep again when they were changing out the IVs.

John felt a lot more awake by the next day, and while taking the bandages off his hands, Dr. Biro filled in some more details for him about the past week.

Sergeant Stackhouse, returned safely from his trading mis-

sion, had taken a large and heavily armed team back into the
repository three days ago. They had recovered Kolesnikova's
and Boerne's bodies, and also let McKay do a brief survey of
Dorane's labs. Now that McKay knew what he was looking
for, he was able to distinguish between Dorane's altered gene
technology and the real ATA. He had concluded in disgust
that most of the equipment that might have been useful in
Atlantis was too tainted with the altered gene to risk using.
They had taken the drained ZPMs on the chance that some
day McKay might figure out how the things were recharged,
collected as many spent cartridges as they could so the techs
could use them for making new ammo, and managed to sal-
vage Ford's P-90 and John's tac vest from the wreckage the
Koan had made of their supplies and equipment. Then they
had planted C-4 in several strategic locations and blown up
the labs.

Biro also told him that Dorane had never had a chance to
send jumpers to the mainland for the Athosians, so they had
fortunately missed the whole thing. Teyla was out there now,
letting them know what had happened, or what had almost
happened.

John had also missed the memorial services for Dr. Kolesnikova, Boerne, and Masterson, the Marine who had been
killed in the 'gate room.

McKay stopped by later, either out of genuine concern or
because he heard John was getting solid food for breakfast, or
more probably a combination of both. This actually worked
out for the best, since John could handle most of what the
medlab considered food, but he didn't even want to be in the
same room with the powdered eggs, and McKay was a con-
venient means of disposal.

Tucking into the yellow egg mush, McKay told him a lot
more about John's initial treatment and recovery than Beckett
or Biro had. The first few days had been much worse than any
of the medical staff had implied. The way McKay described
it, it had been all out war: Carson Beckett, Earth's foremost

xenobiologist and the man who had invented the ATA gene therapy, against Dorane, the Dr. Mengele of the Pegasus Galaxy. The first day Beckett had just struggled to keep John alive, while Zelenka had hurried to finish reconstructing the damaged portion of the memory core and McKay had set up a copy of Dorane's database to get Beckett the information he needed. About midway through the third day Beckett had managed to produce the right drugs, and the lab mice he had tested them on had mostly survived, so he had started John on the full treatment. By that night John was breathing on his own again and the antennae spines had started to fall out, and Beckett had collapsed in the next bed over and snored for eight hours.

McKay also filled him in on what the rest of the city had been up to. "Sergeant Bates had your job for a whole day, during which a petition started circulating in the science team demanding that we hold free elections for the position of acting military commander. Apparently Sergeant Stackhouse was a favored candidate. Then Lieutenant Ford was cleared for duty, so things settled down."

John decided not commenting on that was best, so he just said, "So everybody missed me."

"Let's say they prefer your slacker laissez-faire style to Bates' 'guilty until proven innocent' strategy."

"At least you guys didn't try to form a separatist commune again. I don't think that would look good on my record."

Scraping the bowl for the last of the egg mush, Rodney lifted his brows. "And did they tell you about the operation? Personally, I don't believe in it for cats, but after you shredded a diagnostic bed, we thought—"

"Sorry to disappoint you but yes, Carson told me how I got declawed, and we've already made all the 'Dr. Beckett, Extragalactic Vet' and *All Creatures Great and Small* jokes." John self-consciously tucked his hands under his armpits.

Dr. Biro picked that moment to swoop in, saying breezily, "It really was fascinating. You can see if you like, we filmed the whole procedure."

John stared at her. "You're kidding."

"Of course she's not kidding," McKay assured him.

"Why?"

"Oh, because Biology thought it would be fun to show at the Christmas party." McKay rolled his eyes. "If we can ever contact Earth again, Carson wants the first Nobel Prize awarded in xenobiology. Do you really think he'd pass up this opportunity?"

John looked at Dr. Biro for help, which was probably a mistake. She smiled winningly. "Oh, don't worry, you can't really see your face. You were intubated."

"Oh, well, that's good."

McKay looked at him pityingly. "Right, no one's going to figure out who 'Patient X, Major, Acting Military Commander, Atlantis Expedition' was."

"Rodney, shut up and go away."

Ford came by later to see how John was, and to report that the Koan who had fled the fighting after Dorane's death were more interested in running away than in attacking anybody, so on Dr. Weir's advice he had implemented a 'catch and release' policy where the security details stunned and collected them to toss back through the Stargate to the repository's planet. He was pretty sure they had found all of them by now, though you never knew. With a regretful shrug, he added, "Dr. Weir and Dr. Beckett talked about trying to give them some assistance, but we don't have the resources to do much more than throw a few crates of food through the 'gate after them. And Dr. Beckett thinks trying to mess around any more with their genetics would just make it worse, that now that Dorane's not there to mess with their minds that they've got a good chance of being okay."

John had to agree. "I think they've had about all the 'help' they can stand."

Ford also wanted to apologize for anything he had done while under the influence. He said there was a lot of mutual apologizing going around the city for things people had done to friends and co-workers during the situation. John said in that case he was dropping the charges, so that was okay.

The next day, John got to say goodbye to all the IV stands and escape from the medlab. He was supposed to go to his quarters and rest, but he didn't think anybody really expected that to happen, so he headed up to the operations tower. John was willing to admit he needed another day or two to recover and he kind of liked padding around in a t-shirt, sweatpants, and old sneakers while everybody else was in uniform and working. But Beckett didn't want to clear him for duty for another week, which was ridiculous.

Beckett had also told him that he didn't think anything that had happened would affect the way John's natural Ancient gene worked, the way the ATA responded to him. John knew he should go up to the jumper bay and make certain, but instead he found himself stopping off in Elizabeth's office. And once there it seemed like a good time to talk her out of this crazy off-duty for a whole week idea.

Elizabeth, however, refused to budge. John tried everything from rational and pragmatic arguments to wheedling to the cute but wounded puppy expression that had gotten him the go-ahead to do some really crazy things in the past, but nothing worked.

They were in her office, one transparent wall providing a view over the control gallery. Elizabeth was sitting at her desk, her head propped on one hand, and when John realized she was watching his performance as if this was the most entertainment she had had in a month, he decided to give in for now.

"So how's Dr. Kavanagh? Is McKay riding him into the ground with this?" John noticed Sergeant Bates standing on the gallery outside with a clipboard tucked under one arm, apparently waiting to talk to Elizabeth. John gave him a *she likes me best* smirk and settled into the chair a little more comfortably, intending to take his time.

"I'm a little concerned about that," Elizabeth admitted cautiously, from which John inferred that for the past few days that section of the labs had been like a combination snake pit and bear-baiting show. She eyed him a moment. "I've recommended that everyone who was affected see Dr. Heightmeyer."

Kate Heightmeyer was the expedition's psychologist; John decided not to take the broad hint. He suggested helpfully, "We could all go together, and do that encounter group thing where we talk to each other with hand puppets."

"That would make a great threat, wouldn't it?" Elizabeth looked thoughtful. "By the way, I never bought the story that you were cooperating with Dorane. Neither did Peter." Lifting a brow, she added ruefully, "For one thing, it was exactly the kind of plan you and Rodney would have come up with, like something out of a movie."

John was actually kind of touched to hear that, but all he said was, "Which movie? One of those old ones with Sydney Poitier and Tony Curtis?"

Her mouth quirked. "I have no idea. But you're lucky you didn't have to fool anyone who knew you well and still had possession of their critical faculties."

John nodded seriously. "So if you ever decide to take over Atlantis, we'll have to come up with a new and completely innovative plan to thwart you. I'll put McKay right on that."

Teyla walked in then, saying, "Dr. Weir, they said you wished to—" Flustered, she halted abruptly, and started to back out of the room. "I'm sorry, I did not realize—"

By the time John said, "Hey, Teyla," Elizabeth was already on her feet and at the door.

She took Teyla's arm, drawing her back inside, saying, "Teyla, I just have to— If you could wait for me here—"

Teyla obviously didn't want to stay but was too polite to just bolt for freedom. In another moment Elizabeth was out the door and Teyla was left standing uncomfortably in the office.

Bemused, John watched her, trying to figure out what was wrong. Teyla was avoiding his eyes, her brow furrowed and her cheeks flushed with embarrassment. He said, "I thought you were on the mainland, catching up with everybody." If Beckett was actually serious about this no active duty for a week thing, John was half thinking of going out there himself. Watching the kids play, lying on the beach, getting drunk with Halling and the others around the campfire let you remember that there were places somewhere in the universe where people lived normal lives, without fear, without being hunted. As far as they could tell, none of those places were in this galaxy, but at least it was nice to think that they existed somewhere.

Teyla frowned at the floor. "I was, but I was told Dr. Weir wanted to see me today."

John was starting to get an inkling of what this might be about. Though one office wall was transparent, Teyla had come from the direction where the curve of the gallery blocked a full view of the room until the last instant; she obviously hadn't expected to see John here, and Elizabeth had just as obviously lured her back to the city hoping she would. He pushed to his feet so he could face her, perching on the edge of the desk and folding his arms. "Okay. Would you like to tell me what's wrong?"

Teyla lifted her chin, saying stiffly, "I thought perhaps you would need time... I did not know how these things were done among your people."

John sighed. "So you went to the mainland to make it easier for me to be incredibly unfair and fire you for the exact same thing that happened to half the Marines and a dozen or so scientists and techs, who are all back on duty now including Kavanagh, who nearly cracked Ford's skull?"

Distracted, she asked warily, "Why is it called 'fire?'"

"It's a figure of speech." John shook his head. "Look, that wasn't you."

Her voice hardened. "That was me. I could feel myself doing it." Then she shook her head, her expression turning rueful. "And I did not think you would 'fire' me. But... I cannot ask you to trust me if I do not feel I can trust myself." She gestured a little wearily. "I thought I might want to fire me."

"But Dorane didn't give you a choice; none of what happened was your idea." John noticed Bates again, watching them with a line of suspicion between his brows, as if hoping to catch them at something, like making out in the glass-walled office in full view of half the operations staff. *He obviously thinks being on my 'gate team is a lot more fun than it actually is*. And Teyla had probably reported in detail what Dorane had made her do, which Bates would file away as material to use against her eventually. John had never been able to convince Teyla that selectively leaving items out of your mission reports in order to make life easier for your team leader was not the same thing as lying. "You didn't have any control over what you were doing."

"To my people, leaving a companion in that kind of danger—" Teyla's lips thinned with disgust. "It is as bad as abandoning someone to the Wraith."

"My people aren't real thrilled about that either," John pointed out.

"And it was my hand that gave you the poison that almost killed you. If I could not prevent myself from doing that—"

"Look, at one point I went nuts and ran off and left McKay alone in the repository. He was just lucky the Koan weren't around." John could tell he wasn't going to be able to talk her through this. It was something she was going to have to get through on her own. "I'm not going to argue with you, because you're too stubborn and we'd be here all day. You're not fired and that's final." He pushed off the desk, straightening up. "Now come here and do the head-butt thing with me."

"It is not called the head-butt thing," she said, but her voice roughened and she stepped forward. The Athosian embrace had different shades of meaning John hadn't entirely figured out yet, though respect was one of them and mutual forgiveness another, as well as expressing simple relief that you were both still alive. He had also never gotten the hang of who put whose hands on the other person's shoulders and in what order and who bent their head to touch foreheads first. He managed to fumble the process enough that Teyla actually snorted in amusement.

John led her outside the office after that, so Elizabeth could have it back and Bates could get on with his life. Teyla asked, "Did Dr. Weir really want to see me or was this a trick?"

Rodney was standing at the gallery railing, looking over the 'gate room with the air of a minor tyrant overseeing his domain. John said, loud enough for him to hear, "Elizabeth probably wants you to guilt McKay into not using this to drive Kavanagh over the edge."

Getting the hint, Teyla widened her eyes innocently at Rodney. "Surely Dr. McKay would not do that."

"Surely Dr. McKay would."

Rodney gave them a superior smile. "It's amusing when you plot against me. Oh, I want to show you something." He headed off toward the rear of the gallery.

John hesitated. Teyla had been trying to avoid what had happened to her by avoiding him, and John had just realized he was avoiding something too. But realizing it wasn't enough to make him stop doing it, and he followed Rodney and Teyla over to a laptop set up on one of the consoles.

Rodney sat down and typed rapidly, bringing up a video program. "Zelenka managed to pull this off the memory core while he was reconstructing the data."

Teyla took one of the other seats, scooting over to see the screen, and John leaned on the back of Rodney's chair.

A video clip started to play, and Rodney tipped the screen back so John could see it. "It's too badly damaged to be significant and we have much better visual images of actual Ancients. The best ones, aside from the photos of the Ancient woman they found frozen in Antarctica, are probably the holographic recordings we've found here. But this is interesting for one key factor."

John frowned at the screen, not sure what he was looking for. He recognized the poorly lit underground corridor leading toward Dorane's shielded lab area. Then three people came into view, a woman with two men flanking her. They were dressed in black and between that, the bad lighting, and the fact that the image hadn't been meant to display in this format, it was hard to make out much detail. The man closest to the camera looked directly at it and Rodney hit a keystroke, freezing the picture. John started to say, "So what's the key factor we're— What the hell?" The image was grainy but John could see that the man looked like him. For an instant the resemblance was uncanny, then he realized part of that was the light and shadow. It was still a little spooky.

Rodney said, "Because of the poor quality of the image, the resemblance seems closer than it actually is. Fortunately he looks directly at the recording device so I was able to do a point by point comparison with the photo in your personnel file—"

"Oh, well, good to know that's not actually me." John dropped into the chair next to Rodney and stared at him, incredulous and indignant. "It's not like you could take my word for it that I'm not a ten thousand year old Ancient who thought it would be fun to hang out here playing tag with the Wraith and watching you guys scramble for answers. And how many times have I asked you to stay out of my personnel file?"

"I did not think it was actually you," McKay said witheringly. Under John's suspicious scrutiny, he admitted reluctantly, "Well, not after the first few minutes or so."

John put his head down on the console. *Kavanagh and McKay, with Dr. Heightmeyer and the hand puppets. I am so going to find a way to arrange that.*

"Your resemblance to him is obviously a genetic throwback, like the gene itself. But the point is," Rodney continued blithely, "that it explains a lot."

"It does not," John muttered.

"It does." Teyla sat up straight, staring at Rodney in startled comprehension. "When Dorane first woke from the stasis container, he looked at the Major, and said, 'you're human.'"

"Exactly," Rodney told her. "We thought he was reacting in surprise at seeing us, but he must have been talking specifically to the Major." He turned to John. "Even though he was tracking our movements, that must have been the first time he got a good look at you. He may have thought, just for an instant, that he was looking at the man from this recording. Or that you were an Ascendant. According to Dr. Jackson's experiences, they can appear in their original corporeal forms. Then he realized you were human."

"It must have brought back the memories of his battle with the Ancestors," Teyla said thoughtfully.

"It explains why he wanted to kill you at first sight," McKay added. "As opposed to the usual reasons why people want to kill you at first sight."

John sat up, admitting reluctantly, "Okay, it does explain that. Is there anything else on the recording?"

"No, it fuzzes out right after this." Rodney frowned at the screen. "I think he must have blown up the camera with his mind, or something."

John looked at the screen again, wondering at the motives of those people, so long dead. Or Ascended, or whatever. Maybe part of Dorane's desire for revenge had come from the fact that the Ancients had left him to rot in the repository. Faced with the Wraith advance, they had just filed him away as not important enough to bother with. Unless making it clear to Dorane that he was a minor irritant at best had been some Ancient's idea of the ultimate punishment. Considering the effect it had evidently had on him, it just might have been.

John left Rodney and Teyla still searching through the few damaged images from the core's display. It was time to stop avoiding this.

He went up to the jumper bay. It was quiet and unoccupied, which was perfect. He wanted to do this alone, just in case Beckett was wrong. Half the expedition either didn't have the Ancient gene or the ATA therapy, and losing it wouldn't mean he couldn't do his job. But it would mean he couldn't fly the jumpers. If they weren't able to contact Earth, it might mean he could never fly again. It would mean a lot of things he wasn't willing to give up.

He picked Jumper One for luck; it was the one he had first tried to fly, the one that had gotten him to the hive ship and back when he had barely known what he was doing with it.

But when he stepped into the cockpit and sat down, it happily powered up, adjusted the seat and the lighting for him, popped up several sensor screens when he thought about them and then tried to hand him a life sign detector. It was in its way as big a relief as Jumper Five carrying the bioweapon away through the 'gate; Atlantis still knew him, and everything was all right.

About the author

Martha Wells is the author of seven fantasy novels, including *Wheel of the Infinite*, *City of Bones*, *The Element of Fire*, and the Nebula-nominated *The Death of the Necromancer*. Her most recent novels are a fantasy trilogy: *The Wizard Hunters*, *The Ships of Air*, and *The Gate of Gods*, published in hardcover by HarperCollins Eos in November 2005. She has had short stories in the magazines *Realms of Fantasy* , *Black Gate*, and *Stargate Magazine*, and in the anthology *Elemental* by Steven Savile and Alethea Kontis. She also has essays in the nonfiction anthologies *Farscape Forever* and *Mapping the World of Harry Potter* from BenBella Books. Her books have been published in eight languages, including French, Spanish, German, Russian, Italian, Polish, and Dutch, and her web site is www.marthawells.com.

SNEAK PREVIEW

STARGATE SG-1: SURVIVAL OF THE FITTEST

By Sabine C. Bauer
Publication date: 15 May 2006

Daniel watched the anchor-like metal contraption reach its zenith and stall. It hovered for a moment, then it flipped downward and nosed into yet another plunge, trailing rope. He clamped his hands over his ears, winced. The noise of a grappling hook striking concrete, amplified by God knew how many thousand cubic feet of empty space, was cataclysmic. It seemed to drill through his hands and into his ears, after which it converged somewhere behind his shiner to pound around a bit. Wonderful. By the end of this he'd probably be deaf *and* blind.

Eventually the echo died down, and Sam shouted, "That was great, Teal'c! Nearly there. Try again!"

Oh for cryin' out loud... to coin a phrase. "Sam, I really—"

"Major Carter." Teal'c actually looked frazzled. "A Tauri scientist named Albert Einstein devised a most apposite definition of insanity. Are you familiar with it?"

"Yes. 'Doing the same thing over and over again and expecting different results.'"

"I assure you, the result will be no different however many times I attempt this." And this was the sound of a Jaffa digging in his heels.

Cross-legged on the floor, Sam hunched over her laptop, keying stuff that presumably made sense to her. Now she gazed up. Just how she did it was a mystery to Daniel, but her smile lit up the gloomy factory hall and raised ambient temperatures by several degrees. A select few had been known to say 'no' to the killer beam. Jack, for instance, though he probably practiced in front of the mirror. On this occasion, the full force of it was directed at Teal'c, who wasn't in training. His resistance wilted, and he wordlessly began coiling the zip line attached to the grappling hook. Take umpteen.

"Your last two tries were really close," she said, faintly apologetic. "I've computed the kilopond necessary to get that hook up there. That's easy, just a function of weight and distance, with the aerodynamic drag of the rope factored in. I've also downloaded your biometric profile from Janet's databank, which allows me to calculate the force you put into a throw like this. Now, given that the differential between—"

"Major Carter. I am ready, and it is getting late. We shall not be able to continue after sunset."

Teal'c's methods were somewhat more gracious than Jack's but equally effective. Sam abandoned a lecture, which, in the simplest of terms, came down to *If a Jaffa can't get the damn hook up there, nobody can.* She nodded. "Go ahead."

After a glance at the girder thirty meters above, Teal'c stepped back and measured out some slack on the zip line. Then he began swinging rope and hook in a diagonal circle over his head. Once, twice. The third time he let go, his body extending as if he meant to take flight himself. The grappling hook soared upward and did what it'd been doing for the past hour. Five meters or so short of the girder it ran out of steam and stalled. Crash-bang-boom.

"Well, I think that settles it." The words mixed with the echo still caroming through Daniel's sinuses, and he yawned to ease the pressure. Then his mouth snapped shut with an audible clack. "Uh-oh."

The man stood motionless just inside the open gate, outlined by a wedge of copper evening light. Terrific! If not entirely unexpected. The ongoing racket was bound to have brought security guards on the plan sooner or later. Of course they'd hoped to be out of here sooner. Strictly speaking, what they were doing could be considered trespassing at best, breaking and entering at worst.

"We've just come to collect some leftover equipment." Sam had risen, arms slightly spread to indicate that she was unarmed. "There was a military exercise here a few days ago. If you want to—"

"I *know* there was an exercise here, Carter. I got you killed, remember?"

"Sir!" Chiseled by a sharp breath, it sounded like a sob.

"O'Neill," said Teal'c.

"The one and only."

Fists sunk into the pockets of a leather jacket, he started walking toward them, affecting the nonchalance of a tourist at some historical site. *Gee, that's a real neat battlefield!* Except, it didn't quite come off as planned. He moved as though somebody had strapped him into a corset, and when he finally stepped out of that glaring backlight, Daniel was startled to see how drained he looked. Drained and wound more tightly than a wristwatch.

"What the hell are you doing here, Jack?"

"The perp always returns to the scene of the crime. Never heard of it? We also tend to turn up at funerals."

By Jack O'Neill's standards this was a whole encyclopedia of information, although Daniel was willing to bet a month's paycheck that Jack had had no real intention of carrying the conversation even this far. If they hadn't noticed him, he'd have beat a quiet retreat until after they were gone. And then? He'd have come in here and made himself relive every second of the exercise, compulsively listing and re-listing everything he thought he'd done wrong.

"Where's the crime?" Daniel asked, aware that it was the next best thing to poking a tiger's abscessed tooth.

"We've had this discussion. We're not having it again," snarled the tiger. Then his curiosity asserted itself, and he took in the zip line, the hook, the laptop, and the piece of equipment sitting next to it. "What the hell are *you* doing here?"

"Sir, we—"

"Observe, O'Neill."

Obviously Teal'c had concluded that a demonstration would be more beneficial than Sam's treatise on kilopond and differentials. The grappling hook flew, stalled, plunged, and made that infernal noise.

Jack never even twitched. "You missed."

"That's precisely our point, sir." Sam allowed herself a small, hopeful grin. "If Teal'c's throwing short, Norris' team—Marines or no—wouldn't have had a prayer of catching the girders. Unless"—she picked up a bulky gun that had the business end of a hook sticking out its nose—"they had launchers."

Settling the device against her shoulder, she took aim, fired. The hook soared, rope rippling after it, and neatly wrapped itself around a girder. Just like that, and with considerably less noise, too.

"That's the only way they could have got up there, Colonel," she added. "And we both know that launchers weren't permitted. Norris didn't play by the rules, sir. Nobody can blame you for not anticipating that they'd cheat."

"Oh no?" Jack's voice could have cut glass. "Tell me something, Major. When the Goa'uld pull the next new and improved doomsday machine out of their collective hat you gonna come running to me and bawl, 'They're cheating! They're not permitted those, so I don't wanna play!'?"

"No, sir." Her jaws worked, but she refused to be drawn into a fight.

Sensing it, Jack wouldn't let up. "That's what the enemy do. They cheat. If you haven't grasped that by now, you're in the wrong job, Major! They cheat because it gives them an advantage. We do the same damn thing, and anybody who doesn't anticipate that is a liability."

"Your comparison is flawed, O'Neill."

"Is it?" Jack whirled around, grimacing when the abrupt move jarred his ribs.

"Indeed." Slowly and methodically, Teal'c was coiling his zip line. Each coil punctuated a sentence. "It was a game. Games have rules. You abided by these rules and expected your opponent to do the same, because you *knew* it was a game. But the rules were broken. Who is to blame? You or the one who broke them?"

As so often, Teal'c's unshakeable calm deflated Jack. Sighing softly, he hunched his shoulders. "I *know* it was a game. What I *don't* know is that I'd have done anything different if it'd hadn't been. If it'd been for real... Sergeant Chen's wife had a little girl two weeks ago. If it'd been for real, that kid would grow up without a father because of me. You'd be dead, too, Carter, and I'd rather not think about the ways in which Jacob would rearrange my anatomy. As for you"—he tossed a wry grin at Daniel—"you'd probably have got your head in the way of some obstacle no matter what, so I won't plead to that."

"Jack—"

"Ah!" One hand held up, he wandered away, aimless until he was caught in the gravitational pull of the cotton bales and veered toward those. His left hand slipped from the pocket and started picking fluff. At last he turned back. "I appreciate what you're trying to do, kids. I... Look, I'm sure Carter could get Norris sent down for grand larceny, but it's not gonna change anything. So do me a favor and forget about it, okay? I'd like get out of this with a few shreds of dignity intact."

The *get out of this* part was unequivocal and triggered something of a flashback. As far as thoroughly miserable conversations went, that one had been a doozy. "That's... uh... that's funny, because I didn't figure you for the early retirement type anymore," Daniel said quietly.

Jack shot him a sharp glance. He remembered it too. Those words and what had come next.

"So, this friendship thing we've been working on the last few years..."

And he stares at Daniel point blank and finishes that half-formed question, "Apparently not much of a foundation, huh?"

He had the same steady, determined, goddamn implacable look now, though the veneer of arrogance was missing completely. "This is different, Daniel, and you know it."

It was. This time it wasn't a lie. This time it was for real. The question was if it'd be worth fighting. For a split-second, Daniel saw Reese's dead face and asked himself if things weren't just dandy the way they seemed to pan out now. Then he banished the thought to where it'd come from, ashamed of himself. Twisted and battered and bent out of shape, yes, but that friendship was still there, still for real, and as long as—

"Sir, you can't!" Sam had gone white as a sheet. "Not over this. Not when—"

"*When* what, Carter?" Jack asked almost gently. "Always boils down to the same thing, see? Liability. In every sense of the word. Besides, I already have. The letter should be on Hammond's desk tomorrow. The only alternative would be me pushing paper till the end of my days. You can see that working? No, wouldn't have thought so. I can't either."

Bits of cotton floated in the air, and he caught one, picked at it, blew it away again. Abruptly he turned and headed for the door. He looked surprisingly small in the vastness of the room, a black silhouette outlined by a wedge of light that had deepened from copper to burgundy.

"That's pathetic!" yelled Daniel, furious at him, Norris, the world at large. "The hero walking off into the sunset! It's such a cliché, Jack!"

For once there was no comeback. He just kept going. Daniel started after him, and was stopped by Teal'c's large, strong hand clasping his arm.

"Not now. You will not dissuade him now, Daniel Jackson."

The team battles the Hounds of Hell

STARGATE ATLANTIS

HALCYON
James Swallow

Based on the hit television series created by
Brad Wright and Robert C. Cooper

Series number: SGA-4

STARGATE ATLANTIS: HALCYON

by James Swallow
Price: £6.99 UK | $7.95 US
ISBN: 1-905586-01-9

In their ongoing quest for new allies, Atlantis's flagship team travel to Halcyon, a grim industrial world where the Wraith are no longer feared — they are hunted.

Horrified by the brutality of Halcyon's warlike people, Lieutenant Colonel John Sheppard soon becomes caught in the political machinations of Halcyon's aristocracy. In a feudal society where strength means power, he realizes the nobles will stop at nothing to ensure victory over their rivals. Meanwhile, Dr. Rodney McKay enlists the aid of the ruler's daughter to investigate a powerful Ancient structure, but McKay's scientific brilliance has aroused the interest of the planet's most powerful man — a man with a problem he desperately needs McKay to solve.

As Halcyon plunges into a catastrophe of its own making the team must join forces with the warlords — or die at the hands of their bitterest enemy…

Order your copy directly from the publisher today by going to www.stargatenovels.com or send a check or money order made payable to "Fandemonium" to:

USA orders: $10.82 ($7.95 + $2.87 P&P). Send payment to: Fandemonium Books, PO Box 2178, Decatur, GA 30031-2178.

UK orders: £8.30 (£6.99 + £1.31 P&P). **Rest of the World orders:** £9.70 (£6.99 + £2.71 P&P). Send payment to: Fandemonium Books, PO Box 795A, Surbiton KT5 8YB, United Kingdom.

Or check your local bookshop – available on special order if they are out of stock (quote the ISBN number listed above).

STARGATE ATLANTIS: THE CHOSEN

by Sonny Whitelaw & Elizabeth
Christensen
Price: £6.99 UK | $7.95 US
ISBN: 0-9547343-8-6

With Ancient technology scattered across
the Pegasus galaxy, the Atlantis team is not
surprised to find it in use on a world once
defended by Dalera, an Ancient who was
cast out of her society for falling in love
with a human.

But in the millennia since Dalera's departure much has changed. Her
strict rules have been broken, leaving her people open to Wraith attack.
Only a few of the Chosen remain to operate Ancient technology vital to
their defense and tensions are running high. Revolution simmers close
to the surface.

When Major Sheppard and Rodney McKay are revealed as members of the Chosen, Daleran society convulses into chaos. Wanting to
help resolve the crisis and yet refusing to prop up an autocratic regime,
Sheppard is forced to act when Teyla and Lieutenant Ford are taken
hostage by the rebels...

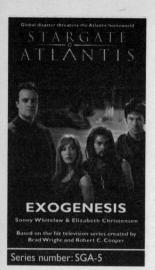

Global disaster threatens the Atlantis homeworld

STARGATE
ATLANTIS

EXOGENESIS

Sonny Whitelaw & Elizabeth Christensen

Based on the hit television series created by
Brad Wright and Robert C. Cooper

Series number: SGA-5

STARGATE ATLANTIS: EXOGENESIS

by Sonny Whitelaw & Elizabeth Christensen
Price: £6.99 UK | $7.95 US
ISBN: 1-905586-02-7

When Dr. Carson Beckett disturbs the rest of two long-dead Ancients, he unleashes devastating consequences of global proportions.

With the very existence of Lantea at risk, Colonel John Sheppard leads his team on a desperate search for the long lost Ancient device that could save Atlantis. While Teyla Emmagan and Dr. Elizabeth Weir battle the ecological meltdown consuming their world, Colonel Sheppard, Dr. Rodney McKay and Dr. Zelenka travel to a world created by the Ancients themselves. There they discover a human experiment that could mean their salvation…

But the truth is never as simple as it seems, and the team's prejudices lead them to make a fatal error—an error that could slaughter thousands, including their own Dr. McKay.

STARGATE SG-1: ALLIANCES

by Karen Miller
Price: £6.99 UK | $7.95 US
ISBN: 978-1-905586-00-4

All SG-1 wanted was technology to save Earth from the Goa'uld ... but the mission to Euronda was a terrible failure. Now the dogs of Washington are baying for Jack O'Neill's blood—and Senator Robert Kinsey is leading the pack.

Series number: SG1-8

When Jacob Carter asks General Hammond for SG-1's participation in mission for the Tok'ra, it seems like the answer to O'Neill's dilemma. The secretive Tok'ra are running out of hosts. Jacob believes he's found the answer—but it means O'Neill and his team must risk their lives infiltrating a Goa'uld slave breeding farm to recruit humans willing to join the Tok'ra.

It's a risky proposition ... especially since the fallout from Euronda has strained the team's bond almost to breaking. If they can't find a way to put their differences behind them, they might not make it home alive ...

Order your copy directly from the publisher today by going to www.stargatenovels.com or send a check or money order made payable to "Fandemonium" to:

USA orders: $10.82 ($7.95 + $2.87 P&P). Send payment to: Fandemonium Books, PO Box 2178, Decatur, GA 30031-2178.

UK orders: £8.30 (£6.99 + £1.31 P&P). **Rest of the World orders:** £9.70 (£6.99 + £2.71 P&P). Send payment to: Fandemonium Books, PO Box 795A, Surbiton KT5 8YB, United Kingdom.

Or check your local bookshop – available on special order if they are out of stock (quote the ISBN number listed above).

Their darkest hour may be their last

STARGATE
SG·1

SURVIVAL OF
THE FITTEST
Sabine C. Bauer

Based on the hit television series developed by
Brad Wright and Jonathan Glassner

Series number: SG1-7

STARGATE SG-1: SURVIVAL OF THE FITTEST

by Sabine C. Bauer
Price: £6.99 UK | $7.95 US
ISBN: 0-9547343-9-4

Colonel Frank Simmons has never been a friend to SG-1. Working for the shadowy government organisation, the NID, he has hatched a horrifying plan to create an army as devastatingly effective as that of any Goa'uld.

And he will stop at nothing to fulfil his ruthless ambition, even if that means forfeiting the life of the SGC's Chief Medical Officer, Dr. Janet Fraiser. But Simmons underestimates the bond between Stargate Command's officers. When Fraiser, Major Samantha Carter and Teal'c disappear, Colonel Jack O'Neill and Dr. Daniel Jackson are forced to put aside personal differences to follow their trail into a world of savagery and death.

In this complex story of revenge, sacrifice and betrayal, SG-1 must endure their greatest ordeal...

Order your copy directly from the publisher today by going to www.stargatenovels.com or send a check or money order made payable to "Fandemonium" to:

<u>USA orders</u>: $10.82 ($7.95 + $2.87 P&P). Send payment to: Fandemonium Books, PO Box 2178, Decatur, GA 30031-2178.

<u>UK orders</u>: £8.30 (£6.99 + £1.31 P&P). <u>Rest of the World orders</u>: £9.70 (£6.99 + £2.71 P&P). Send payment to: Fandemonium Books, PO Box 795A, Surbiton KT5 8YB, United Kingdom.

Or check your local bookshop – available on special order if they are out of stock (quote the ISBN number listed above).

STARGATE SG-1: SACRIFICE MOON

By Julie Fortune
Price: £6.99 UK | $7.95 US
ISBN: 0-9547343-1-9

Series number: SG1-2

Sacrifice Moon follows the newly commissioned SG-1 on their first mission through the Stargate.

Their destination is Chalcis, a peaceful society at the heart of the Helos Confederacy of planets. But Chalcis harbors a dark secret, one that pitches SG-1 into a world of bloody chaos, betrayal and madness. Battling to escape the living nightmare, Dr. Daniel Jackson and Captain Samantha Carter soon begin to realize that more than their lives are at stake. They are fighting for their very souls.

But while Col Jack O'Neill and Teal'c struggle to keep the team together, Daniel is hatching a desperate plan that will test SG-1's fledgling bonds of trust and friendship to the limit...

Order your copy directly from the publisher today by going to www.stargatenovels.com or send a check or money order made payable to "Fandemonium" to:

USA orders: $10.82 ($7.95 + $2.87 P&P). Send payment to: Fandemonium Books, PO Box 2178, Decatur, GA 30031-2178.

UK orders: £8.30 (£6.99 + £1.31 P&P). Rest of the World orders: £9.70 (£6.99 + £2.71 P&P). Send payment to: Fandemonium Books, PO Box 795A, Surbiton KT5 8YB, United Kingdom.

Or check your local bookshop – available on special order if they are out of stock (quote the ISBN number listed above).

O'Neill faces a nightmare from his past

STARGATE
SG·1

A MATTER OF HONOR
Book One
Sally Malcolm

Based on the hit television series developed by
Brad Wright and Jonathan Glassner

Series number: SG1-3

STARGATE SG-1: A MATTER OF HONOR

Part one of two parts
by Sally Malcolm
Price: £6.99 UK | $7.95 US
ISBN: 0-9547343-2-7

Five years after Major Henry Boyd and his team, SG-10, were trapped on the edge of a black hole, Colonel Jack O'Neill discovers a device that could bring them home.

But it's owned by the Kinahhi, an advanced and paranoid people, besieged by a ruthless foe. Unwilling to share the technology, the Kinahhi are pursuing their own agenda in the negotiations with Earth's diplomatic delegation. Maneuvering through a maze of tyranny, terrorism and deceit, Dr. Daniel Jackson, Major Samantha Carter and Teal'c unravel a startling truth — a revelation that throws the team into chaos and forces O'Neill to face a nightmare he is determined to forget.

Resolved to rescue Boyd, O'Neill marches back into the hell he swore never to revisit. Only this time, he's taking SG-1 with him...